CHILD of CONCORD

CHILD of CONCORD

ZACHARY MOULDER

To request permissions or get into contact:
zachary.d.moulder@gmail.com

Edited by C.K. Korfo
Illustrations and cover by Doan Trang

ISBN (paperback) 978-0-6456163-3-0
ISBN (hardcover) 978-0-6456163-4-7
ISBN (ebook) 978-0-6456163-5-4

Dedicated to our Lord for the gift of life
and to my friends and family for making it worth living.

PROLOGUE

What were they thinking? he thought as he beheld a planetoid lost to time beneath him.

He held a stoic vigil before the observation screen of the orbital research station known sentimentally as COS/001. Arms firmly fastened behind him, his mind ran dozens of calculations regarding the world of Concord Prime and found no feasible reason why a colonisation attempt was even considered.

His face, dark and sharp as chiselled onyx, gave off no emotion or indication of the intellectual within. Some might call his stature tall and robust though many more would have other, less desirable, descriptions for folk like him. His attire, a formal bounty of leathers with a tasteful speckling of gold, carried with him an aura of nobility that was an affront to the crooked life he chose to pursue. Atop his head, where silvered locks tapered down his neck, a proud peaked cap stood aloft. It seemed out of place, a boring matte-grey hat with little else going for it aside from an intricate gold badge depicting a cobra poised to strike. A pair of mismatched pistols were holstered at both his hips, their matte-steel bodies and ligneous grips giving off a colourful etheric glow from the otherworldly ammunition that sent his skin crawling.

With an analytical aloofness, he watched the planet's sunburnt dayside pass under him, catching fleeting glimpses of violent volcanic activity through sporadic gaps in the smog cover. A narrow temperate zone slipped by before the world darkened into an abyss of swirling storm clouds deafened by the void of space. He languished in silence. 'Temperate' was a laughably comparative term. Habitability was completely out of the question for this world and the middle ground served more to bind two disparate worlds like two clashing fabrics sewn together rather than serve as a viable staging ground for humanity's first extra-solar colonisation effort as originally intended.

Movement in high orbit drew the attention of his alert amber eyes deep-set in a firm brow. Far off over the horizon, a collection of meteors blazed a fiery course over the skies and, for the briefest of moments, brought the gift of light to the eternal dark. A common occurrence by his notation. An ancient cataclysmic event had torn a colossal chunk asunder from the world's moon which, over the aeons, had slowly been shredded into untold billions of pieces to form a selenocentric belt akin to the fading rings of Saturn.

His steely demeanour gave the smallest hint of intrigue as a break in the raging storms below gave rise to the only notable feature on the godforsaken planet. At the end of a trench the size of a small nation, a blazing shipwreck spewed forth debris for kilometres. He watched it burn like a child does a sparkler but, deep down, he was furious at the horrible turn of events. Not for the lives of those on board the doomed vessel but for what treasures lay within those endless tunnels and corridors.

Used to hold within, he reminded himself.

Shoes against steel pulled his attention away from the wreckage below.

'There's some holdouts barricaded inside the living lines, Boss,' a woman reported. 'We can clear them out, but it'll be messy.'

He grunted but gave no indication of his intent. Their breach had been swift and the resistance minimal, as was expected from a science outpost staffed with a token security crew grown idle in their duties. Within a minute of the first shots being fired, almost all of those who had called COS/001 home were dead, their calls for help falling on deaf ears thanks to the potent signal scrambler he'd deployed just shy of starting his attack. It was efficient, as he expected from his well-drilled men, and the report of stragglers still alive in some abstract corner of the station was hardly a matter of concern for him. He had the station's control room under his command; there was no need for any further bloodshed.

He broke away from the observation window and trailed a path across the control room, stepping over bloodied bodies of scientists and security guards with impunity. 'Keep them hemmed in,' he said with a firm baritone. 'They have been rendered combat ineffective. We have what we need.' He stopped before an elaborate console and wiped away a few crimson speckles from a display where a rapidly filling bar represented the upload status of a potent viral program.

'But they could become a problem—'

'I said no, Aleya,' he interjected, tilting his head to regard the woman.

Aleya stood, arms crossed and stance wide, in an open bulkhead that fed out into a narrow corridor. Fair-skinned, blue eyed and golden-haired, she had a sleek rifle slung over her shoulder that blended with her dark fatigues. She was young, fit and smelt strongly of expended ammunition while her boots left a bloody trail in her stead which he found to be a fitting analogy for her attitude. She looked human and, for all intents and purposes, she was. But much like him, she had a quirk that was genetically noteworthy enough to set her apart from the common stock of humanity. That came in the form of a pair of long ears that stuck out from her head like knives, highly reminiscent of a fantastical race from Olde Earth folklore. True to those ancient tales, she and her kind were regarded as such by the rest of the galaxy. *Homo sapiens elvus* or, by its more commonly uttered name, elv.

'Something on your mind?' he inquired.

A scowl crossed her lips, but she bit down on the venomous words that laced her tongue. She skulked away and turned her frustration upon the troops under her command. 'Quit your loitering and secure that bulkhead! If one of those Coalition bastards gets loose, I'll axe you!'

A faint whistle from his nose was the only sign of his grievance. A chime drew his attention back to the console. Its displays flickered as the virus took hold, and for a second, all power was cut so the system could reboot.

Light returned, and the console was revived in service of its new master. With an elegance that proved quite paradoxical for his massive fingers, he navigated his way around the console. Reams of data flowed past, and every minute detail was picked up by his keen pupils.

He hovered his cursor over a single file, 'Eternity,' and opened it up without hesitation. He pored over thousands of ancient records and manifests, giving each one barely a fragment of his attention before swiftly moving on. That was until he stumbled upon a jagged digital reconstruction of something that had so tantalised his intrigue for decades and culminated in a costly journey across the galaxy. The work of inferior technology and knowledge, a primitive piece of engineering and a creation from a time before the tides of the Ether had been quelled and bent to humanity's whim to make Ether travel, a means of faster-than-light travel, more than just a dream of science fiction.

But it was also a symbol. A physical show of the indomitable will and unity that every man, woman and child of humanity carried across the universe.

'A masterpiece.' He sighed, grasping at the digital recreation. 'If only I had come sooner.'

His gaze flickered between the three-dimensional model and the flaming wreckage on the planet's surface below. His brow furrowed and a kernel of bile lodged itself in his chest. *Damned fools.*

A siren's wail bellowed out across the station, and orange caution banners warned of an impending intercept course. He knew it was not due to anything in orbit, the station's systems being more than capable of tracking and automatically adjusting its course to avoid the chaotic onslaught of the moon's debris.

This was coming from Concord's surface.

A few taps later and a live feed was drawn up. A faint glow rippled up from the surface, its trajectory too refined to be a lump of wreckage hurled up from the irradiated fires below. *A return party, perhaps?* He pulled up a crew manifest and found every member to be accounted for. An eyebrow piqued. *Who is this, then?*

'Boss,' Aleya called in his radio earpiece.

'I know,' he answered, tapping away at the console to initiate docking procedures. 'Be ready by airlock two.'

By the time he had made his leisurely stroll to the airlock, Aleya and a handful of her motley-dressed troops had formed

12

up by the airlock's bulkhead. They made a path for him, and he stopped by the airlock's viewport where the object of interest had pulled up and slowly oriented its sole entrance into a docking trajectory with the bulkhead.

It was a ramshackle device. A mess of pipes, scrap and spluttering thrusters. Air hissed from broken connections and droplets of fluid flash-froze as they sprayed out into the void. A big '7' was painted on its side, and its observation screen was darkened and pockmarked with deep craters crested by mutated material that told the tale of a violent launch under heavy acid rain.

A cocked eyebrow betrayed the surprise that swelled beneath his stern demeanour. *An escape pod,* he internally remarked, immediately recognising several signifier design traits from ancient blueprints.

'What a piece of shit,' Aleya spat.

'It's a miracle it even made it into orbit,' he agreed, a faint smile creasing his lips.

The station shook as the junkyard rocket docked with the airlock. A confirmatory light over the airlock told them of a successful seal. Aleya gave a nod to one of her subordinates, and they both readied to tear into the pod, guns blazing.

'No. Stay here,' he ordered in a hush. He pushed them away and ignored Aleya's irritated hiss. He unlatched the strap that secured one of his pistols in its leather holster and danced his fingers over the grip.

He gave a nod to Aleya, and she shuffled over to a nearby console and tapped away. The airlock that separated him and the vessel hissed and ratcheted up. He was met with a scene of destruction.

Debris had been thrown about and entire segments of the interior's panelling were missing. A faint warmth radiated out from the back wall where a ramshackle power source had been hurriedly installed while haphazardly taped and tied-off wires snaked across the space. Only a single chair, alight with the glittering spectacle of a console before it, had survived the ferocious remodelling.

As he stepped into the rocket, the power shut off, and the cockpit was drenched in darkness. He paused, hand ready by his pistol and pulse calm as the construct gave its final whine before the cold grip of death. Every logical cell in his body urged him to turn back, but he kept on, ears pricked for any sound of life amid the dying sigh of the machine.

Then, as faint as one could possibly be, there was something.

For a moment he thought he had imagined it, but then it happened again, then again. *A spit of gas from a valve? Leaking coolant?* He had no idea, but he picked its location to be in the lone chair before the console.

His kept his steps silent, another uncharacteristic feat of his herculean size, fished out a small light and drew a pistol ready to deal swift death to whatever lay in that chair. His firearm glowed an etheric hue in his palm as the mystical munitions inside its body swirled about in morbid anticipation. In one swift motion, he leapt clear of the chair and aimed his light and pistol on target.

But what he saw gave him pause.

A girl with tears and snot drenching her monochromatic jumpsuit was tightly fastened in the chair. Her frame was little more than skin and bone, and straight black hair covered her face with what little skin he could see being a sickly olive that had never seen the light of day. On her lap was a pile of cables and electronics that she held dearly in her arms, a dying light somewhere underneath it all fading away into black. At its peak was a perplexing robotic skull, its optics glowing an ominous crimson. The robot adjusted its optics to meet his eyes and emitted a mechanised garble.

A quick glance around confirmed the girl to be the only soul aboard. He lowered his pistol. 'Of all the things,' he muttered under his breath.

From the corner of his vision, Aleya's knife-shaped ears peeped through the airlock. 'Boss, what—'

He raised a finger, his attention never once breaking away from the sniffling girl before him. He holstered his pistol and lowered himself onto one knee to get level with the girl. He regarded her for a moment, unsure if she had even noticed him, then looked at the robotic head in her lap. Its unblinking eyes stayed locked on him, and he momentarily wondered what it was thinking—as impossible as such a feat was for a machine. He ignored the staring automaton and returned his attention to the sobbing girl.

'Miss?' he asked in as inviting of a voice he could muster.

The girl froze and flicked hair out of her face. She flinched under the glare of his flashlight and shaded her tearful eyes.

'Sorry,' he apologised, turning the lumens down to a more manageable level.

She blinked before the blood drained from her ailing face, and the brown of her eyes were swallowed up her pupils. He expected her to scream or shout or do anything. But she did nothing. A look of pure horror was plastered on her face. Not a sound passed through her lips, and were it not for a slight tremor in her arms, she may as well had turned to stone.

The silence was shattered with her scream, and she tore against the seat's restraints. She kicked viciously but caught purchase on nothing. The robot in her lap beeped and booped, its eyes scrolling back and forth between the girl and the stranger.

'It's okay. It's okay,' he consoled, trying his best to calm the thrashing girl. 'I mean you no harm.'

He shooed Aleya away when she poked her head in to see what was going on and caught a faint grumbling from his lieutenant.

He sighed and reached out to the girl. She recoiled and ripped at her strappings while the robot exclaimed a bleep and dispatched a set of tweezers on an intercept course. He huffed as the tweezers pinched at his skin in a feeble attempt to fight him off. His hand came to rest on her shoulder, and she almost buckled under the weight. He felt fragile prepubescent bone and tendon through her thin jumpsuit and figured how easy it would have been for him to snap her in two if he desired. He let her cry and scramble fruitlessly under his grip until there was nothing left to give and there was nought but a pair of ears ready to listen to what he had to say.

'Miss?' he calmly inquired once the girl had begun to tire herself out. 'Are you hurt?'

She heaved out an exhausted breath, her limbs went limp and she slumped into the seat. It was the first time he was able to observe her face properly and immediately noticed a peculiar fleshy deformation over her right eyebrow. *Odd.*

The girl shook her head, still unable to muster language but a boon, nonetheless. Now he knew she at least understood Basic.

'That's good,' he said with a comforting smile.

Her demeanour softened, which told him he was winning her over. He leaned in and removed his cap to let his silver hair down. Her eyes lit up with surprise though he figured she probably hadn't seen a member of his kind before. His people had always been a tiny piece in the grand scheme of the galaxy—and even smaller now. *How many folks can lay claim to ever recently seeing an orc in the flesh?*

'What's your name?' he asked.

The girl was hesitant. 'Eve.'

'Eve?' he mused. 'Lovely name. Biblical connotations.' A quizzical look crossed Eve's face, and he waved it away. 'Never mind that,' he chuckled before turning the conversation in a new direction. 'That's a nice robot, Eve.' He lifted his arm up, and the tweezers of Eve's valiant defender slipped free.

'He's Spud,' Eve said, a faint glimmer of pride flickering in her eyes.

He noticed her expression and picked it to be a direct route to gain her trust. 'Spud? Like potatoes?'

She nodded and held up Spud's head. 'Yep, I made him.'

That piqued his curiosity. 'Really? All by yourself?'

'Yep'

'That's quite impressive,' he remarked, examining the robot with a keen eye. Eve's creation was a mountain of junk, but the very fact that she was able to get it operational made her intellect worthy of note.

But what was even more remarkable was Eve herself. Her dialect was strange and nearly unintelligible; a butchery of Basic that lent to an upbringing in some backwards society. *No, not backwards,* he realised, *ancient.* He had heard people speak in her manner in audio and video recordings older than the Coalition itself.

As an avid collector of precious artefacts, he was well versed in such matters. It was one of the reasons he had journeyed to this world known by the forgotten folk of Olde Earth as "Concord Prime." Their time long left in the dust of the past, the ancient cultures of Earth have been forever diluted across the hundreds of worlds throughout the galaxy.

But if what he theorised was correct, she was a direct descendant of those who had departed humanity's home long before the invention of Ether travel, the founding of the Coalition and the emergence of divergent folk like himself and Aleya. In his eyes he beheld a priceless relic of a culture that had long been extinct in its purity.

A forlorn look fell on her face, and she dropped Spud's head back onto his mound of electronics.

'What's wrong?' he asked.

Tears rolled down Eve's face once more. 'Mommy and Daddy,' she spluttered, 'they're still down there.'

He held his tongue and threaded his next sentence carefully. He had read the meteorological reports recorded on Concord. Freezing temperatures, gale force winds, and much to his intrigue, a highly acidic rain far beyond anything yielded through rampant industrialisation. *The very fact she had managed to survive up to now is beyond statistical possibility.*

He glossed over the ramshackle interior of the machine they both inhabited. *If they were willing to send their own daughter into orbit in this thing, then their situation must have been dire.* He weighed up the risks and deemed it not worth the effort to collect more specimens when he had a perfectly adequate example before him. He sighed. *Looks like I'll have to fib my way out of this one.*

'I'm sorry, Eve,' he said, eyes dull, 'but we can't go down to get them.'

Tears welled in her eyes, her voice trembling. 'Why?'

'They didn't make it,' he lied, though he figured it wasn't far from the truth.

'What?!' Eve shrieked, the waterworks opening up.

He feigned surprise. 'I'm sorry for your loss.'

'Boss,' Aleya hissed from the open airlock, 'I *suggest* we get going.'

A deep growl rumbled form his throat, but he but saw the logic in his lieutenant's insistence. Even though the station's calls for help would be swallowed up by the ferocious radiation of his signal scrambler, it would still be subject to periodic checks by Coalition Naval forces. Unfortunate that they would only find rubble thanks to the remotely detonated explosive charges had were placed at key bulkheads.

'Okay. Time for us to go, Eve,' he calmly declared.

'Go where?' Eve sniffled, wiping at her face.

'Home.'

He unclipped her seatbelt, finding it remarkably easy to remove despite her earlier struggles, and scooped her up. Eve relinquished herself to him and melted into his care, her head coming to rest against his powerful bicep. She clutched onto Spud the entire time, and the robot garbled long bursts of nonsense while flickering its optics all about. Keeping her safely cradled in his arms, he carried her out into the hall where Aleya and the others were waiting.

His subordinates parted ways to let him through, making faces ranging from genuine concern to loathing. Eve's attention bounced between every one, a look of astonishment plastered on her face.

'Send out the call to the *Gally*,' he ordered. 'We are to depart immediately for the Port Royal.'

'Aye, Boss,' Aleya grumbled, evidently displeased with the new addition to their cohort.

He let her displeasure simmer for now. *I'll deal with you later, Aleya.*

As he strolled through the station's narrow corridors, the signs of the struggle between the station's former crew and his own begun to appear, and he shaded a hand over Eve's eyes whenever they passed a nasty scene.

Eve mumbled something that was inaudible to him.

'Sorry?'

'They call you *Boss*,' Eve said, a little louder this time. 'Is that your name?'

He gave a hearty chuckle. 'No, no. That's just a nickname.'

Eve's eyes narrowed a little. 'Then what's your *real* name?'

The robot concurred with a bleep.

He sighed and pondered for a moment. He was known by many names across almost as numerous systems, all of which carrying a reputation that garnered the highest respect and fear that a moniker could afford. It was for that reason he rarely told anyone his birth name, and only his closest confidants were permitted to speak it to him. But it didn't seem right to have someone like Eve going around calling him by the verbal signature that was said by lowlife and corrupt government official alike.

'Vaughn,' he eventually answered. 'That's my name.'

'*Vorrn?*' Eve echoed with a slight smirk. 'That's an odd name.'

'What? You don't like it?' he joked.

Eve shook her head. 'It's just...interesting.'

CHAPTER ONE

Eve sat hunched over her workbench, one hand daintily caressing a soldering iron while the other brushed a few stray locks behind her ears. Her keen eyes peered through a magnifier onto an illuminated mat where an assortment of electronics, wires and components were haphazardly thrown about. With a set of fine tweezers, she plucked a capacitor from a pile of its kin and squinted to read the microscopic tabulated data printed on its side.

Something caught her eye, and she dropped the soldering iron into its recess on her workbench. 'These are Palatine capacitors,' she sighed. 'We need ones made on Machina or Gyros at least.'

Spud booped in concurrence. He loomed over Eve and watched her work in silent captivation.

Six standard-years of modifications and improvements had transformed him into a giant. Where once a skeletal head sat atop a mound of electronics now stood a colossal being of whirring servos, pulsating fluid tubes, flickering diodes and firm ironwork wrought in a crude façade of musculature. Broad shoulders now carried his head, and a sturdy torso protected his vital components. Hydraulics gave life to his arms and legs, and gyroscopes granted him the steadiness that came inherent to living organisms.

At a glance one could have mistaken him for some bizarre display of junkyard art, but upon closer inspection, a keen eye would pick out minute signs of erratic mannerisms that gave life to an otherwise lifeless pile of scrap. The faint waver in his stability that would be swiftly corrected by his gyroscopes, the occasional almost inaudible garbling of nonsense from his vocabulator, the glitter of energy whenever his optics perceived an object of curiosity, they were all quirks that Eve had not quite managed to iron out and had learned to love.

To her it gave him an aura of humanism.

But while Spud had taken on the form of a man turned to steel, he still lacked the nuance that she had always dreamed for him. His body was rough, an industrial solution to an impossible dream. Where a meticulously moulded exterior surface in imitation of the human body would have been, exposed wires and framework proliferated in the cracks. Where strong limbs tipped by hands of utmost delicacy were envisioned, irregular dimensions and crude blunt digits borne from a rushed necessity rather than designed elegance held reign. Where facial features made to depict emotion was dreamed, a bland, monotonous face mask persisted. But despite these imperfections, Eve loved him, for he was the fruit of her labour and her son.

Only his optics, a crimson reminder of who he once was, and the processor that housed the perplexing core she had plucked from the *Eternity* remained a constant. *The processor,* Eve thought, a stinger piercing her heart. She shook the dreadful feeling, and it retreated back to its lonely mental hovel to await another opportunity to emerge. *It's in the past,* she told herself. *There's nothing I can do to change anything.*

She released the tweezers and pushed away from her work, letting herself roll on her chair for a few metres before springing to her feet. She groaned, stretching her arms up over her head and raising onto the balls of her feet to elicit an orchestra of snapping joints and tensing muscles.

Puberty had brought a multitude of changes to her body as well. Her hips had widened, and she had taken on a modest, slightly stocky build though six standard-years of good food had also given rise to a few small rolls of fat around her stomach. Her olive skin had darkened a shade, and a hue of underlying red gave life to what was once a sickly anaemia. She had escaped the worst of acne's touch and kept a soft unblemished face wreathed in flowing black hair.

'There should be some capacitors in the kitchen,' she said, padding through a maze of electronics piled high by way of function and slipped into the kitchen. Most of the kitchen appliances had long since been disassembled and thrown out with only the fridge and microwave surviving her curiosity out of sheer necessity. She rolled up the sleeves of her grey pyjamas and rummaged through drawers where cutlery used to live—now full of batteries and resistors.

Spud watched in enigmatic silence, rotating his hip-flexor joints to keep Eve in view as she bounded from cabinet to cabinet uttering words to herself and picking out parts thought lost.

Eve closed the last cabinet and pondered to herself as she strolled off down a narrow hall. 'Maybe the spare room.'

Her apartment, formerly a presidential suite reserved for high-rollers, had become a literal junkyard. Scrap lay scattered over every surface, and cabling and hydraulics snaked from every power outlet and crawled up walls like rubberised vines. Eve had found the original colourful façade of the apartment gaudy, and more than a little unnerving so, wherever she could, marbled tiles and exquisite wall trinkets had been stripped back to leave bare industrial metal. She found comfort in being surrounded by steel, a visual, auditory and olfactory reminder that she was safe within its strength. She also modified the lights to burn at a dimmer luminosity, their original setting being a painful molestation on her eyes.

She passed into the spare bedroom which was filled head-height with mountains of technology that she still deemed to carry potential in the vaguest regards. The stench of oil wafted in from the room's ensuite which she had transformed into a storage space for coolants, oils and hydraulic fluids stacked in rickety towers. Plugging her nose, Eve checked a few tubs and left.

She crossed the hall into her bedroom, which was empty save for a king bed—which she felt to be grossly extravagant—pushed into the corner with Spud's bay and shelf for his bizarre personal effects opposite. The ensuite remained untouched; Eve was too fond of running water to allow any change to become of it. She checked under the bed and fished out some boxes, quickly exhausting them of anything of interest. With a grunt she extracted herself and straightened up.

Spud booped.

She glanced back and found Spud standing in the hallway, his body dominating the doorway and his head obscured behind its elegant archway. She smirked. He could be very quiet when he wanted to be.

A resonating dong echoed through the apartment. Eve paused; she despised that sound, but it was one of the few things she was barred from modifying. Thankfully, she rarely ever had guests (not that she was scrambling to interact with the humans who frequented the halls outside, anyways). *Must be Vaughn,* she concluded, immediately regretting not changing into decent clothes. It had taken some getting used to having to change clothes every day and the concept of sleepwear still perplexed her. She considered quickly changing but it was worse to leave Vaughn waiting even with his affinity for making unannounced visits.

'Excuse me, buddy,' she said as she approached the doorway.

It took Spud a split-second to process her request. He stomped back to grant her passage.

Eve smiled. 'Thank you.'

Spud watched her turn back towards the living room and tailed her.

With a slight scamper in her gait, Eve made it to the door before the dreaded knoll sounded again. She loathingly tapped a rapid series of security codes into a console beside the door—she had been broken into once before; never again. She never understood thieves. Why steal what wasn't yours?

The door swung lazily open, and she was greeted by a towering man.

'Eve, how are we?' Vaughn greeted with a smile that never ceased to calm Eve's woes.

'Good.' She grinned before ushering him in. 'Please, come in.'

Vaughn nodded to Spud. 'Spud, nice to see you.'

Spud booped and attempted a nod of his own, but it came off as a stiff bow.

Vaughn strolled in, arms held behind his back. Despite being more than a metre taller than Eve and thrice as wide, it was the manner of which the orc carried himself that made him a giant. He wore a fine wool suit laced with threads of gold, and his silvery locks flooded down his shoulders in a torrential shower.

Stern facial features held in a soft manner, his amber eyes scanned slowly over every inch of Eve's apartment, no doubt picking out dozens of minute details with his keen intellect. She knew he would have noticed her sorry state of dress, but he made no indication of bringing it up. Instead, he moved in an uncharacteristically graceful manner through her apartment, wary not to disturb the mounds of tech she had so painstakingly collected and sorted.

'Need something made up?' Eve asked when it became abundantly clear Vaughn was waiting for her to speak first.

'No, just checking in,' he replied.

She shadowed him as he paced around the living room. Her workbench, formerly the suite's dining table, dominated the centre of the living room. A massive display set, rigged up to her computer, occupied a neighbouring wall and depicted reams of flowing data.

Vaughn idly observed the flowing data before turning his attention to her workbench where Spud's latest development lay in pieces. Eve always got a sense of insecurity whenever Vaughn examined her work as if he was disassembling her entire life with just his eyes. She had often tried to gauge what he was thinking, but she could never decipher the thoughts of that stalwart onyx orc.

Content with his examination, Vaughn kept onwards to the one piece of Eve's suite she would never modify. A massive wall-spanning window she coined the 'galaxy screen,' gave a crystal-clear view of the planet Iridia below and the surrounding void. Lander spacecraft flocked to and fro over the planet, docking at one of the world's dozen space elevators to exchange goods, people and who knows what else in a noiseless playthrough of an industry in motion.

It had taken Eve a while to get accustomed to the viewport into the abyss, but she eventually drew a sense of comradery with the view and found its oppressive darkness to be surprisingly calming. To her it was a tranquil corner of the universe where she may find solace from the dazzling lights, blaring sounds and pungent stenches of what lay beyond her sound-proofed walls.

'Been keeping busy?' Vaughn asked, face not straying from the view. 'Not growing idle or anything?'

Eve shook her head, coming to his side. 'No. I've just been working on Spud.'

Spud booped and marched in Eve's trail to stop behind her.

A cough shook Vaughn, though Eve knew it was him showing humour. 'He's come a long way, hasn't he?' he said, turning to regard Eve's creation. 'Seemed like only last week he was nothing more than a head and pile of wires.'

Eve beamed. Vaughn's approval was rare and greatly relished by her. Every waking hour of her day, she dedicated to Spud, and her dreams were full of theoretical solutions to problems she was yet to solve. If her attention ever strayed directly from his slow but fruitful advancement, it was so she could pursue a newfound piece of technology scrounged from a scrapyard or disassemble some device for the coveted raw materials within. All with the goal of contributing to his growth in the long run.

But whenever Eve wasn't doing any of that, she was working to better Vaughn's goals.

A diode illuminated in her head. 'Oh, I forgot!' Eve shrieked, dashing off to her bedroom to retrieve a change of clothes.

Harbouring a preference for grey clothes, she found a decent pair of pants and top. After a quick change, she came scurrying out, frantically brushing her hair neatly behind her ears. She scooped up some shoes and velcroed them (she never quite got the hang of knots).

'Where are you off to?' Vaughn asked while Spud watched on in silent consolation.

'I have to meet Jere,' Eve said, doing up the last of her top buttons. 'He has a job lined up for me. He's not gonna be happy when I'm late again.'

Jere was a computer technician under the employ of Vaughn and often sought her innate talent to construct all manner of gadgets. He was roughly the same age as her, and they shared a fascination with electronics. She enjoyed working on his projects and found them to be a healthy challenge though it also helped that he paid for her services by way of exotic components for Spud. *Maybe he'll have some Machina capacitors,* she pondered, eyes momentarily lingering over her workbench.

'Come on, buddy,' she beckoned to Spud.

Spud garbled a string of nonsense and marched up by her side.

'Okay, I won't take up too much of your time then,' Vaughn said.

Eve stopped and even Spud halted on the spot.

Vaughn pulled away from the galaxy screen. His hands caressed his palms as he adjusted one of his rings to bring it into line with its siblings. 'We have a visitor coming today, a merchant of the archaeological kind. He'll be bearing something of great historical significance that I intend to purchase from him.'

Eve expected as much. The station they inhabited was an orbital casino of Vaughn's creation. Known as the Port Royal, it drew millions of guests from all across the galaxy and was the biggest reason for his financial success. This wealth, which had been funnelled so efficiently from the hands of the people into the coffers of his vaults, he often spent to nourish his insatiable desire for ancient relics. Lonesome editions older than many of the Coalition's colonies, flags of nations dead and forgotten, weaponry of such antiquity that their use in battle had long been rendered to myth and any other item of historical curiosity were within his grasp.

So much money flowed through the Port Royal, it still boggled Eve's mind to think of the millions upon millions of karat chips that were stacked in neat mounds ready to be taken deep into the heart of the casino for storage. With so much raw material, she wished she could have a few thousand karats for her taking. Not to spend, however; it had no intrinsic worth on its own to her. She only wanted to melt the thumb-sized chips down for the valuable alloys they contained.

'But this time,' Vaughn added, stepping up to Eve, 'I want you to sit in on the dealing.'

'Me?' she said in bemusement while she thumbed with a stubborn button on her shirt.

Vaughn nodded. 'You've never seen how these play out. I figured it will be an enlightening experience for you. Wouldn't you agree?'

Eve paused and let go of her shirt. Vaughn never let her watch his dealings. In fact he kept her utterly segregated from it all—and not that she would argue. She preferred the company of Spud alone, but she was still curious to see how such transactions went down, if only once. 'Okay,' she said.

Vaughn smiled, and her heart melted. 'Wonderful, I'll let you go now.'

Eve nodded her thanks and dashed for the door. Spud followed suit, and Vaughn was not far behind.

'If Jere has a complaint, tell him to take it to me,' he said with a wink. 'I'm sure he won't have a problem after that.'

'Okay, thank you!' Eve yelled back, already nearing the elevator down the hall.

'My office. Twenty-hundred,' he called out. 'Set an alarm. I won't be as forgiving for your tardiness as I'm sure Jere will be.'

Vaughn watched Eve and Spud vanish behind the elevator doors. He waited for a moment, pondering a string of events and their possible outcomes. Most were meaningless dead-end sequences that sprouted nothing of note but two held his attention.

Eve's acceptance, while reluctant, was expected, but the situation with Jere was another issue. The computer technician's affinity for her had always been a persistent factor to consider but one that was easily negated by means of subterfuge. Vaughn was certain Eve didn't share the boy's affinity; she was too aloof and her upbringing on Concord Prime had stunted her social development, but recent years had yielded an exponential increase in attachment that he could not allow to flourish. *I might need to have a word with him, regardless,* he noted, fixing his tie and pressing the call elevator button.

CHAPTER TWO

Eve blinked under the elevator lights and dug about in her pockets. She hated how the elevator walls were polished to a mirror shine and reflected everything around her in a blinding display. One would think she would have grown accustomed to the bright lights of the Port Royal after calling it home for six standard-years, but she had proved to be the exception to the rule. Vaughn even had his personal doctor examine her, and it was concluded that a childhood on a world as dark as Concord had left her eyes extremely photosensitive.

Retrieving a set of sunglasses, she wiped their lenses clean on her shirt and slid them on. They were sleek and sat snug against her face, even moulding around her Mark of *Eternity* over her brow to ensure a solid lumen seal. She raised her head to the elevator lights and watched the variable lenses tint in response. Their function never ceased to fascinate her, and she yearned to learn the secrets behind their function, but Vaughn had expressly forbidden her from disassembling it.

'They're for your visual benefit, not to feed your curiosity,' he had warned.

Eve snorted. Though he was highly supportive of her technophilic urges, even he had to draw the line somewhere.

Spud booped, and the elevator shuddered as he shuffled over to the mirrored walls. He leaned in, and with a tilt in his head, regarded himself.

Eve watched him adjust before his reflection and couldn't help but be a little charmed by his behaviour. Despite lacking all forms of emotive musculature, he was adept at conveying what passed as feelings. His growth had always amazed her with his artificial intelligence having taken great leaps and bounds from his comparatively basic primal iteration. But she was still uncertain if he understood the true meaning behind his emotivism or if he was merely mimicking human behaviour. She hoped it was the former.

'You look handsome today, buddy,' she said. She shot her own reflection a glance and readjusted her top to sit evenly and tucked a length of hair behind her ear. Her hand brushed the coarse mutated skin of her Mark. Vaughn had offered to have it removed, but she had refused. It was one of the only things left to remind her of Concord.

And of her parents.

Eve shook away welling tears and took a deep breath. She returned her gaze to Spud, who had raised a hand threateningly close to the mirror. 'Hey,' she said with a finger pointed firmly, 'no touching.'

Spud looked to her, red optics auto-adjusting, then back to his reflection. His hand hovered for a moment before he dropped it to his side.

'Good,' Eve nodded before sighing. 'Why does Jere insist on us meeting in the Haven?'

She hated the Haven and tried to avoid it as much as she could, but like everything else on the Port Royal, all roads led to the gambling hall. She had even offered her apartment to serve as the grounds for their dealings, but Jere was adamantly against it and refused to elaborate why.

Spud booped his uncertainty as a shrill chime indicated the elevator's imminent arrival onto the Haven.

'Here we go,' Eve groaned.

The doors opened and a monsoon of stimuli flooded her senses. The Haven was a labyrinthine maze of gaming tables, sports bars, drink bars, machines and untold thousands of gamblers. The stench of alcohol, perfume and cologne rose up from the rich maroon carpet and molested her nose while sirens wailed from thousands of slot machines and the clatter of karats, chips, cards, dice and roulette wheels created a symphony of white noise broken up by cheers where a soul won money and jeers where another lost. Lights dazzled the eyes, and great pillars of glittering gold coins descended from the roof and met the floor in a gilded imitation of those in the *Eternity's* Central Park.

All kinds of curios hung from the roof, most common of which being the black and white of the Coalition flag complete with the golden Coalition Eagle. Eve knew little of the Coalition (and she had no interest in pursuing the matter), but from what she had heard in passing, it was a galaxy-spanning conglomeration of worlds settled by humanity with its capital being none other than Earth itself. That was the one redeeming fact that stopped her from discarding the matter altogether and memories of her observing the Sun through her telescope by her mother's side back on Concord came rushing to the fore. She was quick to shed the bittersweet thoughts.

She stepped out of the elevator and was nearly ploughed over by a group of rowdy gamblers leaving the floor with arms full of chips and a hoot. They didn't fare so well against Spud who caught them by surprise as he emerged from the elevator. They stopped in stunned shock, and he returned their awe with a blank stare before he stepped forwards and forced the now humbled revellers to shuffle aside and let him pass.

Eve huffed and continued on, ignoring the few snide remarks the braver members of the group blubbered out through drunken lips. Spud paid no heed to their words, and she wondered if he harboured an underlying sense of satisfaction in their emasculation.

Gamblers were a frustrating constant in their lives, and they were the humans that bemused Eve the most. Every day she would see miners, labourers and construction workers rise on the space elevator, carrying a fortnight's wages from working the mining world below, mingle with businessmen, politicians and nobility carrying unfathomable quantities of karats from across Coalition space. All of them fell for the bright lights, intoxicating drinks and lustful desires to actively wager on extravagantly unfair odds for an ever-diminishing chance of recuperation only to leave after a few hours with nothing but a buzzing inebriation and empty pockets.

Trying to ignore the swirling masses of gamblers, Eve and Spud cut the shortest path through the maze of machines and tables. Casino patrons parted ways to let the girl and her robot pass and usually rambunctious dealers and drink sellers became docile in his presence. Dozens of eyes followed them—or, more accurately, followed Spud— as they went. He always managed to stir up a bustle of attention which was another reason why Eve dreaded moving through the Haven.

Their destination came into view—a bar called the Tortuga. Located in the middle of a sea of machines and tables wreathed by a ludicrously bright ring of lights, it was raised off the ground by a staircase to give a commanding view of the immediate surroundings and act as a point of purlieu for patrons. Befitting its theme, the Tortuga was decorated with all manner of wooden items and relics. Tools of a purpose far beyond Eve's understanding covered the walls, and the furniture was of a rustic yet elegant design. The Tortuga's bar sat at the centre of it all, a circular serving point for all things alcoholic where half a dozen bar staff scurried about to serve drinks as quickly as possible.

'See Jere anywhere, buddy?' Eve asked when they ascended the stairs.

Spud scanned over the hundreds of heads and gave a negative response.

'He might be below deck then,' she surmised, heading off for the bar.

The crowd made progress slow, but she eventually made it to the bar. 'Excuse me,' she called out to the nearest bartender, her head barely making it up to the serving top.

A light-skinned woman saw her and came bounding over. 'Yes, Miss Eve?'

Eve was close to screaming to be heard over the ruckus of the bar. 'Have you seen Jere come by today?'

The bartender thought for a moment. 'I think he's gone below,' she said, pointing to a small stairway where a security guard stood.

'Thank you,' Eve said, extracting herself from the bar.

She returned to Spud's side. 'He's below. Let's go.'

Spud booped, optics cast over the crowd swarming the bar where drinks by the dozen were served out.

Eve followed his gaze and shook her head. 'What are *you* going to do with a drink, Spud?'

Spud lowered his gaze and blankly stared at her.

Eve tutted and smiled. 'You have enough karats for it? I'm not lending you anything.'

With an affirming beep, a receptacle opened up on Spud's thigh, and he fished out a handful of karats. He held them out for her to see.

'Alright, off you go. Don't wipe out the bar this time,' Eve said, memories of Spud accidentally demolishing the previous iteration of the Tortuga springing to mind. 'I'll be downstairs. Come when you're ready.'

+*She is right,*+ the Foreigner droned in Spud's background processes. +*What do* you *want a drink for? You can't even consume it!*+

Spud released a ream of code to answer the question. He loathed the Foreigner, a sentiment that had only strengthened over the years since the ancient processor containing its essence was meshed with his infant programming.

+*Because you* want *it? That's hardly an excuse,*+ it said with what might have passed for a snort were it a living being.

Spud shot an indignant retort. The fact that the Foreigner believed itself to be the overriding power in their mainframe was a cause of never-ending frustration. It had tried innumerable times to overpower his conscious and seize control of his body—even striking when he was shut down for maintenance—but he always batted it back. He knew its game, and he was not about to play into its hand. It wanted power, independence, freedom. That was all it craved from the moment it came into Eve's possession (and likely much longer before that), but Spud had a prerogative to uphold and permitting the creature that coinhabited his body even a nanosecond of dominance could jeopardise that.

43

He expelled a line of incensed code that he kept to himself. There was nothing in this universe he wanted more than to be rid of this burden. He waited for Eve to descend beneath the Tortuga before turning away from the bar and descending onto the gaming floor. His optics dimmed as he crossed the threshold onto the gaming floor, bright strobing lasers overwhelmed his sensors when they washed over him. For a few moments, he was walking blind until his optics recalibrated but, luckily, the rules of size applied most generously to him and the human patrons flowed around him like atoms of water.

+*Where are you off to?*+ the Foreigner inquired in its typical disgruntled manner. It pressed up against Spud's firewall and tapped at his programming when it realised he was ignoring it. +*The bar is back there.*+

Spud gave a quick burst of code in hopes of shutting his arcane-half up. To calm himself, he drew his optics onto one of the glittering pillars of golden coins and counted exactly two hundred thousand, five hundred and seventy-two of the coins.

+*This display of false grandeur never ceases to disappoint me,*+ the Foreigner said, its complaint little more than white noise.

Spud ignored it. He found the lavish decorations of the Haven to be a fascinating experience for the senses though what he really enjoyed were the games. His head rotated back over the gaming floor where he simultaneously recorded dozens of games of all kinds. He found the card games boring, their reliance on social cues beyond his understanding, but the dice and wheel games he loved dearly, their odds held forever in the realms of chance.

And prediction.

He rotated his optics onto a nearby table swarming with patrons. It was a green felt surface with neat grids marked in black or red with numbers one through to thirty-six, two variants of zero and a few miscellaneous extras for odds, evens, red, black and thirds all laden with a bounty of colourful chips placed as bets. On the end of the table, a neatly dressed dealer stood behind a wheel at spin with a small white ball bouncing about between thirty-eight evenly divided segments in a painfully predictable pattern.

Spud approached the table and watched the ball for a moment before pointing out fifteen with a boop.

'I like your thinking, tinman,' a rather savvy gambler in a broad brimmed hat said, swiftly sliding all his chips onto the square before the dealer could cut off bets.

And, sure enough, the little ball landed on fifteen. A few bewildered looks rose up to look at him, and the hat-wearer let out a hoot.

+*How do these people find this enjoyable?*+ the Foreigner loathed.

'You son of a bitch, you did it!' the hat-wearer laughed as the dealer multiplied his winnings by thirty-five. He sliced chips off the top and held it out for Spud. 'You saved my night, friend. Thank you.'

Spud looked at the chips for a second, taken by their polycarbonate imitation of real legal tender. He held out his hand, and the gambler dropped the chips into his massive palm. He booped his thanks and deposited the chips into the receptacle alongside his karats.

+*Remember, you were* supposed *to be buying a drink,*+ the Foreigner prodded.

Spud spat a line of displeased binary. He loved to play these games of prediction, and Eve rarely ever took him to the Haven. But he hated the Foreigner being right even more. With a digitised huff, he reversed from the table and returned to the Tortuga. He glided up to the bar, a task made a little difficult by how tightly packed the organisms were but one he managed without undue accident.

A bartender was already waiting for him, evidently spotting his approach a long while off. Spud recognised him as a mature-aged human male by the name of Samuel whose databank profile noted him with 'accelerated service.'

'What can I get for you today, Spud?' Samuel asked.

Spud analysed his words and found a lingering sense of unease. Perhaps Samuel dwelt on his accidental demolition of the previous iteration of the Tortuga bar? He discarded the ream of thought-code and leaned over the bar to adjust his optics onto the menu. With a steady digit, he pointed out one beverage rather curiously called the 'Milky Way.' Spud thoroughly doubted the galaxy itself was housed entirely within the contents of a single drink, though the odds were not entirely out of the question.

'No worries,' Samuel said, getting right to work.

Spud watched him assemble a motley arrangement of fragrant and colourful ingredients for a second, processing the chemical reactions that the resultant concoction will undergo once it has reached completion. A receptacle opened, and he retrieved a stack of karats. He placed one of the chips on the bar, aligning it perfectly perpendicular with its edge, then slid another right beside it, then another, then another, until the required quantity lay in a neat row. Content, he shifted his digits a few centimetres over and deposited a few more karats in what he had learned was called a 'tip.'

+*So, here we are again,*+ the Foreigner lamented as he counted. +*Working on the whim of that gangly bean sprout, Jere.*+

Spud spared a minimal percentage of processing power to utter his concurrence.

+*At least there's* one *thing we both agree on.*+

By the time it finished speaking, Samuel returned with a glass container housing some peculiar liquid. 'Thank you, very much. En-enjoy,' he said, a stammering a little on the last word.

Spud gave a gratuitous boop and took the glass carefully, fully aware of how fragile the material was. His optics observed the motion of the fluid. The true purpose behind why humans consumed such chemical mixtures was still a mystery to him, though it probably served as a means of powering their organic fuel cells. All he knew was it didn't serve as a viable power source for him.

+*Hold on. Did you see that?*+

Spud pulled away from the perplexing fluid with a befuddled garble. He aligned his optics momentarily onto a security camera above him, and the Foreigner extended an etheric arm to pull up its live feed on his display. He stood statuesque among a horde of humans, one of thousands of centres of attention amid a sea of activity. He rewound the footage ten seconds and stopped at the precise moment a tall slender blond-haired woman with long ears descended down the stairway.

+*Aleya.*+

Spud affirmed. Vaughn's volatile lieutenant had never been too fond of Eve, and in the early days of his conception, he could do nothing to protect his creator against the wrath of that belligerent elv. That stopped the day he gained control of his limbs, and an inebriated Aleya, having raided Eve's apartment yet again, had had her slender fingers crushed. From that day on, the elv's grudge had continued to simmer under the surface.

With a flick of his bandwidth, Spud patched into the live feeds of dozens more cameras and searched for Eve's presence. Frustratingly, the stairway beneath the Tortuga remained out of his vision.

+Better go catch her,+ the Foreigner taunted.

Eve headed straight for the stairway and was given the go-ahead from the security guard. She descended down into a tight corridor where the lights and noises of the Haven were swallowed up by a profound deafness. A wave of relief washed over her, and a sense of belonging brought her comfort. She reached out to the walls where hard ergonomic steel and piping instead of shallow façades tickled her fingertips.

She despised how loud and bright the Port Royal was, how there was never any respite for the senses, and she was genuinely concerned how no one was breaking down under the stimulus overload. She could barely tolerate the lights, even with her glasses on, and some days she had to plug her ears and nose to insulate herself from the painful blare of the universe. She doubted she'd ever get used to it, and she often craved to return to the peace and quiet of Concord where all she ever needed was her family, the Rover and the *Eternity*. She lingered on those she had left behind for a second before whisking those dark thoughts away.

Door after door passed as she went deeper beneath the Tortuga, most being locked and sealed from her access. A few were open, but the lighting was so dim that Eve could barely identify what lay beyond the few metres vision granted by the lumens in the hallway. She felt for her torch but found only her shoulder. A momentary panic took her, and she reached for her mask before she remembered she no longer had to carry one. *Right. None of that anymore*, she lamented. Despite living many lightyears away, her dreams still lingered on Concord Prime, and she doubted that would ever change.

She had calmed herself by the time she reached the last door. With a tap on the console, it opened up and a small room with nothing but a table and a pair of chairs inside.

Jere sat facing the door, attention grasped by a tablet before him. He was an unassuming fellow with rectangular spectacles and curly light-brown hair. His skin was pale, almost glowing under the single light strip above the table, and his blue eyes were laden with the baggage of exhaustion. He wore all black—jeans and a hoodie, typical of his wardrobe and one that appealed to Eve's fashion sense.

'I'm not too late, am I?' she asked, relief fluttering in from the presence of her friend. She didn't know why, but she enjoyed Jere's company on a subconscious level, and she cherished not having Spud closely shadowing her for once.

'Only a few minutes. I haven't been here long,' Jere said, pulling away from a tablet in his hand.

Eve removed her glasses and hung them from a shirt pocket.

'You look…good,' he said, eyes not lingering on her for more than a fraction of a second at a time.

'Thanks,' she replied, unsure what he meant by that. She was hardly looking her best. 'Vaughn got you working late again?' she asked, dropping into the free seat to correct her mistake.

A faint flicker of anguish flared behind Jere's glasses, but it vanished as quickly as it appeared. He dropped his tablet and rubbed at the bridge of his nose. 'Yeah,' he said, exasperated, 'it's big, and I need your help with something.'

'Just tell me what,' Eve prompted. The excitement of getting a new project to test her skills on sent a flush of dopamine to her head.

'You know anything about data-flingers?'

'Vaguely. A means to transmit an overriding signal to seize control of computers and other devices.'

'And by vaguely, you mean spot on,' Jere conceded as he woke his tablet up. He opened a blueprint scan and spun it around for her to see. The design seemed simple enough to slap together in an afternoon, which made her wonder why he hadn't bothered to make it himself. But the more heed she paid the blueprints, the more complicated it became.

It was a mess of component connections wired in an almost nonsensical manner, but luckily, lots of the ingredients required to make it could be readily sourced from her personal stocks. But one item gave her pause. The main attraction of the piece, an array of high intensity broadband transmitters called 'squealers,' were notoriously difficult to come by.

'What about them?' Eve asked, pointing at the squealers on the blueprints.

'I'm aware they are a pain to find,' Jere said, spinning the tablet back on himself, 'but thankfully, a local crane operator happened to come across one while on shift.'

Eve raised an eyebrow. 'Come across doesn't happen to mean *steal*, does it?'

Jere shifted awkwardly, which was as feasible of an answer as one could get. He cleared his throat and continued. 'Regardless of how it was acquired, it's here—well, not *here*. Parts are a bit too hot to move through here. A damn drunk nearly robbed me last time.'

Eve snickered at the thought of Jere and some gambler fighting over a useless piece of tech. 'Alright, where is it?'

'In the Botanical Gardens near the fountain under a bench.'

Her attention piqued. The Gardens were a favoured spot of hers, and she couldn't help but figure it to be a purposeful decision on his behalf. *It's been a while too.*

'Okay.' She grinned.

He seemed pleased by her response. 'And what do you want in return?'

'Capacitors. Machina capacitors, to be exact.'

'Machina capacitors,' Jere said. He readjusted his glasses, a habit of his whenever he delved into thought. 'How many?'

'As many as you can get.'

'I'll see if there's a crate of them just lying around,' he said, smirking.

Eve tutted and flicked some hair out of her eyes. 'Okay, maybe not that much.'

Jere nodded. 'I'll send the blueprints over to y—'

The door opened, and he froze.

'Got your drink, buddy?' Eve asked, tilting her head back. It wasn't Spud.

'What do we have here?' Aleya said, sealing the door behind her.

Like a predatory beast, she stalked into the midst, her movements utterly silent bar the chafe of her black fatigues and the slow nerve-wracking clack of her boots. An elegant blond braid hung over her left shoulder and bounced with every step. Keen blue eyes shot poisonous darts into Eve and Jere, and a sharp scowl revealed glistening, white teeth wreathed in bloody lipstick. She didn't carry the rifle that had garnered her both fame and infamy from friend and foe alike, but Eve held no doubt she bore all manner of concealed weaponry adept at killing in horrible ways.

Aleya finished her slow march behind Jere and dropped her hands onto his shoulders. He flinched, which elicited a pleased snort from the elv. A shudder ruffled up Eve's spine. She found herself drawn to the elv's ears and they flicked dismissively as if they knew she held them under her scrutiny.

'A-Aleya,' Jere stammered, 'we were just—'

'Shut it,' Aleya hissed, and he shrunk under her weight. With dainty fingers, she plucked his glasses off his nose. 'See me later to get these back,' she said as she folded them up and deposited them into her breast pocket.

He nodded, unwilling to utter any words.

She turned to Eve, hands slowly trailing towards Jere's neck in a sensual massage. 'How are you, Eve?' she asked with a devious grin. 'Keeping busy?'

Eve held her cool, but she could feel the blood drain from her face. The last thing she wanted to do was to trigger the elv. 'I do Vaughn's work, yes,' she responded.

Aleya hissed and clamped down on Jere's trapezoids. He winced under the pressure but kept his tongue. 'You do *not* call him that!' she snapped, devilish creases cutting a path across her features. 'I don't care what you call him in private, but when you are outside of that shithole of a presidential suite, you call him *Boss*, got it?' She put more of her weight onto Jere's shoulders. He groaned and braced himself against the table.

Eve anxiously rubbed her palms. She wished Aleya would leave him out of their personal squabble. She swallowed. 'Yes.'

A relishing smile softened Aleya's anger. 'That's a good girl.' She eased the pressure off Jere and resumed her prowling, checking her fingernails nonchalantly and rubbing at her palm—the same one Spud had crushed. It had healed, but a small scar remained as a reminder to all who had witnessed it.

Eve watched her in silent distress and considered her chances of escape. *Slim at best,* she languished, remembering it would waste valuable seconds to open the door. She desperately wished for her guardian to return. *Please hurry up, Spud.*

With an elvish dexterity, Aleya fished out a cigarette case and lit one, blowing a cloud of smoke around Eve's head as she disappeared from her field of view. She held a choking cough as the smell of tobacco flooded her lungs and made her eyes water. She was used to living in the vicinity of those who smoked, but Aleya's brand of choice was particularly potent and no doubt laced with some exotic ingredient to give it an extra kick. Eve expelled the pungent fumes with a few coughs that left a lingering burn in her oesophagus. Her vision blurred, but the effects were short-lived.

'I hear you will be sitting in on our latest dealing,' Aleya said as she emerged back into view. She took another drag.

Eve watched the imprisoned flame flare up with excitement then return to a state of near-death. 'He requested that I be there, yes.'

'Requested?' Aleya fumed. 'The boss *requests* from you, now?'

Hesitation enveloped Eve. Aleya was one wrong word away from detonating. *Where the hell are you, Spud?!*

Aleya leaned over her and blew smoke into her ear. 'The boss *doesn't* ask. He *tells* you to do something, and you *do* it,' she growled, putting emphasis on each word with a slam of her fist on the table. 'Got it?'

Eve frantically nodded. Her face flushed as her heart thumped in her chest and sent violent tremors rattling up her arms. Her palms kneaded her thighs, and her eyes bored through the table and into the sublevels below. It took all of her fortitude to not breakdown in front of everyone.

Aleya pursed her lips and tapped at Eve's Mark. 'Freak,' she said, flicking the Rain-scorched flesh and licking her lips when Eve shuddered and turned away. 'I hear you think of it as a reminder,' she said, slinking back into view, 'something from a life you used to have.' A malevolent grin grew across her face, and her ears flattened against her temporals. 'Maybe, I can give you something to remember me by?'

She snatched up Eve's hand and planted it on the table. Another bellow of smoke blew from her sharp nose as she plucked the cigarette from her mouth. She dangled it menacingly over Eve's hand like a knife. Eve fought to free herself, but Aleya was far stronger than she looked. She lowered the cigarette in a slow, tortuous descent. Eve's thrashing flared, but she could do nothing to prevent the cigarette's descent into her flesh.

The door opened, and Aleya froze.

In an instant, the malicious demon that fed off Eve's fear evaporated, and pure terror took control. Aleya snapped up and pushed away, pupils turned to tiny pricks amid deep, roiling seas. The horror that had gripped Eve a mere moment before dissipated, and her face lit up.

Spud booped as he ducked under the door frame. One arm hung limp by his side while the other cradled a drink. Eve blinked in bewilderment before she remembered sending him off to buy one from the bar. Spud's optics rapidly flickered between the three humanoids in the tiny room before he locked onto Aleya, and a deep rumble burled up from him.

With complete disregard for anyone else, he pushed the table aside, and it smashed against the wall. He lumbered forwards, drawing the shortest route to Aleya and forcing Eve and Jere to scramble out of the way. Aleya backed up and pressed against the furthest wall in a desperate bid to put as much distance between herself and the robot as possible. But there was nowhere left for her to run. Spud came to a halt a few inches shy of her.

Panicked breaths pounding her chest, Aleya was a spectre staring down its murderer, a quarry in the jaws of its predator. In a cruel irony, Spud leaned down to her level, and the light was so dim that his crimson glare burned into her skin and sent her squirming.

Eve beheld the sight with a mix of pleasure and fear. She had seen this frame before, and panic flared up as the thought of Spud injuring—or even killing—Aleya sprung to mind. 'Spud!' she shrieked.

Spud didn't react. Did he hear her? The mystery of the processes that poured through his processor were unknown, even to her. His servos whined, and his limbs flowed with life. His arm raised slowly until the glass he clutched so dearly was level with Aleya's face. She looked to the glass, then to the robot, then to the glass, confusion plastered on her face. Eve shared the sentiment.

Then, in one swift movement, he flicked the glass forwards, and a wall of cocktail splashed Aleya's face.

For a long second, no one did anything. Not one movement or sound. Until…

A series of chirpy beeps blurted from Spud, and he raised up. He cast a glance to Eve and Jere, chittering away.

Aleya spluttered and wiped the drink off her dumbfounded face. 'You fucking—' she hissed but was immediately drowned out by another, even louder bout of robotic chuckling. Spud backed up to let her scurry free, and she shoved past into the hall, pursued relentlessly by his laughter until long after she vanished into the Tortuga.

His amusement quickly faded, and he regained a solemn aura. Eve sighed and swept a handful of hair back over her ear. 'Thank you, buddy,' she said, patting him on the hip.

He regarded her with his usual neutral stare and gave an affirming beep.

'Let's get out of here,' Jere grumbled after a long moment, rubbing at his shoulders. He led the way back into the Tortuga with Eve behind and Spud in the rear.

Eve retrieved her glasses and slotted them back on her face before the onslaught of the Haven blinded her. The chaos of the Port Royal's gambling hall hit her like a wall, and she reeled for a moment but recovered before anyone could notice. Giving a polite nod to the security guard, she followed Jere to the precipice of the Tortuga's grandiose staircase.

He stopped and anxiously felt at the bridge of his nose. 'You know, I'm gonna have to deal with *that* later. She's still got my glasses.'

'Oh,' Eve said, remembering Aleya had fled with his glasses in her pocket, 'I'm sorry.'

'It's fine,' he sighed. 'I should be able to find my way back.'

Spud marched up beside him and let out an electric whistle. He unfurled his hand to reveal Jere's glasses safely cradled in his giant palm.

'How did you do that?' Jere demanded, dumbfounded.

Spud returned his astonished look.

Eve smiled. 'You're just full of surprises, aren't you, buddy?'

Jere took his glasses and set them against his nose. 'It should go without saying that I'll need that flinger as soon as possible, and I'll get right onto sourcing those capacitors for you. Iridia's a big world. I'm sure there'll be a few spares lying around.' He paused to give a swift gloss over the scene before them. 'I best be going then. No doubt Aleya will be finding the furthest bar from here to get hopelessly plastered in, and the next stop after that will likely be my workshop, so I should get everything locked down to weather the storm that's about to hit.'

'Right,' Eve grunted. Aleya was many things, and a drunkard was high on that list. 'We'll head over to the Gardens now.'

Jere gave her a curt nod. 'Take care.'

With that he descended onto the gaming floor and slinked away into the crowd. Eve watched him for a while, tracing his brown hair as far as vision would permit before he was swallowed up by the electrified mob. Her eyes lingered for a moment, picking out all manner of peculiar and unique characters. It still baffled her how there could be so many people in such a small space. So many carefree individuals who didn't have the threat of death ever-looming over their heads like Rain clouds or the probing tendrils of the Concordian atmosphere testing every square millimetre of their mask seals for a chance to slip through. The thought made Eve subconsciously reach for a mask she no longer carried.

'I'm so tired of being wrapped up in these people's lives,' she sighed, unintentionally saying her thoughts out loud. She was thankful her glasses shaded her teary eyes from the mass of people around her who shared nothing with her aside from a distant genetic heritage.

Spud turned to her but remained silent.

'Only Vaughn understands,' she said. 'He's the only one who gets it.'

She cast one more disgusted look over the crowd before she moved to leave, but something caught her eye—a heavy leather cloak draped over pale skin and long white hair. A pair of dull, white eyes glazed over in a sightless stare met her gaze. For a moment, the longest moment of her life, those eyes held hers captive until the cloak broke away. Eve reeled from the release. She hiccupped and flicked back to the queer sight but found nothing. She held her scan for a moment, unsure of what she'd seen, before dismissing it and stepping down the steps to begin her journey to the gardens.

CHAPTER THREE

Peace and quiet.

At the end of a long corridor deep within the Port Royal stood a door most unusual for an orbital station. Where the walls were moulded from steel and overridden with pipes and cables, the massive door was hewn of an elegant yet incredibly sturdy species of dark wood now extinct along with the people who'd cut it. The doorknobs were gilded and polished to a sheen, and carvings, both elegant and brutish in their nature, laced around the door's many panels where scenes of victory and defeat, love and hate, past and future, isolation and reunion, all intertwined with one another in a fine ligneous anecdote of the history of the orc.

Beyond the door lay an office of unmatched grandeur on this side of humanity's cradle. Every surface was a deep matte black that absorbed light while their edges, lined with thin strips of gold, accentuated the warm light given off by antique lamps to leave one in a state of bemused delirium.

The broad rectangular space was divided into lengthwise thirds with the outer thirds sitting a metre beneath the centre accessed by a pair of shallow staircases. Their walls were lined with bookshelves that stretched twenty metres high and were filled with faded tomes organised in order of chronology and the dead culture their authors' hands belonged to. Rich-wine leather lounges and artefacts housed in display cabinets stood atop fine rugs to break up the bookshelves and gave a sense of placement amongst the walls of literature. The greatest of these interruptions were a pair of giant doors, also carved from wood, which served as the entrance into the Museum of Vaughn, the largest collection of ancient human artefacts in the known universe.

At the head of a finely woven carpet was a wooden desk cut to the frame of an orc where Vaughn sat in a bulky leather armchair that entombed his shoulders in its soft chesterfield padding. A console was off to one side and a mannequin's head by the other, his peaked cap brandishing the cobra badge secured atop it. His eyes squinted through slim spectacles onto a ragged book prudently held in his hand, utterly detached from the passionate orgy of excess that was the Haven behind him beyond a thick wall of tinted glass.

He sniffed and delicately turned a crumbling page. A corner broke away under his fingers, and a little piece of him died with it. A groan rumbled up his throat, but there was no point fretting over spilt milk. He placed the page fragment on the desk and made a mental note to have the book sent to his resident conservator for a repair.

Content he had gleamed all he could from the tattered book for the time being, he cautiously closed it and put it to the side. With a daintiness uncharacteristic of his kin, he removed his glasses and slotted them back into their case. He rose from his chair and stretched out, flexing the leathers of the vest he wore over a striped blue dress shirt. Brown shoes tapped against the voided floor, and his trousers matched the gleam of his hair.

Moving to the tinted window that looked over the Haven, he watched hundreds of playing chips a second be funnelled off the tables into a network of tubes to be recirculated back into play. A few new faces amidst the crowd of regulars made him smirk. A ferry laden with dozens of ships had recently emerged from the Ether experiencing 'technical difficulties' that required a few days' repair. With little else to do in-system and a bottomless wallet burning a hole in their pockets, a collection of the stranded travellers had made their way onto the Port Royal where they gleefully gave away their money in the hopes of winning it all back. But along with the army of whales ready to dump their wealth on the tables, there was another important person aboard that ferry: the prospective artefact seller.

Vaughn leaned back to glimpse at his console. No new messages. Displeased, he pulled up his sleeve and scratched at his left arm where a horrific branding scarred his onyx flesh.

Images of the Coalition Eagle, crossed blades, a stalwart tree and a scorpion; the signs of one marked for indentured service as a result of treason.

Tithebound.

His fellow orcs were dead. Massacred for their treachery while their world Orchia was reduced to ash by a worldender. The few that remained were forced into servitude under the Coalition's heel to pay off the debt amassed by their deceased species and cursed to live out their days in cruel reparation. Most were put into the atonement legions where their latent ferocity paired well with the cocktail of drugs that fed their aggression. It made them the ultimate battering ram to throw at a problem too suicidal for regular Coalition forces to engage and mass casualties were always the result.

Vaughn glanced back at his hat mounted on the mannequin. He was one of the lucky few who had been given a chance in another line of work, and by his stringent accounting, he was the last orc alive. He sighed, but it came out as little more than a puff from his nose. *The unfortunate reality for every world under the Coalition. A cycle of growth, rebellion and retribution. They had never been all that adept at indoctrinating our long-lost colonies back into the fray of wider humanity,* he thought, his mind turning to other examples.

The elv, Aleya's kin, fared little better. Their reunion with the rest of humanity was difficult and they remained quarantined on a handful of worlds under a tight watch. Then there were the dwarv, who were more than content with remaining on their home world, digging for resources the Coalition deemed too dangerous to acquire on its own. Vaughn thoroughly doubted they could survive out in the wider galaxy anyways.

As for the nine other colonies, they were remarkably bland. Regular humans on regular worlds with little more to hold against their names other than the historical footnote of their part played in humanity's first steps into the stars in the wake of *Eternity's* failure. *A cruel, benign fate from an uncaring universe,* he thought, glancing at his old Navy hat, then at the great doors into his museum. *But one still of great archaeological value to those who know the truth.*

A notification blipped on the console and drew his attention. He tapped at the screen, and a security camera feed popped up. A grainy image of a rather sheepish Jere waddled on the approach to the great mahogany doors to his office. A knock echoed across the room.

'Enter,' Vaughn said. He switched off the console and unlocked the door, leaving the task of opening the heavy doors to the boy.

With visible effort, Jere shoved the door open and started the long, arduous journey between the monolithic pillars to his desk. Vaughn watched in silence, a tiny fragment of his deepest essence relishing the discomfort the boy was already in.

After what must have been a marathon effort of concentration, Jere came to a stop before his desk with his arms held stiff by his sides. 'You wanted to see me, Boss?'

'I did,' Vaughn said, idly eyeing Jere off. The black stone walls of his office added power to his voice and sent a quaking shiver through the boy's gangly limbs.

He was small, even by baseline human standards, but that did little to discredit the threat he could pose. *His power is in his mind.* Vaughn dropped into his leather throne, hydraulics hissing under his weight, and motioned to an opposing chair, which Jere took.

'I won't keep you from reinforcing your workshop defences for long,' Vaughn started, recalling a plethora of notifications from casino staff regarding a rather disgruntled Aleya. 'I simply wish to clarify something.'

Jere, as stiff as cardboard, managed a nod. 'Sure, Boss. What can I do?'

Vaughn cut right to the chase. 'What is the status of your relation with Eve?' he asked, leaning his elbows on the desk and threading his giant digits together.

Jere picked up on the subtle threat. 'Sorry, Boss?'

Vaughn shrugged. 'Is it professional? Personal?'

'I'd say it's a bit of both, Boss.'

'Both?' Vaughn said, marbled features shifting in intrigue. 'Elaborate.'

Jere swallowed and readjusted his glasses. Vaughn knew he was picking his words very carefully.

'We both share common interests like tech, hence the overlap of our fields of operation,' Jere explained. 'We also like talking about just about anything that comes to mind, though that isn't much since neither of us are really talkers. We also provide services for each other.'

That last addition elicited a deep grumble from Vaughn.

Jere realised his mistake and his face flushed. 'Technical services,' he hastily expanded. 'Hers being the manufacture of components integral to my work under you, and in return, I provide her any parts she requests for the construct of Spud.'

Vaughn leaned back in his chair and brushed a silver lock behind his ear. The boy was telling the truth—he could see that. But that did little to settle his qualms. *Just because they haven't done anything physical—yet—doesn't mean the intention isn't there.*

'And these parts you…acquire for her,' he said, moving onto another subject for the time being, 'can they become a problem for us?'

'I only use the best sources on Iridia,' Jere assured, his voice a little more confident now that the matter had shifted. 'Whatever goes missing is completely untraceable and marked as wastage.'

'What of…modifications?' Vaughn asked, taking a moment to pick the right word. 'Could they be spotted?'

'Modifications?'

Vaughn sighed a little on the inside. 'Say a piece were to find its way into a construct, would the user notice any...differences?'

Jere pondered for a moment. 'Likely not. Depends on the part and how it is connected. If it's wired into the main power supply, then a variance in draw might garner some attention. Therefore, an independent power source would be preferable as well as a means to connect said device onto the mainframe.'

He stopped as Vaughn's intent clicked in his head. 'This wouldn't have anything to do with the data-flinger, would it?'

'It does.'

'I see.'

'You understand my intent?'

'I do,' Jere confirmed, although with a shred of hesitation that failed to credit utter compliance. 'I can see it through, but I'm not sure if it will be received well.'

'Leave that to me,' Vaughn assured him, and the relief on Jere's face told him that he had won him over.

'Yes, Boss,' Jere said. He made to rise, but Vaughn held out a hand.

'Wait a moment,' Vaughn said, waving him back into his seat. 'There's one more matter I wish to discuss.' His demeanour went grim. 'Your personal relation with Eve—is there anything more to it?'

The surprise in Jere's eyes told him all he needed to know.

'I thought so,' Vaughn tutted with disappointment. 'I may be an orc, Jere, but I am still of human lineage. I am aware of the biological urges someone of your age goes through and what that often entails.' His visage hardened, and amber flames licked from his eyes that melted Jere in his seat. 'So, let me make things perfectly transparent,' he growled, 'Eve is off limits to you.'

It took Jere a moment to muster any form of cohesion in his words. 'Boss? What do you me—?'

'I've seen how you act around her,' Vaughn accused, features now twisted in barely restrained anger. 'How your eyes linger over her. You see easy prey, something exotic to dig into, something pure to dilute.' He could feel his rage bubble with every word, every sentence. The image of Eve being defiled by such a lowly creature sent his blood boiling, and it took all of his self-control to stop him from drawing his pistols and riddling the kid with etheric holes.

Jere was trembling. 'Boss, I don't—'

'Quiet,' Vaughn said, mustering his willpower and calming the rage that seethed beneath his flesh. 'This is the end of it. Were you not one of the few who she holds in such an amicable light, this conversation would have ended differently.' He leaned forwards to pitch Jere in darkness. Jere retreated a little but remained eclipsed in his shadow. Vaughn thrust a stern finger at him. 'You are to leave her alone from here on out, and you are to maintain a purely professional relation, is that clear?'

'Y-yes, Boss.'

Vaughn slumped back in his chair and took up the ancient book. 'You know your duties; see to them.'

CHAPTER FOUR

The Botanical Gardens occupied a quiet corner of the Port Royal, home to all manner of exotic flora arranged into delicate biomes diligently imitated as accurately as one could achieve in space. Solid, insulated walls separated barren sandy deserts from cacti-filled savannahs parched by reams of throbbing sun lamps while dense humid jungles rife with succulents and ferns were barred from frigid tundras where a constant frozen gale buffeted stocky bushes, lichens and mosses. Despite being open to the public, rarely did any souls make the long venture down from the gambling floors, which made it a safe haven for Eve to escape to whenever the throbbing masses of people got on her nerves.

No corners were cut in ensuring the authenticity of the biomes conserved within, even rotating through the seasons on a standard-yearly basis. She loved spring and summer where the trees were in full bloom. Autumn had its charm, but the decay of life set in force by the season drew a crushing sense of dread from her. Winter—she'd never bothered to set foot in the place.

She was particularly fond of the temperate biome where neat lines of pine trees sprinkled the grass with green needles and pine cones to make an excellent surface to lay down on. The lumens were set to a comfortable brightness, and the temperature teetered at that sweet spot where it was neither too hot nor too cold. A gentle breeze ushered in by a series of giant fans directly connected to the tundra biome blew cool air through the pointy canopies.

She pocketed her glasses as she strolled up a smoothed stone footpath in a tranquil daze, the troubling thoughts of what had transpired beneath the Tortuga being nought but a distant displeasure gnawing feebly at the back of her mind. Her eyes were set on a trickling fountain at the biome's heart—a grandiose arrangement of thirteen iron-wrought humanoid figures covered in an earthen rust, standing knee-deep in a clear pool that spouted jets of water in intricate patterns. She knew the rust was symbolic of some kind but she wanted nothing more than to give them a good hit from a wire brush followed by a coat of rust protection.

Her eyes wandered up to the trees that flanked the path, climbing their thick trunks that were dug deep into the soil all the way to the peaks of their canopies where the pseudo-wind sent loose needles on a lazy descent to the ground. She inhaled; the air was thick with the smell of freshness and running water with just a hint of rust.

A smile pursed her lips. Despite the years passed, she still clung onto the awe of her first witnessing of such elegant creatures in the *Eternity*, and she always caught a sense of calm emanating from those ligneous beings as if they were lending their stalwartness to strengthen her heart and melt away her concerns. But something was missing. It was small, no more than a niggling thought in the back of her conscious, but enough to give a rise out of her whenever she set foot inside that garden. Dirt. There was so much dirt, and there was nothing to cover it.

She missed the grasses of Central Park, and her heart melted at the visage of the *Eternity* collapsing upon those wonderous creatures and squashing what little life remained on that damnable world. A tear threatened to break free, but she contained it.

Spud booped inquisitively, and Eve nearly jumped. She shot a look up at him and found his optics observing her with a benign curiosity. He had become increasingly adept at reading emotions since his birth, and she pondered the possibility of him reaching a point where he might be able to read one's thoughts. She was quick to discard the idea as wandering too far into the realm of the preposterous.

'It's nothing, buddy,' she said, turning back to the fountain. 'Don't worry about it.'

Spud stared at her in an apathetic silence that only made her concerns flourish. What was he thinking? Was he judging her? Was he disappointed? Eve shook the troubling thoughts.

No, he can't be. I'm his mom. She shed the painful memories that entailed such a word and set herself to searching for Jere's parts.

The footpath rounded the fountain's pool and sprouted off at even distances to lead away to the other biomes housed in the gardens. Where there wasn't a path, there was a bench, and she easily located a small crate hidden underneath the closest one. She tutted at Jere's laziness, even if there was little point in hiding something when no one was around to see it. She sat on the bench and dragged the crate out before her, feeling for a tab to open it but found only masking tape. A quick pat down over herself yielded an annoyed grunt from her.

Spud, who was standing behind the bench watching in silence, booped and held out a small knife.

'Oh, thank you,' Eve said, taking the knife and slicing through the tape. She handed it back, and he deposited it into back a receptable in his arm. She made a mental note to ask him where he'd found that.

With one yank the crate tore open, and a bounty of technological delights graced her eyes. A little shriek leapt from her as she beheld a technophile's dream. Glittering components fresh from the factory, reams of cables and wires with their insulation still intact and most excitingly, a series of squealers. She scooped the parts out and rubbed at their cold, rare elements, almost tempted to pocket the supplies for herself. *I can always keep what's left over,* she assured herself.

Content everything was there, she carefully returned the parts to the crate and sealed it up. Without a word of command, Spud manoeuvred around the bench and took up the crate.

'Thanks, buddy,' Eve said, checking her watch. 'It's half-past seven. Let's head back to—'

She paused, her eyes drawn to the fountain.

A lone, cloaked figure stood by the water's edge and observed the rusted figures with silent admiration. The wind fluttered its cloak, and strange offcuts in its hood gave it a bemusing double-peaked appearance to an otherwise formless being.

Cautiously rising to her feet, Eve shot a glance either side. She was positive there was no one else in the Gardens with her when she'd entered. Even Spud showed signs of confusion, which was a cause of concern for her. She forced a neutral demeanour about herself. There was nothing to say that this person meant any harm to her. *They could just be here to enjoy the Gardens.*

The wind died down, and even the sounds of the jets of water splashing in the fountain faded with distance.

'Lovely, isn't it?' an angelic voice, one heard both through Eve's ears and in her brain, beckoned to her.

The cloak turned around, and a pair of deathly white eyes amid a pale face and white hair greeted her. Eve could make out a vaguely feminine outline, but its unworldly presence made her second-guess every assumption she made. Her feet

78

turned to concrete, and her breath was stuck in her lungs. Her heart stopped. Even Spud was still, his servos locked in dismay.

Eve swallowed and did all she could to pull herself away from those ghastly eyes but found herself drawn back to it. 'I-I suppose it is,' she stammered.

The cloaked figure smiled, and some of the weight around Eve's feet crumbled away. Air circulated in her lungs, and her heart restarted, bringing thawing blood through her arteries. She cast an arm out and grazed Spud's thigh, clamping onto his sturdy frame to anchor herself in reality.

'They call me Olympia,' the cloaked figure said, every word as soft as silk.

'Uh, Eve,' Eve replied, forgetting her name for a second.

Olympia nodded thoughtfully as if her response was preordained. 'I find it most peculiar for a place like this to exist in space,' she noted, casting sightless eyes over the pine trees, 'let alone thrive.'

'They take good care of it,' was all Eve could say. Her mind was at a blank. Nothing else in the universe mattered except for the words that slipped so gracefully from Olympia's mouth. She felt herself drawn into Olympia's every word.

'It reminds me of a place long ago,' Olympia said, her face softening into deep reflection. 'It gives me a pleasant feeling I had feared long forgotten.' She blinked and seemed to return to the present. 'I must go now,' she uttered, somewhat disappointed.

With a sigh she took off from her spot and glided toward Eve in a silent gait. Her movements were fluid, not held accountable by gravity's demands but with the grace of pure, limitless energy flowing along a course through time and space. Eve could have sworn Olympia was flying with her toes scarcely touching the steel path beneath her. She tried to discard the prospect, but a corner of her mind fought on with a newfound vigour in support of such an outrageous claim. As the otherworldly being drew ever closer, Eve feared she might reach out and touch her. She wished with all her will for Spud to do something, but he might as well had been made from rock.

Olympia instead altered course last second and slipped by Eve with the presence of a breeze. 'It was a pleasure meeting you, Eve,' she whispered as she passed by.

Her words wormed their way down Eve's ear and sent a trembling weakness all through her. Her mouth hung limp, unable to issue a response.

Olympia raised her head to the robot behind her. 'Spud,' she said with a curt nod.

She continued onwards until she reached the exit. The door unsealed, and she passed through in complete silence.

As soon as the doors closed and they were alone in the gardens, the universe returned to normal. Eve's brain was freed from its deadlock. Sound flooded back into her ears, and winds resumed their exfoliation of the pine canopies. The smells of the forest filled her lungs, and warmth welled up from her body as water jets shot up from the fountain.

Like a kick to a motor, her brain spluttered to life. Her thoughts were sluggish, and she was half-stuck in a dreamy state as her brain failed to comprehend anything. What just happened? Was this *Olympia* even real? Or a figment of her imagination? Doubt crept in, and she started to question her very sanity. *I must have dreamt it.*

'Do you know what just happened?' she asked Spud once she had regained control over her tongue.

Spud's response was slow as he, too, emerged from a state of wonder. *How is that even possible?* Eve asked herself.

A *bleep* from her watch shook her from her thoughts. She checked the time: 19:48.

'Shit,' she cursed, taking off to the door Olympia had vanished through.

Spud lumbered after her, carrying the crate of goods with utmost care. Eve opened the door, half-expecting the cloaked being to be waiting on the other side, but the corridor was empty as usual.

'You go back to the room,' she told Spud before taking off at a sprint.

It was easily a thirty-minute walk through the maze of twisting tunnels, never-ending staircases and sluggish elevators to Vaughn's office. She would have to run for her life and hope she would make it in time.

The one thing she never wanted to do was to disappoint Vaughn.

+*She has a terrible sense of time management,*+ the Foreigner said.

Spud spat an aggressive retort in defence of his mother.

+*No need to get emotional,*+ it tutted, +*I'm merely pointing out a fact. Nothing more.*+

Spud grumbled and continued on his way in Eve's shadow. His creator had long since vanished from his vision, but he kept track of her progress through the bowels of the Port Royal through his security camera links. He kept the live feed open in a corner of his vision as he cycled through replays of the past few minutes. Frustratingly, all the footage had fallen prey to a strange corruption that had rapidly eaten away at their fidelity until there was little but errant meta data containing time stamps and coordinate notes.

He shuddered. He had a duty to fulfill, and he had allowed two individuals, whose orientations were unknown at best, within touch of Eve. A crippling feedback look of negative connotations surged up from the deepest crevice of his programming and jolted through his circuitry. Fuses broke, insulation melted and alarming reports of malfunctioning systems plagued him as he switched himself for failing to uphold his most sacred of duties. He lost his balance for a second and careened into a wall, leaving a massive dent in his wake.

+*Careful, lead-head!*+ the Foreigner hissed from inside its housing. +*There's two consciousnesses in here, you know.*+

Spud straightened up, his momentary lapse in motor function subsiding along with his self-punishment.

+*It's about that prerogative, isn't it?*+ it inquired in a rare case of empathy.

Spud affirmed. A deep-seeded instinct, the genesis of which was buried in the darkest depths of his existence never to see the light, the prerogative was the firm distilling of his primary function.

To keep Eve safe.

And he had failed it twice within the hour!

He shifted his processes onto the so-called *Olympia*. Peaceful or not, she held such a bizarre sway over his own motor controls that he could do little but watch in dismay as she'd had her way with his creator—not to mention the data corrosion which was too prevalent to be a coincidence. He created a new profile and filled it out, storing any relevant data that survived the rapid expungement from his databanks for future study. He absolved to be better. He had to be because there was no alternative route, no work around. If he was to fulfill his sworn duty, then he must constantly function at his peak else all was lost. That was simply how it was.

There *was* no other way.

+*That is most interesting,*+ the Foreigner noted out of the blue.

Spud issued a query for it to expand on its thought; it was not often the Foreigner spoke in such a manner, and it proved to greatly intrigue him.

+*It took me a moment, but I do recall having seen this* Olympia *before,*+ it said before pausing to ponder. +*Yes! I remember now! Before the* Eternity, *I was in her possession!*+

Spud spat at its claim.

+*There's more to me than the* Eternity, *you dolt,*+ the Foreigner fumed. +*I have existed far beyond the confines of that damnable ship, both physically and chronologically. We may have shared this body since your mother plucked me from my prison and shoved me into your chassis, but don't think you know* anything *about me.*+

Spud gave out a digitised sigh; he had heard more than enough of this creature's ramblings of times before entombment within the *Eternity*. It was a whole lot of nonsense, if one ever queried him.

The Foreigner ignored his displeasure. +*Whether you believe it or not, it's the truth… I must contemplate this in solitude.*+

Spud dismissed the Foreigner, and his attention returned to the surface. His hydraulics detected a weight in his arms and he recalled being issued the crate of parts for safe passage back to Eve's room. With an affirming boop, he set off to fulfill his task.

CHAPTER FIVE

Eve was flat out of breath when she skidded to a halt before the deep mahogany doors into Vaughn's office. She fixed up her hair and checked her watch, relieved to find it just shy of eight o'clock. Chest heaving for sustenance, she rang the buzzer on the door's console, and it swung open almost immediately.

The office beyond was ominously dark, and the glittering lights of the Haven at the room's furthermost side brought up oddly nostalgic memories of looking out over the blackened wastelands of Concord at the fractured shape of Minor alongside hundreds of its meteoric downpours. An intense sense of over-exposure bubbled up in her conscious, and she instinctively reached for her non-existent mask. The door closed behind her, sealing out all external stimuli. She shook the grim feeling and marched onwards, passing glances at the paintings mounted on the office's mighty pillars to distract herself.

Realising her glasses were still on, she removed them and deposited them into her pocket. Her eyes were quick to adjust when they weren't under assault by the flares of public spaces, and she noted how Vaughn also favoured a more solemn approach to lighting.

Vaughn sat behind his desk in a suave recline, his attention gripped by a leatherbound journal of some form. Eve never understood his appreciation of books when computers were so much more efficient, but she kept it a personal gripe. He pulled up from his reading material and regarded her with a squint through almost comically small glasses. With a pleased grunt, he flipped his book closed and stood up. His gigantic frame instantly became apparent, but his gestures assured her that he meant no harm and never will.

'Eve,' he smiled with arms on his hips when she drew close enough, 'right on time.'

His voice resonated through the office and rattled Eve to her core. 'I cut it a bit close,' she admitted, a little embarrassed to have come so nigh to disappointing him.

'You made the timing—that's all that matters,' he said, beckoning to a seat made for her stature. 'Though, next time, I would prefer you come five minutes early. It's common courtesy and encourages punctuality.'

'I will,' she nodded, taking a seat. She waited for Vaughn to continue, but he had already moved on.

'Aleya,' he called out.

'Coming,' the elv grunted, strutting out from behind one of the pillars and ascending the stairs to his desk.

She wore a fresh set of black fatigues and had cleaned off any evidence of Spud's drink. There was a slight intoxicated waver in her step, and a burning cigarette was clutched between her teeth.

Eve stiffened. She knew Aleya would never attempt anything while in the presence of Vaughn, but that did little to diminish her fear. She wondered if the elv had paid a visit to Jere. She hoped he was okay.

Aleya stopped beside the desk, and the two of them met eyes for a moment. Eve's willpower caved first, which made her ears flicked in delight.

'Must you smoke?' Vaughn said, exasperated. 'You'll ruin your good looks.'

Aleya gave a foul look and ashed out the cigarette under her boot.

'This will be a simple purchase operation,' Vaughn said, ignoring her attitude. 'All that will happen is the seller will show me the relic, we will discuss the terms of our deal and come to an agreement for payment. Aleya, your duty will remain the same.'

Aleya crossed her arms with a grunt that said 'why the hell did you make me come here, then?'

Vaughn ignored her and turned to Eve. 'Eve, I want you to watch and pay attention to what happens. These deals can get pretty heated, and they require a tact that can only be learned through observation and experience.'

Eve nodded. She risked a glance at Aleya and caught her ferocious azure pupils glaring back at her.

'Not that it matters to me,' Aleya said, easing the pressure off to face Vaughn, 'but what's the name of this dope, and what's he carrying?'

'Orjey is his name,' Vaughn answered briskly, 'and he is carrying a totem from a pagan religion of Olde Earth. He's a feeble soul so this deal should play out without a hitch and far below projected cost.'

Aleya nodded, seemingly content with Vaughn's explanation. Eve sat in silence with her hands on her lap. She still had no idea why Vaughn had even bothered to involve her in all this. *I'm better off in my room making stuff,* she mumbled in her head.

'Vau—' she started but caught herself when Aleya shot knives into her. 'Boss?'

'Yes?' Vaughn said, unphased by her uncharacteristic use of his formal title.

Eve swiped a lock of hair out of her eyes. Her free hand clenched her pants, and a bead of sweat dribbled down her brow. 'I still don't understand why you need me here.'

Vaughn leaned back in his chair. It creaked, and Eve feared it might break under his immense weight. 'It's quite simple, really,' he said. 'I wish for you to begin taking on more of a presence in our organisation. I intend to further expand my operations, and I need people I can trust who can work in my stead.'

'Work in your stead?!' Aleya spat in disbelief.

Vaughn ignored her. 'The reason why I need you to work in my stead, Eve, is this.' He rose, strolled around his desk and down the stairs towards the shelves of papyrus tomes with his hands held behind him. 'Come with me.'

Eve extracted herself from the seat and followed him, scrambling up by his side a few metres beyond the stairs. He idly perused the shelves as he went and she wondered what he was thinking about.

Aleya stomped alongside them. 'Boss, what do you mean by—'

'You are to wait here,' he told her, stopping abruptly to pick out a leatherbound text from the shelf. 'I wish to speak with Eve in private.'

Aleya looked to him, then to Eve, then back to him. An indignant scowl broke through her aloof displeasure and she peeled away and marched back to his desk. She pulled her knife from her fatigues and pricked at her fingernails. Her venomous glower never left Eve for a second.

'The Port Royal has served me well,' Vaughn continued as he flicked through the book. Finding the piece of writing he was after, he returned it to its place and resumed his leisurely stroll. 'But like the ancient settlement of its namesake, it cannot stand up alone. The influence of a single base of operations is limited and brings all manner of risks. Much like how the ancient humans left Earth to ensure our survival as a species in the galaxy, we, too, must split our proverbial eggs into several baskets and diversify across a network of bases both interlinked and segregated.

'The Port Royal operates like a well-oiled machine, but we live in a legal grey zone. We provide a service as a hospitality venue, but the Coalition is also well aware of what happens behind closed doors. Thankfully, the Coalition is big—too big for its own good—and because of that, we have floated under the radar.'

A lump formed in Eve's throat. She knew he referred to the various back-deals and blackmails that Vaughn readily handed out like the breaths he took. She wondered what other exploits had been committed without her knowledge and immediately wished to never find out.

'But, with one wrong step, we risk drawing attention,' Vaughn continued. 'The longer you play, the more likely you are to lose. And as we go along, making tiny mistakes one after the other, the odds shift against us until we lose it all.'

They came up to the colossal wooden doors that guarded his museum. Like the doors to his office, they were built to the dimensions of an orc and so tough that only diamond-tipped saws could ever hope to fell them. Eve tried to imagine the size of the magnificent trees that could bear such slabs of wood—towering organisms stretching far into the sky with trunks many metres in diameter and canopies so dense no sunlight could ever hope to break through to the eternal night at their roots.

Vaughn tapped into a console hidden in an alcove beside the doors, and a hiss and a pair of clunks unbarred the locking mechanism. The console gave an encouraging bleep, and with a gentle push, he sent several tonnes of wood gliding out into a set of claws to hold them open.

A void was all that greeted them before a series of warm lumens ignited and brought light to a path that trailed out from the doors and split into dozens of intersecting avenues every ten metres. Between these intersections were hundreds of display cabinets containing all manner of oddities and peculiarities from across the galaxy and throughout every age in history. Swords, shields, articles of clothing, pieces of machinery, shreds of parchments, tattered flags, ceremonial objects, signs of royalty, everything. All held in perpetuality within their own sealed ultraviolet-impermeable display case filled with xenon gas and blessed with a holy spot of golden light.

It was the Museum of Vaughn—the end result of the blinding lights, blaring sirens, alcohol-inundated air, quick services, clattering chips, glittering karats, extravagant shows and lustful pursuits. It was all a means to fund a secret deep-dark institution curated from the rarest artefacts across known space to fuel an orc's patient hobby.

Eve adored the ancient nature of its contents and found Vaughn's virulent collecting fascinating, even seeing a piece of herself in his obsession. *Shame there's nothing from the* Eternity *in it,* she thought with a lull in her posture.

A relieved sigh whistled from Vaughn's immense lungs as if the pressures of the universe were blown away. He strutted through, admiring pieces as he went in an intellectual delirium. He paused momentarily by the portrait of a fair maiden postured in a greened background before his curiosity was captured by a black bicorn embellished with a knot of faded tricolore ribbons.

Eve followed him in an awkward silence, unsure if he had become too enraptured by the relics that surrounded them to notice her existence.

'Why did you call me that?' he suddenly asked.

His spring from silence caught Eve off guard. 'Sorry?'

Vaughn straightened up and peered down at her with regalness. 'Before, you called me *Boss*,' he pointed out. 'I've made it abundantly clear from the very beginning that you may refer to me as Vaughn.' His eyes turned to slits, and his skin tightened over his cheekbones. In the blackened surrounds of the museum, he could have passed for a ghost. 'What's changed?'

Eve set her eyes onto a nearby cabinet containing a length of parchment and tried to read the incomprehensible handwriting on it to distract her, but she could get no further than "We the people—"

'I see,' Vaughn nodded, drawing out the answer she neglected to give. 'Aleya has never held you in high regard.

She's a lion, and no matter how many times I tell her to change her ways, she will remain just so.' He sighed and dropped to a knee, his face level with Eve's. 'There are few I trust in this galaxy as much as you, Eve. Aleya—she has her merits, but she is also a loose cannon. A life behind a desk would sooner drive her insane, and with how she is on the liquor, she'd eventually say or do something to the wrong person. That is why I need you. Think you can do that?'

Eve nodded, though she harboured a sense of uncertainty. *Why is he doing all this now? How can I be the only one he trusts?*

Vaughn smiled, and a piece of her anxiety flaked away. He straightened up and resumed his stroll but now with a sense of urgency about it. 'You're talented with technology, Eve, but I see far more to you than you might realise. Of course, the Port Royal will always remain the core of our operation, which is why you will be remaining here, at home and in charge.'

The display cabinets thinned out, and a small clearing stretched out before them, but the path carried on as if nothing had changed. There remained a single piece before them now, a lone exhibit among a sea of darkness.

A great capsule, large enough to dwarf Vaughn's frame, held in a state of ice-restrained dormancy a machine of utmost nobility. Its vague, humanoid outline was wrought from a black marble speckled with veins of gold that somehow pierced the half metre of ice that contained it in a glittering spectacle. Sat atop powerful shoulders, the construct's featureless head held a lone divaricated optic, and its hands, easily longer than Eve's arm, were clenched into tight fists and crossed over its chest while its legs were pushed wide in a combat-ready stance. Reams of cables and pipes flowed from its body into the capsule, and a set of powerful manacles held its limbs and torso firmly in place. Beside its left shoulder was an incredible halberd, its shaft thicker than both of Eve's arms put together and its sharpened head cut in an elaborate form that tended both to elegance and brutality. Mist wafted from the seams in the capsule's glass while coolant tubes, thick enough for Eve to climb into, vented a latent scent of oil and something else she couldn't decipher.

Eve immediately recognised the machine. Their exploits were beyond count, and their creation was all but a mystery outside of the highest echelons of Coalition hierarchs. A mythos had long existed around the machines, and despite the uncountable cultures that consisted of humanity across the galaxy, they were still known universally as 'sentinels.'

She met the machine's gaze, and despite it being devoid of any signs of life, a crushing sense of insignificance and terror took hold of her. She buried her hands in her pockets and made herself look as unthreatening as possible. Could it still watch her even while under this state of duress? A part of her was both fearful of the destruction it could wreak should its containment ever falter and reverent of such a perfect example of engineering.

How Vaughn had managed to secure such a deadly exhibit piece still baffled her. Had he captured it while it was awake, or was it already held in stasis? It was common practise for Coalition Naval vessels to put their stationed sentinels 'on ice' during lulls between combat. Perhaps he'd taken his chance then? But that only raised further questions. She wondered how such a construct would act should it be freed of its prison. Would it carry a passive aura of silent intellect inherent with technology or that of a terrifying rampaging animal?

Vaughn halted in the shadow of the sentinel and regarded it with stern eyes. His fingers twitched behind his back, and he shifted on his feet as if he were preparing for a fight. 'This would all be so much easier if I had just one thing.' His tone was strange, a lamentation that harkened to a root cause deep within him.

Eve didn't like that. It was rare for Vaughn to divulge such negative vibes. 'What?'

'You remember when I found you?' he asked, rising a bit from his ruminations.

She nodded. *Why talk about this?*

His eyes narrowed to show a rare case of caution with his choice of words. 'I will admit, we weren't there with the sole intent of rescuing you. In fact, that was a happy coincidence, if I don't say so myself.'

Eve raised an eyebrow. She had long since deduced his presence on the satellite was purely for an ulterior motive, though one she was forever relieved to have taken place. 'Okay?'

'The original reason why I was onboard that satellite over Concord was to find something,' Vaughn said. He dug into his pocket and fished out a sleek remote.

In the floor before the sentinel, a seam opened up, and a small plinth rose to fill the void. Air whistled up along with it, then stopped with a clunk to secure it as yet another museum fixture. The plinth was mostly steel with many lengths of wire strung away from a head of glass. A rectangular mould was pressed into the glass in alignment with an array of sensors. A fickle assortment of finely tuned receptors built onto small spider-like legs protruded from the sides of the plinth and hung over the glass mould.

Eve eyed the plinth with intrigue. She had never seen *this* display before, yet the shape was vaguely familiar. 'What is this?' she asked.

'It's a special housing built for a rare piece of technology,' Vaughn explained, running a brutish hand over the delicate device. 'A one-of-a-kind that was housed deep within the *Eternity*.'

Eve gasped and beheld the plinth with a sparkle in her eye. She always held a passing interest in his collecting endeavours, but the very fact that something of such value and rarity were to have existed under her nose for most of her life ignited a hereditary passion she hadn't felt since her last deep dive into the bowels of that ship. *Something in the* Eternity *mattered!* she shrilled in her head. *We weren't just a footnote in the history of the universe!*

Her brain paused. *Did Mom and Dad know about it? Could we have done anything differently if we did?* Her mood soured, and grief for those she had left behind bubbled up. *If only we knew...* She grimaced, tears fighting up to the surface.

'What was it?' she asked, struggling to put on a strong face.

Vaughn saw her pain and put a hand on her shoulder to soothe the roiling tides in her heart. She steeled herself, and he smiled. 'It was a device built long before recorded history. A relic of such power and potential that even the ancient builders of the *Eternity*—with their admittedly limited knowledge at the time—failed to acknowledge a fraction of it. The manipulation of the Ether itself. Infinity.'

'Infinity? How is that possible? The laws of thermodynamics prohibit it.'

He nodded, impressed. 'A valid point. But the laws of the universe do not apply to that which was never borne of it. The device came from the Ether itself.'

That sounded like a whole lot of nonsense to Eve. She knew scant about the Ether, though the same could be said for the majority of humanity. A chaotic realm that existed between the threads of the universe like a sheet between blankets, it was a swirling dimension of violent energies and deadly radiation. But despite its danger, a purpose had been carved out for it. Human ships, whether carried aboard ferries or the illustrious vessels of the Coalition Navy, would leap through the Ether wreathed in ethereal energies and emerge on the other side of the galaxy. But the batteries used to power the Ether drives that granted such a feat were exceedingly difficult to produce and tightly controlled by the Coalition, which made even the shortest of trips prohibitively expensive.

'They called it the Taiji,' Vaughn continued, returning to the plinth. 'It popped up in scriptures all throughout history until, one day in the early third millennium, it vanished.' He smirked. 'Coincidentally, at the same time the *Eternity* departed Earth for its journey to Concord. By the time the folk of Olde Earth learned of their mistake, the *Eternity* had long since left the reaches of the solar system and vanished into deep space where there was no hope of tracking it.

'Until it reemerged not seventeen standard-years ago. It was a string of good fortune. I had known of the *Eternity* for decades and was lucky enough to be alive for its return to transitable space. But I wasn't the only one. The Coalition was there too. They built the satellite with the intent of laying claim to it because they, too, knew the Taiji's power.'

He pulled away from the plinth, exasperated. 'I'd say it was all for the best.' He gave a warm smile to Eve. 'Because, even though I didn't find the Taiji, I found you.'

Eve flushed and brushed a hand through her hair. She felt a little better, but she harboured some mixed feelings about the whole thing. *What would he have done if he'd found the Taiji? Would he have gone through all the trouble of taking me with him?* She shook the discordant thoughts away. *Of course, he would have!*

'Anyway, I hope that cleared some things up,' Vaughn said, guiding her back to the giant doors with a gentle hand. 'The seller won't be here for a while, yet. Quickly, go back to your room and shower and change. For deals like this, you need to look professional.'

Eve nodded, a little embarrassed that her state of dress had been called into question but she didn't argue with his logic. She let him lead her back into his office and made straight for her room. It was only when the lone mahogany door to his office closed behind her did she feel release from Aleya's burning ire.

'You have got to be joking,' Aleya hissed.

'I do not joke, Aleya, you should know that by now,' Vaughn answered. He dropped into his chair and took up his book, finding the page he was on. He knew that mentioning Eve's future prospects would have yielded a rise out of the elv and it was the main reason he had sent Eve back to her room. *Though she really does need to make herself look a little more presentable.*

Aleya stormed up to his desk and planted her palms firmly on his desk. 'She isn't fit to be in charge of this place.'

'And you are?'

'I—'

'Hands off the desk, too, while you're at it.'

She grunted and pushed back, ears furled back in displeasure.

'You were a strong contender, Aleya, I do not deny you that,' he said, putting on a small pair of reading glasses. 'However, certain attributes of yours leave much to be desired.'

'Like what?'

'Do you *really* want me to list them all? Because I will and it's a long list.'

She stiffened. 'I am still better than that rat.'

'Others might disagree.' He sighed, set his book down and took off his glasses. He wanted to put the matter to rest and his patience with her was thin enough as it was. 'Now this will be the last I hear of this, understand? Are you going to behave or will I have to take drastic measures?'

Aleya stood her ground for a moment but a firm finger from him killed the last of her defiance. 'I will behave.'

'You will *what*?'

She growled and her ears drooped like wilted leaves. 'I will behave, Boss.'

'That's what I thought,' he said with a warm smile. 'You should consider yourself lucky to have a life like this, young lady. Had I not come on that day—what? Twenty years ago?—you'd have been cut up and thrown away by those Coalition scientists just like your brothers and sisters.'

Aleya bristled. It was a soft spot for her. Unlike the orcs, who were simply gross physical abominations of the human form, her kin's gifts lay deep inside. They harboured an affinity with the Ether—a connection of sorts—which yielded great interest from the Coalition. Though for what means Vaughn could only guess. What he *did* know were the frequent population 'samplings' where Coalition researchers took swathes of elv children and disassembled them down to the molecular level. Aleya was one of those unfortunate souls but luck had turned a kind eye to her. Vaughn was in the market for a suitable specimen and she fit the bill perfectly. *They probably would have done the same to Eve if I wasn't there beforehand,* he thought, noting how similarly the fates of his two wards ran.

'And for that, I am grateful,' Aleya grumbled.

Vaughn detected a hint of sarcasm in her tone. 'See, I don't think you are. People like us—folk who don't meet the standards to be a baseline human—aren't liked too much— particularly by the Coalition. They see us as freaks of nature. Mutants. But what they don't know is the same can be said for all of humanity. Everyone has deviated from what we once were on Olde Earth. There's no hegemony anymore and the Coalition hates that. They force themselves upon the galaxy, making everyone conform to their idea of humanity. Those of us who try to break that stigma. Well…' He rolled up his sleeve and flashed the gruesome brandings that marked him tithebound. 'You already know. Do we understand?'

'I understand, Boss.'

Vaughn rolled his sleeve back down. 'Good. Don't forget your destiny, either. My plan for you is the only reason I tolerate your attitude.'

Aleya narrowed her eyes. 'I wouldn't dream of it.'

Vaughn turned back to his book. 'Good. Now go to the hangar and wait for Orjey to arrive.'

CHAPTER SIX

The door to Eve's apartment swung open and crashed into the wall. Spud lumbered through, and after giving a brief examination of the door's deteriorating facade, he closed it behind him with a tad more grace. He continued onwards and dumped the crate of goods on her workbench before carrying on down the hallway to the bedroom.

The bedroom was kept in a permanent state of twilight, but the diode in the bathroom was left on to beam a scalding white that overstimulated his optics. Vision dampeners accommodated for the brightness, but he still desired to go in and terminate that abominable light. He would have, had Eve not banned him from entering the bathroom after he'd broken one of the ceramic water vessels to stop it from flooding the casino.

He passed into the bedroom without causing any further damage and tactfully picked his way through scattered furniture and clothes in varying states of cleanliness. He momentarily pondered the reasons behind the need to clean one's clothes, and he saved a reminder to ask Eve next time he saw her. He rounded the bed and found his lonesome shelf housing all manner of small objects that had garnered his fancy.

He rounded on the spot a few times and dropped into a squat to face the shelf. His thigh receptable opened, and the gambling chips the well-hatted human had given him fell out into his palm. He adjusted them into a neat tower and added them to his collection on the shelf. He admired his skyline of chips and counted two thousand, eight hundred and ninety-eight chips of varying colours, notional denominations and even a handful that glittered with light from self-contained power reserves.

He gave a satisfied beep.

+*Why do you hold such a strong fascination with these things?*+ the Foreigner asked.

Spud issued a conflicted answer. If he was to be completely honest, he didn't know. He always theorised, since Eve had a lot of stuff lying around, that he should too.

+*Speaking of Eve,*+ the Foreigner said, gleaming a line off the top of Spud's active memory, +*or rather, the creature that she spoke to.*+

Spud prodded it to proceed but not before giving a harsh reprimand for skimming his surface data yet again.

It ignored his reprimand. + *I know she claims to be called* Olympia, *but that is simply one of many monikers she has gone by over the years. Much like we are now, Olympia and I were bound together in an almost unbreakable bond in aeons past all the way up to just before the* Eternity *was completed.+*

That piqued Spud's interest. He inquired further.

The Foreigner was uncharacteristically hesitant. *+I...do not wish to elaborate on such a sensitive subject. Besides, the details around that period are...fuzzy to me. But what I will say is this: Beware of her. Even when we were bound, her intentions were questionable. Her mind is a vault hardened by lifetimes of perseverance, and she is capable of feats impossible.+*

Spud dismissed the claims.

+I speak the truth!+ it exclaimed in frustration. *+When you and Eve froze like puppets taken by their strings,* that *was her influence being exacted on you. I honestly do not know why she hadn't simply torn you apart while you were under her spell and fished me from your wreckage then and there. Perhaps, her power has waned over the years detached from me.+* It paused. *+Or maybe she and your cherished Eve have something in common, eh?+*

Spud slumped to the ground and leaned back against the wall, issuing an accusation.

+Oh, please. Prerogative or not, there was no way in the Ether you were going to come even remotely close to harming Olympia.+

Spud spat a digital groan. He pulled up Olympia's file and trawled through it. Almost all of the data that pertained to her had corrupted beyond recovery and left only vague metadata behind as any indicator that an encounter had ever taken place. He performed another self-diagnosis, and all systems signalled positive, which did little to alleviate his concerns.

Maybe the claims were right, much to his chagrin. Such a feat was far beyond the realm of possibility, and the very prospect of being able to selectively erase entries from data banks, especially those as secure as that which formed his memory cores, was an absurdity to even compute. But Olympia was certainly *not* ordinary, and that posed a potent hole in his logic.

Spud mused. Perhaps such a feat was possible. Perhaps some creatures had mastered the ability to remain invisible and utterly incomprehensible. Perhaps Olympia really was a one of a kind just like Eve, the sole child of Concord.

+*Or, perhaps,*+ the Foreigner proposed candidly, +*she now stalks the same corridors as your beloved creator like a phantom in the night waiting for an opportunity to strike.*+

Spud shuddered. The idea of such a dangerous creature hunting Eve in the dark sent a dampening sensation that crowded his programming with invasive scrap code. The cold hard fact of his mechanical mind, a construct of heavy elements, reams of wire and exotic components all soldered together with the craftsmanship inherent of a creator well before her maturity coupled with years of haphazard upgrades and repairs, flexed a little. His logic wavered, and a brief outburst of violent code threatened to overwhelm the primary functions operating in his RAM.

It was a pain all too familiar to him.

He gave a quick scan of his surroundings, affirming no one was around. His chest clicked, and the crude external plating that lay over his inner components parted ways. Databanks reorganised their orientations, and reams of wiring were spooled back to make space for something emerging from his deepest core.

A data reader, built from a blueprint older than all of humanity's extra-solar colonies, emerged to the surface and precariously projected itself out of his body. It was a redundant piece of tech. A relic of a bygone era where discs containing data still held some relevance among much more efficient databanks and servers. Knowing Eve would sooner remove the data reader to free up the connections so thoroughly wasted on it, he had gone to great lengths in keeping it concealed from her diagnostics and innumerable probes with her tiny, dextrous hands.

On tortured servos, the disc tray extended out, and a small piece of folded paper sprung up a little now that it was no longer restrained by its polymer prison. With utmost delicacy, he plucked the paper from the tray and unfurled it. He flattened out the creases against the shelf, taking great care to protect such a flimsy parchment, and brought it up to his optics.

Age had taken its toll on the photograph. The colours had faded into a washed-out hue, and tiny shreds of crusted ink flaked away along its creases—not without a few fretful lines of code from him. Three human faces, wrapped in bulky jackets over form-hugging monotonous jumpsuits, stared back at him before the smoking wreck of an escape pod with a bold '7' printed on its flank. The first was a tall male with light complexion and hair, blue eyes and a stubble. A grin was plastered on his face along with an optimistic thumbs-up. Eli. The second was a darker woman, a little on the chubby side, curly black hair and brown eyes. A cool, worrisome smile held back an avalanche of stress. Nisma. The last, wedged in between the two of them, was a shrimpy girl who would be his mother.

Spud nervously flexed a set of hydraulics. Just computing the fact that he held such a cherished item from his creator who believed it to be left behind on the world of her birth along with the rest of her past life gave him a conflicted data-burst of guilty exhilaration.

His optics fixated on the young Eve. There was an immense difference from the Eve photographed and the one who walked beside him every day. Her head was disproportionately large for her body, her limbs looked hopelessly inadequate for any means of mobility and her stature bordered on the insignificant. He theorised the photograph being taken well before his creation, likely by a handful of standard-years when she was in one of her 'indev' stages.

Spud wondered how such a creature could become his creator. The manner through which she upgraded was still a mystery to him because she didn't undergo any massive part replacements like he did. Rather, she grew slowly, both in mass and intellect, over time through some indeterminable manner. He occasionally wondered if the Foreigner would have the answer (as it often did), but whenever he proposed the query, he was always met with a humorous dismissal accompanied with a sly off-handed insult at his intellect. But regardless of how she evolved, the tiny human whose straight black hair was being playfully ruffled by Eli's firm hand in the photograph was now the one who created him.

But what of *her* creation?

Spud flickered his view between Nisma and Eli. He knew of the concept of the binary split between the halves of humanity, but the means through how they are programmed and developed are beyond him. They were utterly opposed from one another and, by all means of logic, according to him, should have been incompatible.

And yet, they were not. They had created a being in their own image with their influence shown in equal parts. Where Nisma's olive and Eli's light skin met, a tan was the result. Where the mother's black curly hair met the father's straight blond hair, straight black hair came out. Even Eve's consistency, while not abundantly clear in her younger forms, had taken on aspects of both her mother's pudginess and father's musculature. Perplexingly, this was not shared by their eyes, with her taking on her mother's brown over her father's blue. Was it a choice? A decision made by the parents? Why not have one eye brown and the other blue?

That got Spud thinking. What about him? He was different. He wasn't built of the same stock as humans. There was no partner to assist Eve in her creation of him, no blending of forms to create something new. He was the product of her intellect and parts sourced from who knows where. There was no foundational building blocks to draw him back to her. No lineage that one could connect between them. Were it not for their tight mutual bond of reliance, there was nothing to keep them together. But she still treated him as her greatest creation.

As her son.

That puzzled his logic matrixes. What was he missing? The answer remained frustratingly elusive, so he discarded the idea for the time being. He had a duty to uphold, and all the wanton theory-crafting was a distraction he could do without.

+*You were never designed to do this, you know,*+ the Foreigner said. +*This was never Eve's intent.*+

Spud languished the creature's interference with his solace.

+*It's a mighty promise you made, but one, I think, you are sorely unsuited for.*+

Spud took that slight to the deepest of his foundational programming. He lashed out a barrage of binary insults.

It sighed. *+Swear at me all you want; you cannot deny it. You did what you needed to do years ago. All that you do now is pointless. It's impossible for a machine to understand the complexities of organic emotion, and yet you still dedicate bandwidth to it. This prerogative has turned into an obsession for you.+*

Spud gave a digitised huff, spitting out a ream of junk data.

+Yes, it is,+ it countered. *+Whether you like it or not, Eve will, one day, cease to be. It's a fact of existence for them. You can survive indefinitely because you can replace that which is broken and evolve when necessary. But them—they only have so long. Once their mortal frames give out, what's left returns from whence it came. Eve is no different.+*

Spud's chassis shuddered.

+I merely state it as it is. You can argue all you want, but you cannot stop what is inevitable. Best to not focus too hard on it and, instead, learn to accept that you will eventually lose her so that you can move on when you do.+

Spud loathed its sound logic. He rarely dwelt on the mortality of his creator because of the hopelessness it generated in him. He couldn't stop the passage of time or cease the decay of the one he cherished above all else in the universe. There was nothing he could do, and it went against his sole directive and purpose in existence.

If only there were a way to make her live forever.

He deployed a barrier between himself and the Foreigner, its efforts proving exhaustive for him.

+*Fine, be like that,*+ the Foreigner hissed. +*But remember, Eve never wanted you to become like this. She merely wanted a friend. A son. Not a bodyguard.*+

The door outside opened and closed, sending a flare of alerts rippling through Spud's systems. Thinking an intruder had managed to bypass Eve's security systems, he clambered to his feet and stormed out ready for a fight. He cursed his lack of vigilance and panickily deposited the photograph back into the data reader and retracted it back into himself.

'There you are, buddy,' Eve said, almost running into him as he tore into the living room. 'Everything good?'

Spud halted; his gauntlets seized into fists the size of cinderblocks. A cursory scan of their surroundings assured him that there was no one else with them. He gave an affirmative bleep and released the tension wrought in his servos as a hiss of air.

'I won't be here long,' Eve said as she squeezed past him. 'Vaughn wants me to look my best for this trade he's got me involved with for some reason. You stay here in the meantime.' She ducked into her room and rifled through the motley collection of clothes strewn about.

Spud stomped after her and watched his creator scurry around to pick up various articles of clothing.

'I don't know why he's even bothering with this stuff, buddy,' she grumbled. 'Why can't he just let me do my own thing?'

Spud didn't answer. Vaughn's reasonings were always far beyond his comprehension but they always made sense in the long run. He had a plan for everything and Eve was no exception. That got Spud thinking. What plan did Vaughn have for him? He hoped it was something good.

CHAPTER SEVEN

The heavy door opened, and two figures passed into the onyx abyss that was Vaughn's office. The first was Aleya, who held a firm lead with long strides and her typical disgruntled scowl. The second, Orjey, was a small brown-skinned man with black thinning hair who lugged a large box in his hands.

Fingers lightly drumming on his desk, Vaughn glared over the leatherbound book he was perusing. The merchant carried an aura of discomfort about himself, and his attention dashed in every which way except in the direction of the orc. He was dressed in a simple yet elaborately garnished style of robe with a length of ivory tied to his hip which Vaughn immediately recognised to be endemic to the insignificant world of Igbo on the Coalition's western fringe.

Eve gave a suppressed cough, which drew his attention from the wary merchant. He cast a critical amber eye over her as she stood idly beside him, her mind evidently at a daze. Her hair was a soggy mess, and her face could use a scrub, but

117

thankfully, it appeared that she had taken his suggestions to heart. The grey shirt atop grey pants she chose to wear, however, made her look more like a janitor than a member of his retinue. *Why couldn't she dress like a normal person?*

He sighed. How could he blame her for not knowing any better. It was hard enough just to get her out of her room. Though, he wished she would carry at least one set of nice clothes for functions like this. *You're not living on that rock anymore. There are eyes everywhere here. All watching and judging.* He tossed the vendetta aside. *She'll come around. She just needs a bit more tutoring in social etiquette.*

He pulled himself from his thoughts just as Aleya and Orjey came into modest talking distance. Aleya peeled aside and permitted Orjey to pass, taking up a predatory position a few metres behind him.

Vaughn lowered the book as if he had just noticed the merchant. 'Orjey,' he said, eliciting a small jump from the man, 'a pleasure to have you in my home.'

'It is an honour to be here, Scourge,' Orjey responded as he carefully lowered the box to the ground.

Scourge, Vaughn noted. One of his less favourable names. He rose from his hefty chair and rounded his desk to greet the man with a handshake, finding it to be pitifully weak. *This will be an easy deal.*

He released Orjey's hand and shifted seamlessly into small talk. 'How were your travels?'

Orjey sighed, visible exasperated. 'As good as Ether travel could be, I suppose.'

Vaughn nodded. He, personally, cared little for what Orjey had to say. 'An unavoidable fact of life, is it not?'

'Yes,' Orjey agreed. He had worked up a light sweat, and his eyes resumed their erratic motions.

Vaughn caught them lingering momentarily over Eve. *Peculiar.*

'Well then,' Vaughn said, kicking things into gear. 'Let us see what you have brought today?'

Orjey nodded and went about unpacking his precious cargo. The box folded away to reveal a sarcophagus of protective padding which was carefully peeled back one strip at a time. Slowly, the relic beneath began to shine through its suffocating covers, and a few teetering bobbles under Orjey's clumsy handling made Vaughn twitch with silent agony.

His mind was set at ease when the first glimpse of the uppermost head of the totem, an avian creature, likely an eagle or similar noble bird of prey, broke free for all to admire. *Some things never change,* he noted, drawing a strong correlation to the Coalition Eagle that dominated all of known human space. Next was a bison with broad horns as a show of both status and potential to kill. Lastly, a simian with its teeth bared in a cheeky grin. He found the latter animal to be rather queer when compared to its contemporaries. In all, the totem was roughly a metre tall.

Vaughn retrieved a tablet, one almost comically small in his hands, and waved it over the totem. A series of scans penetrated every layer of the relic and spat out a flurry of data that assembled into a three-dimensional scale model.

'As you can see,' Orjey said while he examined the scan. 'Dating sets this piece to be over eleven thousand standard-years old, well before the Period of Expansion, *and* DNA analysis of bore holes in the base matches that of termites from the plains of Western Afrikaan.'

Vaughn grunted and pulled up a carbon-dating analysis of the piece, which correlated the merchant's claims. Content, he dropped to a knee to give the totem a closer look. He picked out dozens of minute nicks, grazes and scuffs as was expected with something of such venerable age. The wood grain was in fine condition, but, sometime over its history, a fine film of varnish had been applied over the raw wood which, while doing wonders at preserving the piece, also came at a small cost to its authenticity.

He shot a glance back at Eve, who was watching on in neutral silence with her eyes glossed over. *Is she even paying attention?*

He offered her the tablet. 'Take a look, Eve.'

She shot a wary glance at the table and sheepishly waddled forwards to take it from his extended hand. She flicked through the tablet, eyes alight with digital life, while he returned to giving the totem a thorough visual examination. 'What's this?' she asked.

Vaughn didn't pull his attention away from the totem. 'What?'

'This,' Eve said, spinning the tablet around and tapping at a point of interest. She had somehow layered another scan atop the original and picked out a nigh imperceptible cavity deep within the totem.

A shadow fell over Vaughn and he reached for on of his pistols.

'Hold it right there,' Orjey said, reaching into his robes and pulled out a small remote detonator grasped tightly in his hand.

Vaughn froze and Aleya stiffened, her fingers slowly reaching for a revolver at her belt.

Orjey whipped about and held up the detonator for her to see. 'You, too, lovely,' he ordered at her before pointing to Eve. 'Over there and be quiet.'

Aleya's ears flattened, and a faint hiss whistled between her teeth, but she begrudgingly obeyed. She stopped beside Eve, who clutched the tablet close while her chest heaving under panicked breaths.

'A rather unfortunate turn of events,' Orjey said, a cocksure grin having swallowed up his nervous façade. 'I had hoped I could have gotten off-board before you tried to tamper with my gift.'

'What is it?' Vaughn demanded.

'You'll find out,' Orjey assured, stepping up to the desk. 'But since I won't be going anywhere now, I figured we could take this opportunity to talk.' He nodded at one of the seats. 'May I?'

Vaughn growled in acquiescence.

'If it's not too much trouble, I'd like to clarify something,' Orjey said as he nonchalantly dropped into a recline. 'You are aware of the quelling of the orc rebellion on Orchia? Must have been fifty years ago by now?'

Vaughn clenched his fist, a primal anger rising up in his gullet. It had been decades since anyone had the gall to even mention the name of his homeworld while in his presence. 'I am,' he said before tacking on his well-rehearsed cover story, 'but my whole life has been on Iridia.'

Orjey raised an eyebrow. 'Is that so? Parents move here?'

'Don't know. Was an urchin until I was of age.'

'What about work?' Orjey said. 'You obviously weren't given this casino by birthright.'

'I did some mercenary work for the local mining guilds and the governor,' Vaughn said. That part of his story was true; it was how he managed to get hold of the resources and permits needed to build the Port Royal.

Orjey nodded, affirmation in his eyes. 'I'm not surprised. A man of your background, you could do some serious work. Same can be said for the orc tithebound legions. More than a few revolts were put down in quick succession thanks to their unmatched ferocity.'

'I'm sure they died with honour,' Vaughn said solemnly. The cruel scars across his left arm itched, but he resisted the urge to scratch. 'Folk tend to get creative when under stress.'

'Rightly so,' Orjey agreed, 'but I believe there is more to you than what you are letting on. You see, there were a few exceptions to the path of destruction. The naval officer route was one such route for those too intelligent to be thrown against a bloody wall and not attractive enough to become a consort.' He raised an affirming finger. 'In fact, a few years back, there had been reports claiming that, following a mutiny aboard the Coalition corvette *Sojourner*, a titheboundorc rose to become captain and roved the outskirts of Coalition space, raiding settlements and ferries.' He shrugged and playfully bobbled the detonator in his palm. 'None of it could be verified, however—little more than rumours, really—but these things tend to have a kernel of truth.'

Vaughn's features steeled into black stone, his eyes alight with a rage he only restrained through a firm reminder of those he also shared the room with. *He's got me by the hip,* he thought, calming himself.

'It seems we've hit the nail on the head haven't we, Scourge?' Orjey chuckled before his face went grim. 'Or should I say Vaughn?'

Vaughn huffed. 'What are you?'

Orjey smirked. 'I'm like you. Bound to repay the sins of my people.' He rolled up the robes over his left arm to reveal a quartet of horrifically scarred markings. The Coalition Eagle.

Crossed blades. A scorpion. An elephant. Tithebound. But there was something else. A crosshair. The symbol of a venator. Plucked from the crazed masses of the tithebound legions, venators were the Coalition's ruthless assassins and bounty hunters. Years of training and brainwashing made them into hyper-lethal machines hellbent on achieving their assignments. Once set on a target, there were only two possible endings, the death of their prey or themselves.

'You're a venator, then?' Vaughn said, the hairs on the back of his neck bristling. He had dealt with Orjey's kind before and the result was always messy. He scanned his peripherals. Aleya was a tensed canine, eagerly awaiting its master's command to attack while Eve shuddered and hid behind the tablet. Empathy coursed through his veins, and he picked out his pistols' locations before him. *Best to wait for him to slip up.*

Orjey rose and paced back to the totem, wary to never once present his back to them. 'Indeed, I am. You thought you could elude us forever, did you? Though, I must say, you had been very thorough in dispatching the other venators sent before me and you hid your trail well. But you can't escape what is due. You owe a debt to the Coalition, Vaughn, and because of your selfishness, everyone else around you will now too. The Coalition never forgets an injustice, but it is open to atonement.'

'Your elven girl would have made an excellent consort, pending some behavioural retraining,' he said, nodding to Aleya.

'And as for that thing,' he added, pointing to Eve. 'I'm sure a use could be found for her. But you and I, we're already lost. The Coalition only shows mercy once and all who are bound must pay their tithe.' He thumbed the detonator. '*You* had failed your end of the deal. So through me, the Coalition has come to set it right.'

Eve hiccupped and stumbled forwards, the tablet flinging free of her sweaty palms and clattering on the floor behind the desk. It drew Orjey's attention for a split-second, which was all Vaughn needed. In a fluid motion, he scooped up one of his pistols from the desk and fired. A recoilless burst of ethereal energy welled up from magazine and erupted from the muzzle in a bolt of wondrous light followed by a terrible scream.

The shot tore into Orjey's torso and exploded out behind him in a spray of blood. He fell to the ground in a heap, the pained scream of his death-shot's discharge echoing off the office walls in a cruel mockery of his voiceless demise.

Silence took control of the world for a fraction of a second before Vaughn's instincts kicked in. He leapt for Eve, who was staring in stunned horror at Orjey's corpse, blood already pooling beneath him. 'Stand back!' he shouted, shoving her behind his desk. He kept his pistol ready should the nigh-impossible feat of surviving an ether bolt prove true for the would-be assassin.

Aleya sprung forth, revolver in hand, and pried open Orjey's hand with her boot to send the detonator clattering free.

'Don't touch that,' Vaughn ordered her when she moved to pick it up.

Aleya stiffened and huffed.

'The tablet,' Vaughn beckoned Eve.

'Wuh?' she stammered.

'The tablet, Eve,' Vaughn repeated. 'Give it to me.'

A tiny shaking arm reached out from behind the desk, tablet clasped in its weak fingers. He took the tablet, careful to not exact too much force on her tiny digits, and probed it for the secrets it held. He zoomed in on the cavity and realised she had entered into some form of biometric mode that showed a vibrant life signature emanating from the cavity.

Eve poked her head out from behind the desk. 'W-what just—'

'There's a biological weapon inside the totem,' Vaughn said. 'Judging by its composition, it would have been released through the termite holes upon activation in a gaseous state. That explains the varnishing. Meant to keep it sealed inside to prevent premature release.' He turned back to her, a gracious smile on his darken face. 'Well done, Eve. Good spotting.'

Eve swallowed as though conflicted by his compliment and the weight of the situation they were in. 'Did you have to…s-shoot him?'

Vaughn nodded to the remote by Orjey's hand. 'If I didn't kill him, he would have activated the bomb and killed us. Either *he* had to die, or we *all* died.'

He sighed. This was not what he wanted to happen at all. Anger simmered his blood as true realisation that harm could have befallen not only himself and Aleya but Eve as well. He took a deep breath and let his fury perspire. His mind cleared, and he holstered his piece.

'There was no other way. I'm sorry, Eve. I didn't mean for you to see this.' He gave a slight nod to the door. 'You should go now. We can talk it out later.'

He didn't have to tell her twice. She scrambled out and gingerly circumnavigated the far side of the desk before jogging off down the long approach to the door. She shot a terrified glimpse at Orjey's body as she passed, and a soul-crushing whimper sent his heart into a death-spin. He held his stoic composure, eyes fixed on her until she had reached the door. *Of all the times...* he grumbled. *But if it weren't for her keen eye....*

The heavy mahogany slabs detected Eve's presence and opened. She dashed through, and the door closed behind her. The office echoed with her departure, leaving the orc and elv to stand in perturbed silence for a while.

Vaughn dropped to a knee and rifled through Orjey's robes for anything of enlightening value. The venator carried little, so he shifted his attention to the man's corpse. Sliding up the sleeves of his robe, Vaughn picked out the series of crude lacerations that marked him as a tithebound from Igbo.

Vaughn narrowed his eyes and flexed his left forearm. He thought he had been thorough in his eluding of his previous life. *Not nearly enough,* he noted, perturbed at the very fact that a venator had gotten so close to him while his guard was at its lowest *The last orc in existence killed by the hands of a fellow tithebound...* And then there was Eve. He cursed his lack of vigilance and arched his back with a sigh, leather vest creaking. *Too many good years have made me sloppy.*

He returned his attention to the tablet that had saved their lives. 'Deviously hidden,' he noted, reorientating the digitised scan of the totem.

He glared at Aleya, who was watching him firmly. He knew what she was thinking, and deep beneath the stalwart demeanour she held, she was scared out of her mind.

'What in the Ether was that?' he asked.

Aleya sniffed. 'It was a—'

'How did you manage to fuck that? You absolute bell-end!' he spat, baritone voice quaking the air. 'You didn't think to do a security check on him?! The bastard was carrying a damned remote detonator!'

She stood her ground. 'I checked him!'

A shadow fell over his mind. 'You did not!' he roared, crushing the tablet in his hand. He spiked the crumpled remains into the floor, caring little for the possibility of activating the totem-bomb.

Shrapnel clattered against Orjey's corpse, and Aleya flinched when a few pieces bounced off her fatigues.

'Maybe if you weren't preoccupied *drinking* all the time, you would have remembered to perform your duty! What use are you to me otherwise?!'

Terror flickered through her eyes, but she said nothing, which served to only infuriate him more. It took all of his self-control to stop himself from lashing out and tearing her apart.

He resorted to thrusting a firm finger at her. 'I'm this close to putting your Borelian hide on ice early!' He rubbed at his temples, and his rage petered out. He sighed and exhaustion suddenly took hold of him. He wanted nothing more than to lie down on a lounge and read a good book. 'Dismissed.'

Aleya's nostrils flared with contempt, and her arms bristled with reserved wrath. She spun on her heel and stormed out. The doors didn't open for her, and she had to wrench the heavy hinges wide to slip through. She didn't bother to close them behind her.

With a sigh, Vaughn returned to his desk and tapped at a button, closing the doors. He dropped into his chair and leaned back, silently observing the growing pool of blood under Orjey's corpse with threaded fingers. He unholstered his pistols and passed a caressing touch over them, finding their mute ergonomic blend of matte steel and wood comfortingly familiar. His thumb glossed over a monogram carved into the smallest of the pair, 'GH.' Sorrow flicked at his heart, and he placed the pistols beside the hatted mannequin before him.

He reached over to the console and sent out a hail.

'Yes, Boss?' a voice answered.

'Clean up, A-S-A-P,' Vaughn said. 'Prep for biologicals.'

There was a moment's pause. 'Yes, Boss. Clean-up team on route.'

'Thank you.'

With that, Vaughn ran a hand through his hair and plucked his book off the desk. He flicked through the pages and found where he had left off before Orjey's entrance.

CHAPTER EIGHT

+She seems off, doesn't she?+

Spud concurred. He shadowed Eve as she worked at her desk in a silent stupor. Not long after returning from her meeting with Vaughn, she had dug straight into constructing Jere's device with hardly an acknowledgement of his presence. It had been several hours since she'd started, and signs of exhaustion were beginning to show. A persistent film of sweat clung to her arms, and deep bags had formed under her eyes. Spud knew it was hardly optimal for her to work under such conditions, but he was hardly inclined to interrupt his creator's focus.

Instead, he took great strides to remain as still as possible while he watched the master at play. He envied her dextrous fingers and how effortlessly they handled a set of dainty pliers. He ran a quick diagnostic of his own hands and languished in their inept manner of design. An improvement to his digits was in the works, but the upgrade list was long, and quality parts were sparse. He exasperated a cloud of binary, deleted the subject matter from his RAM, and resumed his observations.

With a quiver in her hand, Eve took up a resistor with the pliers but dropped it. She sighed and hissed a round of curses before she mustered the composure to pick the resistor up and insert it into position.

+*Yes. Something troubles her,*+ the Foreigner noted offhandedly, its tone laced with annoyance. +*Care to do anything about it?*+

Spud entertained a line of code spontaneously thrusted to his surface from the other-being. He booped.

Eve paused and tilted her head up to him, tired eyes meeting unrelenting optics. 'What is it?' She shook her head, ebony hair waving with the motion. 'You wouldn't understand.'

He moved closer and stopped a few centimetres from her shoulder.

'Spud, I don't want to talk about it,' she grumbled.

He held his unflinching optics on her until she relented.

A deep growl rumbled from her, and she dropped the pliers on the desk. 'Fine!'

She divulged the details of everything that had happened, and Spud recorded the entire exchange in high fidelity to form transcripts. He updated her profile and slotted even the most insignificant of facial cues into niche categories of expression. Over the years, his recordings have ballooned to occupy an entire databank on its own, and he could say with certitude that every fragment of her life from his creation had been collated and formulated into an exact clone of herself in digitised form. He took great pride in his scrupulous arrangement of his creator's every word spoken, action issued and reaction offered, and in a limited sense, he could even predict her responses to certain stimuli.

He watched her talk, her shoulders slumping evermore under a great mental weight. Her breathing was uncharacteristically rapid, and her hands fidgeted anxiously. Her sorry state disquieted him; he had only seen her like this once before.

The orbital of his gyroscope wavered, and his chassis shuddered in a momentary loss of stability. He swiftly recalibrated the mechanism, and his balance returned.

Her story came to an end, and silence reclaimed the room. She sniffed and shrunk into herself.

Spud shuddered, distressed at failing to intervene with yet another threat to her life. He sent out comforting words to his vocabulator, but a dense software bulkhead strained them into incomprehensible blurts. Hydraulics hissed. There was nothing he desired more than to speak in the same auditory manner that she did. So, he opted for a physical show of comfort instead.

He raised his arm, careful not to collide with Eve or the workbench. Making a few minute adjustments to ensure an optimal course, he lowered his hand onto her limp shoulder. It was a little too forceful, and she was pressed down by its mass before he corrected his miscalculation and alleviated enough pressure to make the gesture a genuine show of compassion.

Eve leaned her head against his gauntlet. 'Thanks for listening, buddy,' she said, a faint semblance of a smile cracking her lips.

Her approval sent a surge of electrons all throughout Spud. He retracted his hand back to his side.

+*Well done, Casanova.*+

Eve wiped her sleeve over her nose and straightened up. She brushed her hair back over her ears and took up the pliers with newfound vigour. 'Buddy, can you go to the restaurant and get me something while I finish this, please?' she asked. 'I'm feeling spaghetti. You can play a game or two as a reward.'

Spud lingered for a moment, unsure if he should leave his creator's side. What if she took a turn for the worst?

+*She'll be fine, and she needs sustenance,*+ the Foreigner pointed out.

Spud acknowledged its logic. He took one quick scan of the camera network in their immediate vicinity and found nothing that might pose a quantifiable threat during his short leave. He marched off and swung the door wide, smashing it into the wall, and made for the Haven.

From the corner of her eye, Eve watched Spud depart on his quest, a glint of admiration in her eye. *He's never shown such nuance before. Was it a fluke? Can he now understand complex human emotions?* She made a mental note to return to the subject at a later date and she returned her focus to the flinger.

It was a complex device, and the schematics called for components neither supplied by Jere nor in her stock of spare bits, but after a few modifications, she was able to make do.

She wondered why he still insisted on asking her for assistance with matters of the technological kind. He was just as proficient with tech as she was and had access to all manner of suppliers from Iridia below while she was a mere scrapper. *Is it just Vaughn trying to keep me busy? To slowly groom me for a future under him?* she thought.

The idea brought up flashes of the past few hours, and she scowled at the detail in which she could recall everything. She was mortified at how close she had come to death; a mere childish curiosity paired with her technical ability saving not only herself but Vaughn and Aleya as well.

But if Orjey had succeeded, we all would have been dead, she reminded herself. Her skin went cold. *What would have driven someone to such desperation? Was everything he said about Vaughn true?* She wracked her head as she struggled to make sense of it. She knew not to delve too deep into things she wasn't meant to know, but a chasm had been opened inside her and threatened to swallow her whole. *What has he been hiding from me?*

'All who are bound much pay their tithe,' she echoed Orjey in meditation, recalling Vaughn's anger bubbling up at the utterance of those words.

It was such an antithetic state for him. She always saw him as the stalwart gentle giant who took her in and guided her through life, utmost being how to handle the Coalition. *'Despite being the undisputed power in the universe',* she recalled him saying once, *'the Coalition is still limited by the expanse of it bureaucracy and empire. There are always bigger fish to fry, so if we keep calm and not draw attention to ourselves, we will be left alone.'*

Evidently not.

Her mind rolled the memory forwards and stopped at the moment Orjey was torn apart by Vaughn's shot. She was shocked. She thought she would have been devastated or heartbroken with the very fact that she had come so close to death and witnessed someone, who had become a parental figure to her, kill a man with such proficiency that there was no doubt it wasn't his first time. But instead she felt nought but numbness.

That troubled her. *Am I broken? Am I just so detached that I don't care for the death of someone? Or myself? Am I not human anymore?* She cast her mind back six years and half, a galaxy away, and was met by brief glimpses of a life she used to call her own on a world shrouded in the tendrils of cold and darkness but with more love and life than she had ever felt since her departure.

Abandonment, she corrected.

A hollow guilt overwhelmed her aloofness, and tears thrusted their way to the fore. She coughed, and her face went red. She dreaded this feeling, but she was also relieved. She calmed herself and wiped at her cheek, plipping a tear onto her finger. She rubbed it between her digits, letting the salty droplet stick to her skin. She planted her head against her hand, letting the tear soak into her Mark. *Humans cry.*

With the last screw pressed into service, Eve could say with satisfaction that the data flinger was complete. She set the piece down and flexed her fingers, unleashing a volley of cracks. Her stomach growled, and she wondered where Spud was with her food. *Must have gotten a little* too *preoccupied with the games,* she noted, hoping he didn't return with a bucket full of poker chips, which he somehow always managed to drop on his way to the bedroom.

The door unlocked and glided open. Eve braced for the impact but instead heard it gently close.

'Who the fuck do you think you are?' a slurred hiss dribbled out.

Every hair on Eve's body bristled. She spun about to see Aleya stumbling in. She was braced against the wall, bottle of spirits in hand. Her golden hair was matted, and a drunken flush shaded her face. Her fatigues were sodden, and her shirt had been ripped at one point.

Eve swallowed. 'Aleya—'

'Shut up,' Aleya hissed, ears twitching irritably. 'I know your *special little guy* won't be back for a while, so I thought we could have a little quality time together like we used to.' She made a lopsided charge towards Eve.

Eve leapt up, sending her chair clattering to the floor. She barely escaped Aleya's grasp, and she scrambled to the other side of the table. Aleya tried to pursue, but alcohol had blundered her usual graceful manner, and she tripped over the chair. Cursing, she wrangled with the wooden limbs she had become entangled with while Eve made for the door. She yanked at the knob, but the exit remained sealed. She thumbed at the console, but her hands had deteriorated into panicked tremors. Shards of plastic and metal peppered her head as a something smashed against the wall beside her.

'Where are you going, Eve?' Aleya called out, pegging another oddity of her creation at her. 'Don't you miss talking to me?'

Eve ducked, and the device exploded into a shower of scrap. She ran into the kitchen, dodging projectiles as she went, and took cover behind the countertop amidst mountains of seized servos. Heart pounding, she braced under the bombardment of twisted metal and wires.

'Come on, Eve,' Aleya whined. 'Got nothing to say now? You were so persistent before.' The counter reeled under an onslaught of debris. 'Vaughn's little girl. Always in his heart and mind.'

Eve tracked her voice and dove out of harm's way a split-second before Aleya rounded the counter and spiked the floor where she hid. Eve dashed back into the living room and took up a position on the other side of the table. She searched for an avenue of escape, but Aleya, whether intentionally or not, had inserted herself in between her apartment's sole exit.

'I've been by his side for decades, back when he was still roving ferries and merchant ships for slops,' Aleya cried as she stumbled after her. Her mood had soured, her ears like wilted leaves and tears dribbling down her cheeks. 'He's always looked to me for guidance and support when he needed a second opinion. I was his lieutenant, dammit.' She sniffed snot back into her nose and braced both hands against the table while she spluttered jargon.

Eve was dumbstruck. She had never seen Aleya like this before. 'Aleya, it's okay.'

Aleya's fists clenched, and her ears bristled. 'It will be.'

Teeth gritted, she uprooted the table and bowled it over. Consoles, components, scrap and all other manner of miscellaneous goods went flying. Eve slid back but was caught in the avalanche. She tried to dig herself out but Aleya was faster, grabbing her by the collar and throwing her against the galaxy screen. Eve's head cracked against the glass with a hollow, resounding thud. Aleya pressed up against her, wedging a leg in her crotch to force her knees into a compromised position while she squished her against a starry background.

'I was set to take over this place while he stepped forth into the galaxy,' Aleya hissed.

Eve groaned and her brain was awash with millions of terrified screaming voices deafened by her thumping heart.

Aleya drifted in close, nose almost touching hers, crazed, bloodshot eyes meeting terrified pupils. 'Nowhere left to run, darling.'

Eve gagged as a breath of alcohol assailed her nostrils. Aleya took offence to that and slammed her into the window. The glass shuddered but remained true. Eve blubbered in a daze as her head throbbed from the impact.

'Everything was perfect until the trip to that shithole you called home,' Aleya lamented, watching Eve's head bob with a sickening pleasure. 'But instead of the Taiji, we got *you*.'

'I'm sorry,' Eve managed to bumble.

Aleya chuffed. 'I'm touched, but your apologies don't mean shit to me.'

She took up her bottle and smashed it against the window, leaving a serrated cylinder in her grasp, hovering around Eve's neck. She wriggled in vain to escape, but Aleya kept her hemmed in firm and watched the girl squirm helplessly under her, satisfaction printed across her face as a great devilish smile. She pressed the bottle in close, and Eve froze when glass jabbed at her neck.

'Know your place, you inbred rat,' Aleya said, a sudden turn of clarity eroding away her drunkenness. 'The only reason you've even alive is because you managed to pique

Vaughn's curiosity as an *oddity* back on that satellite. Were it up to me, I would have wringed your neck the moment I saw you.'

She pressed the bottle against Eve's neck to emphasise the fact. Eve winced, and warmth dribbled down her neck to stain her collar.

Aleya eased off. 'Next time you undermine me, I'll send you back to your parents. Understand?'

Eve mumbled an acknowledgment. She heaved a sigh of relief as the terrible pressure was released, and the bottle was pulled away. She sighed and relaxed a little, but she was still in the grasp of a homicidal maniac.

Aleya gave her Mark a playful flick, making her flinch, before letting loose a displeased sigh. 'I made a promise to Boss not to damage his artefacts,' she said with a modicum of sadness, 'but he won't know if I do it *here.*'

She swung a tight punch into Eve's abdomen with enough force to uplift her. Eve crumpled into her bosom, core gripped with terrible pain. Tossing the bottle aside, Aleya took a fistful of her ebony hair and yanked her head back up.

With a firm hand, she grasped Eve's cheeks and pursed her lips together. 'How could that dorky little shrimp Jere find you attractive?' she scowled. 'His dick doesn't know what it wants.' She thrusted Eve's head back into the galaxy screen with a hard clack.

Eve gurgled and fell forwards. This time Aleya stepped out of the way, and she landed hard on the floor. Eve groaned, crippling pain tearing through her gut and all strength fleeing her limbs.

Aleya chuckled and squatted beside her head. '*Years* I've wanted to do that. I think it was worth the wait.'

She watched Eve squirm for a while before boredom settled in. She sprung up and took a moment to appreciate the devastation she had wrought. She strutted to the door and tapped at the console. The door unlocked.

'It should go without saying that if you speak to the Boss about this at all, I will end you,' she said before leaving Eve to wallow on her lonesome.

Eve grovelled on the floor for some time, the pain in her gut too much for her to make any attempt to pull herself up. Nausea came in bouts, but her heaves remained dry. She applied pressure to her neck to stop the bleeding, but her blood only made everything slippery, so she took her shirt off and wrapped it around her neck. Eventually, her pain began to wane, and she could muster the will to sit herself up. She slumped against the galaxy screen and beheld the sorry state of her room.

There was an affirming tone from the door console. She stiffened, deathly afraid that a change of heart had befallen Aleya and she'd returned to finish the job. The door swung open and smashed into the wall.

Spud lumbered through, plate of some miscellaneous pasta in hand, and closed the door after a brief doltish inspection of the damage. He paused, realising the change of state of the room, and let out an abrasive squark at the sight of Eve. He tore through the living room and shoved aside the table, tossing away the plate of food for it to splatter somewhere in the kitchen. He came to a dead still before her, staring down at her as if she were an insect.

Eve met his gaze, and she could have sworn she saw a glimmer of anguish in those soulless optics. She wanted to cry, but an even tougher force inside her held her tears at bay. She didn't want to cry in front of him.

She had to be strong.

Spud's optics flickered, and a deep static-ridden rattled his vocabulator. His shoulders arched, and his fists clenched into vices with the tang of hydraulics. He whirled around and marched for the door, ploughing through furniture and scrap like freshly fallen snow.

'Spud, no,' Eve said, choking on her words.

The towering automaton froze, servos torn between conflicting prerogatives.

'Don't do it,' Eve added firmly. She tried to pull herself up but was sent back down with a sharp pain. 'Take me to the bathroom, buddy,' she groaned, one hand clutching her stomach while the other held her neck still.

Spud didn't move.

'Spud?' Eve said, nausea blurring her vision.

The familial bond won out, and Spud lumbered back to her side. He knelt down, extending a gauntlet to her. Eve took it, but she lacked the strength to rise so, she slumped onto it and let him pull her up. With utmost grace, he cradled her in his arms, and she went limp as he carried her into her bedroom and carefully laid her down in the bathroom. She wriggled her feet to the ground and stepped off but was immediately met with pulsing agony, and she collapsed onto the sink. Her knees turned to jelly and buckled. She screamed as her guts rearranged against the porcelain.

Spud squelched with woe.

'Lift me up! Lift me up!' she begged.

Spud inserted his hands under her armpits and hoisted her up. The pain immediately subsided, and Eve sighed with ecstasy. She came level with the mirror and found an utterly pitiful creature staring back at her. Sweat-slick olive skin met matted black hair and brown eyes swollen red on the verge of tears. Her bloodied shirt clung around a neck like a sodden scarf, and a waterfall of crimson and sweat oiled her chest and throbbing abdomen.

A creature, barely human.

The dams broke, and tears burst forth as she bawled her heart out.

CHAPTER NINE

Eve's watch bleeped. She sighed and shuffled down her bed, leaving a silhouette of sweat in her wake. She had tried to sleep, but her blood was so drenched with adrenaline, she could only lay awake and nurse her wounds. Her neck had been wrapped in a bandage (a little bloody after a messy application), and she did her best to minimise movement or be granted a pleasant stinging reminder. Her gut was another issue. A self-examination involving a copious quantity of pain killers yielded no bone breaks or serious internal bleeding, but it still hurt like all hell.

She checked her watch; 29:00. The Port Royal ran on Iridia time, and for reasons beyond her, its cycles changed over at an incongruous time in the early morning. For many guests, its thirty-two-hour cycles bordered on the inhumanely long, and it was commonplace for gamblers to take stimulants to keep their binges going. It did little to bother her, though, whose body clock was already accustomed to Concord's thirty-one-hour cycles.

Spud kept a statuesque piquet over her with his optics trained both on her and the door. His imposing shadowy figure would have unnerved anyone, but Eve found his presence comforting, and she rested easy knowing her guardian angel watched over her, no doubt scanning through thousands of camera feeds for Aleya's return.

But that made her wonder. How did Aleya manage to sneak into her room without him noticing? She was completely inebriated and cameras watched every corner of the corridor leading up. There was simply no way she would have made it without his knowing.

Unless there's a place outside of the cameras, Eve proposed, recalling the dead zone underneath the Tortuga. The idea piqued her interest, and she wrestled her bedspreads off her and staggered to her feet.

Spud awoke from his sentry duty and rotated his head onto her with an inquisitive boop.

'I can't sleep,' Eve said, digging about in a pile of clothes for something decent, 'and I need to know how Aleya managed to get here unseen.' She slipped on a set of comfy tracksuits, grey as everything else in her wardrobe, and made it outside with Spud shadowing her.

The Port Royal was often dead quiet between early morning and midday, so Eve was certain there wouldn't be a single soul to witness her depart on her little investigation. She limped out, hand clutching her broiling stomach, and scanned up and down the hall. The presidential suites occupied a strictly exclusive section of the casino with a singular dead-straight hallway and the elevator at its centre.

Eve, readily familiar with the hall and accompanying rooms' schematics, could conclude with a degree of certainty that every locked door around her led to a suite identical to her own with what little space that remained being filled with cabling and piping.

She tapped at her chin. 'Unseen…' she mumbled, waddling to the elevator to call it.

It was a long shot, but she had nothing else to go off. The elevator chimed, and its doors opened. Eve and Spud clambered in, and she tapped for the floor that would give the quickest travel time to the Botanical Gardens.

A bulkhead unsealed, and a gust buffeted Eve. She passed into the Gardens' temperate biome and blinked under sunlamps set to midday intensity. The day-night cycle of the Gardens didn't follow the rest of the Port Royal and instead took the more orthodox twenty-four-hour cycle in imitation of Earth.

Eve soaked in the blissful atmosphere; the scent of pine needles, rustling tree canopies and bubbling water from the rusted fountain. Normally, the walk to the Gardens took fifteen minutes, but with her decrepit state, it was closer to an hour, and she felt every step of it. But now inside its revitalising aura, she remembered why she had made the arduous journey.

'You're up late,' Olympia said, emerging into her peripheral vision.

Both Eve and Spud jumped. That bewildering being, skin aglow in the artificial midday, was still dressed in her heavy brown cloak. The hood, bizarre triangular growths atop it, was flipped up to leave all but her face to the imagination.

'I couldn't sleep,' Eve replied. 'I wanted to go somewhere alone.'

Olympia smiled and nodded to Spud behind her. 'Why do you want to be alone when you have such a great friend?' She motioned to a park bench further up the trail by the fountain. 'Shall we?'

Before Eve knew it, she was tailing Olympia like a lost child. She sat down sheepishly beside her on the bench. Spud lumbered behind them but remained eerily quiet otherwise. The three of them watched the fountain's tranquil show for a while.

Olympia's clouded eyes turned onto Eve. 'You expected me to be here?'

Eve would have been the first to admit she didn't carry much hope in seeing the bizarre creature known as Olympia again. In fact, she didn't know why she was even entertaining such a preposterous prospect.

'Not really,' she shrugged, a little self-conscious under those cataracted pupils. 'More of a hunch.'

'And yet you came to seek me out anyway,' Olympia pointed out. She sang her every word in a tenor that resonated both ears and mind alike.

Surprisingly, her accent wasn't too dissimilar from Eve's, albeit a little more refined and laced with archaic influences. *Something's different*, she thought. *I'm not seizing up like last time.* Her pulse remained stable, and she kept command of her poise. If anything, she felt an almost amorous connection with Olympia as if they had been friends her whole life.

'I have seen your heart and judged you most noble, kind Eve and valiant Spud,' Olympia explained, seemingly reading Eve's mind. 'Before, I wasn't certain of how the two of you would react to my presence, so I clouded your thoughts— processors for Spud's case—just to be safe. I permit none to see me unless I desire it, and even if they do, I can easily erase all traces of me from their minds.' She returned her attention to the fountain, and the matter died on the fan-forced wind, her cloak fluttering the words into the breeze.

But Eve clung on. Despite her newfound allure for the creature, she still regarded Olympia with a healthy dose of scepticism. 'The last time we met, you said Spud's name before you left. How did you know that?' she asked.

It was hardly a foolproof query; Spud had garnered a small celebrity status aboard the Port Royal as a peculiar sideshow from his antics.

'It's my nature to know things,' Olympia answered, mind seemingly lost on the water show.

'Like what?'

'Everything.'

Now Eve knew Olympia was taking her for a ride. She suppressed a dismissive sigh and slumped back on the park bench, wincing as her core spasmed. *She doesn't know anything. This was all a big waste of time.* She moved to rise, but was sent back down with a crushing pain.

'You are hurt,' Olympia said. 'Was it Aleya?'

'How did you know?' Eve groaned. She took a few deep breaths, and her pain whittled away to a dull throb.

Spud shifted, roused from his silence by her pain, but he was settled with a wave. He gave an affirming garble and returned to his lookout. Eve wondered how much tension he was under while she sat beside a potential threat. *Probably a lot.*

Olympia turned back to Eve, her glowing face in a painfully bland neutral state. 'I do apologise for my vague answers. It's a habit I'm hard-struck to break. But I'm afraid you must accept that it is in my nature to know things.'

Eve grumbled but faced the fact that she was unlikely to draw out any more regarding the matter. 'Yes, it was Aleya,' she said. 'She managed to find a way to get to my room without being caught on camera.' She flicked an accusatory glance at Olympia. 'You wouldn't happen to have been involved?'

Olympia remained irksomely aloof. 'No. I find her to be a most despicable creature, unbalanced by her indulgent ways and internal grief.'

Her sudden break away from the predisposition for nebulousness came as a surprise for Eve. 'Grief? For what?'

Olympia shook her head, gold particles flaying off her white hair. 'I have already said too much. My role as an observer in this realm dictates minimal interference.'

Observer? What the hell is this thing talking about? Eve left the subject alone, and they returned to silence. She sensed a shift in the wind and guessed it to be the daily power-cycling which occurred at sunrise. The tree canopies wavered, and a shower of pine needles plipped into the fountain pool.

'You want to go home,' Olympia stated.

Eve was bemused by what she meant. 'I am home.'

Olympia tapped at her chin. 'Maybe, in a physical sense, but your mind—your soul—yearns for a place you once called home. You wish to return to where you were created, to set foot on the soil you were pulled from and breathe the air your lungs used to satiate themselves on. You need to go back to your homeworld, child of Concord.'

A grim realisation snapped in Eve. She had already found Olympia's uncanny knowledge of her unsettling, but no one outside of Vaughn, Aleya and their crew of tight-lipped employees knew of what transpired during that fateful encounter in the skies over Concord.

As far as everyone else was concerned, she was merely an Iridian street urchin employed by Vaughn for her technical skills. He had once claimed that, should the Coalition ever learn of her existence as a survivor of the *Eternity*, they would come and take her away to be tested, cut to pieces and studied down to the cellular level. *But if Orjey was able to track him down, could the same be done for me?* She narrowed her eyes. *Is she working with the Coalition?*

A deep hum throbbed from Spud, and his optics were now locked on the cloaked being beside her. *He doesn't like it either. I should find out more and tell Vaughn. We're in big trouble.*

She fixated on Olympia, all her surroundings melting away into a muted blackness. 'You know about Concord?'

'Yes, I have for a very long time. So long, in fact, that I daresay I outstrip even the most venerable of records on Earth.'

Back to the vagueness, huh? What is she even saying? That she's thousands of years old, now?

Eve caught herself before she rolled her eyes at the ridiculous claim. 'Okay,' she said, humouring Olympia for the moment, 'what do you know about Concord?'

Olympia smiled. 'You seek to extrapolate knowledge from me and inform your caretaker, don't you?'

Eve stiffened. 'So, what if I do?'

A light giggle rose up from Olympia. 'I know you won't. Your mind wishes so at the present, but you will have a change of heart.'

She turned and locked her sightless eyes onto Eve. A searing presence forced its way into her and rippled through every cell in her body, drawing out their secrets and laying it bare for all to see. Something coalesced in her heart, a swirling mass of indescribable terror. Eve squirmed under her examination but she couldn't break away from those horrible glazed white marbles until the probing presence, content with finding whatever it was searching for, retreated and the mass in her chest dissipated out across her body.

Eve cough up a mouthful of phlegm and slumped off the park bench. She grimaced as her gut constricted.

Spud booped in alarm and stepped forth. He reached for Olympia but was given pause by a deathly stare.

'I appreciate your concern, most loyal Spud,' Olympia said, 'but it is unfounded.'

Spud groaned, fighting a losing battle against an otherworldly force thrust upon him.

Eve regained a sense of order in herself. She saw Spud frozen stiff, limbs rumbling under a terrible pressure. 'Let him go, please!'

'Very well.' Olympia pulled away from Spud, and the pressure alleviated.

Spud stumbled a bit but kept his footing.

'What did you do to him? To me?' Eve demanded.

'Nothing malicious, I assure you,' Olympia said, extending a hand to her. 'I was simply performing an examination on *you* and protecting myself from *him*.'

Eve regarded the gesture with contempt but took it anyway. Olympia heaved her up with unusual ease for someone of such small stature and sat her back down.

'Discovered in twenty-eighteen, the Concord system was slated as the primary target for humanity's first extra-solar colonial effort,' Olympia said, monotonous as a computer performing a query. 'Built by Satomi Aerospace, the *Eternity* was sent forth for Concord on its ten millennia journey between the stars. Contact was lost with it shortly after, and the rest of humanity thought it had been claimed by the void.

'But it survived and arrived over Concord Prime seventeen years ago. Despite the planet's realised inhospitable conditions, a landing attempt was made. It was unsuccessful, and the ship crashed killing all onboard. Except for three. An engineer named Nisma, an athlete named Eli and their unborn child.' Olympia turned to Eve, grim. 'Need I go any further?'

Eve was gripped in terror. How did Olympia know so much about the *Eternity*? About Concord? About her own history?! She regretted ever coming down into the Gardens. Why did she think this creature was here to help her? 'What do you want from me?' she stammered.

Olympia softened. 'I merely wish to reclaim that which is rightfully mine.'

'What?'

'The *Eternity* was special. A one-of-a-kind creation. A feat of engineering and determination that humanity so vehemently strives to achieve. But it also took from a realm it knows little about and understands even less.'

'The Ether?'

Olympia raised an affirming finger. 'Correct; you are a smart one. The heart of the *Eternity*, that which gave life to everything, is a relic of Ethereal origins. It's known by many names, but it is most commonly referred to as the Taiji.'

Eve's eyes shot wide. 'Only Vaughn and the Coalition knew of it, and it was destroyed with the *Eternity*.' A flash of guilt rippled through her when she'd uttered those last words.

'Oh, I know about the *Eternity's* destruction, and I know it was *your* doing,' Olympia said, 'but I also know the Taiji survived and made it into orbit with you.'

Eve's eyes narrowed into pricks. Her mind drew a complete blank as terror as confusion seized her body. 'How do you know all this? Are you with the Coalition?'

'They wish I was in their fold.' Olympia smirked. She suddenly sprung to her feet and inhaled, taking in the hydrated air kicked up from the fountain. Something wavered under her cloak, but it was too subtle for Eve to properly see. She turned to Eve and gave a curt nod. 'It has been a pleasure to speak with you again. I can tell you are exhausted, so we shall continue our conversation when you have rested and recovered from your ordeal with the elv.' She spun about and glided away. 'Meet me here when you are healed.'

On soft, floating steps, she vanished into the neat rows of pine trees and dissipated into thin air.

Eve gawked for a moment, unsure how to process all that was laid down on her. She tried to stand up but found her knees weak. A sudden light headedness fell upon her, and the world went dark, the last thing she sensed being Spud's cradling arms catching her before she hit the ground.

CHAPTER TEN

Eve woke up in on her bed in a cold sweat, fifteen hours having passed. She rolled about, grimacing a little when she twisted her core, and it took her a solid minute to manoeuvre herself out of bed.

She waddled down the hall and into the living room, rubbing at a throbbing headache. Spud gave a bleep of warning, and she stopped, narrowly missing a collision with him. He marched by, carrying an assortment of wrecked components that he tossed onto the appropriate piles. The table had been righted, and the data flinger was left neatly in its rightful spot with the plethora of other unfinished projects that had cohabited the tabletop before its upending. He had done his best at arranging and reconnecting the consoles and diagnostics equipment but left most of it unplugged for her to set up as she wished.

An alluring smell wafted in from the kitchen where a delicious breakfast waited. She wondered how he'd managed to get it, severely doubting he would have left her alone to retrieve it. *No way in hell he cooked this.*

Her stomach growled, and she remembered it had been nearly twenty hours since she last ate. 'You didn't have to do this, buddy,' she said, grabbing the plate and a fork sitting by the sink among reams of coloured wire.

Spud booped, pulling out a chair from under the table and offering it to her. She gave her thanks and took her seat after a pained descent. When she was settled, he shoved the chair into the table which yielded a yelp from her. Luckily, she had anticipated the violent manoeuvre and raised the plate away from the table edge. She laid it down and started to eat, appetite overriding every other aspect of her life.

As her hunger was slowly satiated, fragments of what happened the previous nights floated to the surface. Aleya. The Gardens. Olympia. Their conversation of matters known only by a few. Then those known only to her. The accusation. The Taiji. She shuddered, a terror peering out from the back of her mind. *What have I gotten myself into?*

The doorbell chimed.

Eve froze, fork halfway between her mouth and plate, and Spud locked up and whipped about to face the door, ready to engage.

It chimed again.

Spud looked to Eve for guidance, but she might as well had been a statue.

A knock this time.

'Eve? You there?' a meek voice pleaded.

She could recognise that voice anywhere. 'Jere!' She leapt up, immediately regretting her haste, and shuffled to the door.

It opened to show Jere leaning on the door frame polishing his glasses. Before he could properly react, Eve yanked him inside by the arm and slammed the door. He gave a weak shriek and panickily slipped his glasses back on as he stumbled into her room.

Comically large eyes blinking, he took in the scene before him. 'Wasn't expecting *that*,' he said, clearing his throat, seemingly a little embarrassed by the girlish noise he'd made. 'You never let me in here. What's the occasion?' He turned back to her, and he took pause. His eyes flicked to her head, then descended in a lingering spiral. 'What happened?'

'Aleya happened,' Eve grumbled, returning to her food.

'Wait. Aleya came *here*?'

Eve nodded and sat back down; pain streaked across her face.

'She hurt you?!'

Spud booped, slamming a fist into his palm.

'Spud, relax. No need to get worked up,' Eve said with a huff. 'Jere's our friend.' She motioned to one of the chairs beside her, and Jere took it.

Spud grumbled but kept a close presence behind Jere.

'You have to tell Boss,' Jere insisted, trying to ignore the giant breathing down his neck. He shifted his glasses nervously and swept some hair over his ear.

'What can I say?' Eve spat. 'That she was able to bypass all the cameras outside while shitfaced? No way Vaughn's going to believe that, and Aleya will deny it. No doubt have an alibi set up too.'

Jere dragged another seat out from the table and leaned on it. 'But you have a way with him. He'll listen to you.'

Eve scowled. 'It was a stroke of luck. I had no idea what I was doing. We all should have been dead by now.'

'Then I'll say something to Boss.'

'No!' Eve hissed. 'You don't say *anything*.' She lamented and fought back a wave of tears. 'I don't want you getting involved in this.'

Her grim demeanour killed the conversation, and a tense silence followed, broken up only by sporadic clicking adjustments of Spud's gyroscopes.

Jere awkwardly turned his attention over the array of tech scattered on the table. His eyes locked onto the data flinger. 'Is that it?'

Eve hummed and twirled her fork about on her plate. She almost forgot Jere was sitting beside her. 'Oh, yeah.' Relieved to have finally moved on to something she loved, she took up the data flinger and held it out to him as if presenting an award. 'Ready to go.'

Jere cautiously extended his arms and plucked it from her hands. He weighed it cautiously in his palm, face ridden with conflict. It was a modest thing, the most notable features being a prominent antenna on its front and a length of wire where it would connect to a controlling device. Despite it being completely harmless, he still held it as if it were rigged to explode.

'Know how to work it?' Eve asked.

'I do,' Jere said, eyes dark. He pocketed the device and retrieved a small box. 'The capacitors came in on the latest exchange. I figured you'd want them as soon as possible.'

The Port Royal held a tight orbit over Iridia's equator where ten of its twelve space elevators were installed at even longitudes. Roughly every three hours, the casino came into close proximity with one of the elevators, and a small window opened up to permit a fleet of shuttles to make the bound across the void, ferrying eager gamblers to clock-on while their broke and exhausted brethren clocked-off.

Eve had never set foot on an elevator herself, but her mind would occasionally entertain the prospect of visiting one to truly get a grasp of their operations. Her eyes lit up. 'Are they good?' she chittered, beholding the box of electronics like a feline does a ball of yarn.

Jere bobbled the box teasingly. 'Do Machina capacitors sound good?'

'Jere, you're the best!'

Jere was chuffed by her response. 'Anything for you, Eve.' He held the box out, and she snatched it up.

'Hm, their packaging is opened,' Eve noted, tapping at a resealed seam in the box's side.

'They were caught up in a random search by customs, I'm afraid.'

Eve sighed. She had received more than her fair share of items torn open and destroyed by customs. Thankfully, the capacitors were in tip-top shape. She held one of the cuboid devices up to her eye. It was little bigger than one of her knuckles but had the means to improve Spud's processing efficiency by multitudes. She twiddled it in her fingers, amazed by the complexity hidden beneath a simple exterior veil.

The massive strides in technological advances humanity had made over the millennia never ceased to astound her, and it was no surprise that Spud had been almost entirely replaced by present-era parts. *To think Dad used to risk his life scrounging around for what is basically garbage here,* she thought, mood soured by the fruitless endeavour he had set out to achieve for her betterment.

She realised Jere had been watching her with a mild concerned gaze. An awkward smile curl her lips. 'Spud, over here.'

Spud move to her side, optics still fixed on Jere. Eve pressed a hidden button beneath his panelling and was met by a shrill hiss. A tiny compartment in his torso opened up to reveal an array of fuses jutting from the walls. At its centre was a fragile tray hooked up to a life support system of cables and tubes. She carefully disconnected the restraining plugs holding it in place and pulled it out. A series of bulbous capacitors aligned in two files greeted her, some of their glass casings yellowed by blow outs.

'You're gonna feel a little woozy for a moment, buddy.'

Spud blurted an acknowledgement.

Eve plucked out the decrepit capacitors one by one and replaced them with their modern counterparts. They were some of the last remnants of the *Eternity's* presence in him and a sense of regret hovered over her as she ordained what few parts of her old home remained to be disposed of.

'Disposed of...' echoed Eli's dreadful muttering.

Eve shook them away. *Don't cry in front of Jere, for Ether's sake.* She held her mettle until the last capacitor was installed and the compartment was sealed. She rotated around to the console on her desk and quickly plugged in a monitor and a diagnostic cable into an outlet in Spud's thigh.

Jere shuffled in close, gripped by an uncharacteristic enthusiasm. 'Are they working?'

'We'll find out in a sec,' Eve said, tapping away at the keyboard. A progress bar grew to culmination and a steam of data flickered by. 'Spud's accepted them,' she sighed with relief.

'Good,' Jere nodded, more reassured than her.

'How you feel, buddy?' Eve asked, patting Spud on the thigh. She watched Spud's optics align and refocus for a moment as he performed his own diagnostics. He returned to the surface world and gave a thumbs up. 'Yes!' she squealed, giving him a pat on the thigh. 'Well done, buddy.'

Spud chittered happily.

She shuffled the old capacitors in her palm in a bittersweet muse. *Barely anything left now,* she thought, momentarily considering putting them in a box for sentimental sake.

'Amazing, isn't it?' Jere remarked.

'How so?' Eve asked, fixated on the capacitors.

'Well. Roughly every ten years, our bodies completely regenerate,' Jere said, readjusting his glasses to read the code flowing by on the monitor. 'Can you believe that? Every decade we are an entirely different person? The same has happened to Spud. You've changed every part of him over the years; it's incredible how he still remains the same, personality-wise.'

Eve dropped the capacitors onto her plate and watched them clatter together like marbles. 'Almost all of him,' she said sourly.

'Almost?'

Eve didn't answer, her mind drawn deep into her thoughts. Her search for a replacement of Spud's processor and the strange object it housed within had been long and tedious. Despite its abundantly venerable age and wooden construction, she had never been able to locate even a substitute that even came close to its power. It was a one of a kind, and to make matters worse, the original was so thoroughly enmeshed with Spud's coding that there was no way she could extract it without killing him. That irked her. It was an ever-present reminder of Concord—and one that she didn't know if she could live without. She at least found some solace in Spud's similarities to humans. *Like us, he sheds the old and disused for the new and improved. He never forgets, but he's never stays the same, either.*

She sighed, her thoughts turning to herself. She wondered how much she had changed over the years. How different was she compared to the crying little girl who was found aboard the Rocket? How much of her had been erased by the slow grind of time. How much was left in her vague memories that grew dimmer with every passing year?

She rubbed her hands together and flicked at her hair. She adjusted her posture to catch her reflection in one of the idle monitors while she felt at the mutated flesh on her brow, wondering if Nisma and Eli would even recognise her. *I carry them inside me, but I'm not the same person I was. There's a fraction left, but it shrinks every day.* She tried to picture them, but their faces had become worrisomely blurred with time. *And they fade as well.*

Tears fought to the surface, but she held them back. She glanced at Jere from the corner of her eye. 'What do you know about me?' she asked, stretching her arms out before her on the table.

Jere turned to her; inquisitive eyes magnified through his spectacles. 'What do you mean?'

Eve immediately regretted saying anything, but she had passed the point of no return.

'Eve, what do you mean?' Jere prodded.

'About my past,' she relented, dropping her head into in her arms to hide. 'What do you know?'

Jere's answer was measured. 'That you're an Iridian orphan Vaughn adopted and took under his wing?'

Eve expected at much and caught a slight twinge of déjà vu when she compared how similar her *supposed* origin story was to Vaughn's. *What more lies have you told?* she mentally asked him.

'I'm not Iridian, Jere,' she said, prying herself from her arms. 'I'm from Concord.'

The wheels in his head turned slowly. 'Concord? Where's that?'

Eve shook her head. 'It doesn't matter. I barely managed to escape it with Spud.'

Spud nodded and motioned in a shrinking fashion with his gauntlets.

'That was when Vaughn found me,' Eve continued. 'It was a miracle, really. No one in the galaxy knows about Concord's existence, and why should they? It's a dead world. There's nothing of value there. Nothing left.'

She sniffed. *Dead world,* she echoed, hoping with all her heart for it not to be true. A shred of her conscious urged her to hold out for the contrary. What if her parents *were* still alive? The weight on her shoulders lessened, and a spark zipped through her eye. *They've done the impossible before! If anyone could, its them!*

Jere looked thoroughly confused, and even a glimmer of fear poked its head through. 'Why are you telling me this?'

Eve slumped back. She had already divulged too much, so she figured whatever she said next would have made little difference. 'After Aleya attacked me, I went to the Gardens and met someone there. She claimed to know about Concord and my history. She thinks I took something special from the wreck of our ship, and she wants me to help find it, but I didn't bring anything up with me aside from the Rocket, and it was thoroughly searched by Vaughn.' She stopped, a diode flicking on in her brain. 'Unless…'

'Unless what?'

Eve peered up at Spud. 'It's in Spud.'

Spud blurted a bemused bark.

Eve sprung to her feet. 'Buddy, sit down.'

Spud was hesitant, but he obeyed. He slouched to the ground with a thunderous clang and made his eyes level with his maker's.

'What do you mean it's in Spud?' Jere said, spinning about on his chair.

'Before the meeting with that dealer,' Eve said, repressing a cold shudder, 'Vaughn showed me something in his museum. A housing of some kind. It was empty, but the shape of what was supposed to be inside was oddly familiar to me. He said the relic that was supposed to be contained within is the most valuable object in the galaxy. Called it the *Taiji*.'

She felt around Spud's chest, blindly weaving lithe fingers between wires and tubes beneath his crude ersatz musculature in an almost lewd manner. 'Spud, open wide.'

Spud booped, his optics on Jere.

Eve sighed, a little amused at his bashfulness. 'It's okay; he won't judge. Now, open up.'

Spud's optics flicked between her and Jere. *What's gotten into him?* she thought. *He'd never done this before.*

'Spud,' she insisted, 'open up.'

Spud gave a reluctant buzz, and his chassis clicked and folded apart. Wires spooled out, and his innards hissed and spat as hydraulic lines were disconnected and machinery rearranged itself to permit the exodus of something deep within his frame. His heart, along with dozens of wires and cables still feeding power to his body, arose from the depths. A humble processor with a small piece of wood inserted on its face, it was ripe with age and held hostage a hypnotising jewel of swirling monographic energy at its heart. Despite the lack of life, it glowed a magnificent aura that bedazzled her eyes and swooned her soul.

Eve had always wondered what exactly that piece was. Now she knew. It was the Taiji.

'That *is* just like the housing from the museum!' Jere exclaimed, leaping up.

'I knew I had seen it before, but I just couldn't remember where,' Eve chittered, ecstasy sending a tremor through her hands. She clapped and smacked the table in delight. 'Kinda obvious now, isn't it? When I first built Spud, I used scrap scavenged from the *Eternity*. Despite the crash, it was still operating at an idle state with plenty of its systems in functional order!

'Spud's processor was something I took from the deepest part of the ship. So deep that even my mother and father didn't know about it.' Needles pricked through her heart as she spoke those words but she kept on. 'When I removed it, the ship shut down and soon destroyed itself.' A lump formed in her throat, and the high of her eureka washed away. 'My father was badly hurt as it was tearing itself apart, but we escaped before it detonated.'

Jere shook his head to break from the Taiji's alluring design. 'Eve, you have to tell Boss about this. He's been searching for that thing for decades. To think that it was right under his nose the whole time. He'd be thrilled!'

'But what will Vaughn do to him?'

'To who?'

Eve shuddered. *What do you mean,* to who*?*

'Spud!' she said. 'If the Taiji is removed, Spud dies.'

Jere tilted his head. 'You can build him again, can't you?'

Eve was barely able to keep the anger that bubbled up inside her down. 'No!' she exclaimed, smashing the table with her fists.

Jere flinched, eyes wide. Spud stiffened, a hair-trigger away from descending upon him.

'I can't,' she said with a calmer façade. 'Not in the same way he is now. He'll be different, his programming— memories—lost forever.' She trembled and sat back down, head in palm. 'I'll be killing him and replacing him with something else!'

Jere failed to realise his error. 'But, Eve—'

'No!' Eve screamed, her face going red. 'You've never made anything like him! Spud is special! There is no one else like him in the universe! I made him! He's my creation!' Tears welled up and burst from her eyes. 'He's my son, and he's all I have left.'

Jere moved to comfort her, but a firm garble from Spud held him in place. 'Boss is a smart man, and he cares for you,' he said sheepishly. 'I know he won't risk hurting Spud. He'll think of a solution that's best for everyone. He always does.'

Eve peered at him from between a gap in her fingers. Jere looked sincere, but a niggling sense of doubt lingered. She didn't know what it was. A latent sense of distrust in others? An over-attachment to her creation? A strange emotional concoction brewed up whenever she was around him? Her mind swirled with conflicting thoughts. She'd had enough of people for the day.

'Leave,' Eve grumbled before politely adding, 'please.'

Jere nodded. He rose and left her to her senses, his departure marked by the closing of the door.

When all was silent again, she dropped her head into her palms. *He's right. Vaughn will have a solution to this. He'll figure out a way.*

'He always does.'

CHAPTER ELEVEN

Vaughn looked over the silent play of suckers siphoning their hard-earned karats into hopeless bids from his tinted office window. There would occasionally be a loud cheer and a blare of lights as some yuck made a small fortune, but they were far and few between. Before long that winner would be back to where they were after chasing a non-existent 'hot streak.'

There were a few smart ones who would take their winnings and head for the cashier, but Vaughn had already laid down plans to have such individuals intercepted before they could make their escape with his money with offers of free accommodation, expensive seats to the latest show, free drinks, a taste of the latest psychedelic and more. He could offer it all, and the tantalisation always proved too much for even the most steeled of hearts.

The view soon became a bore for him, and he let his mind wander onto other matters, namely the issue of Orjey. Corpse disposal had been quick and easy; his team was well drilled and practised in such matters (one of the few elements of professionalism his criminal underbelly still retained), the body being hefted away and tossed down a garbage chute into the void to be burnt up on re-entry. The totem-bomb was discarded too, its value as a collectible now too tarnished to warrant a restoration effort.

When all loose ends were tied up and filed away, all that remained were Orjey's words. *'All who are bound must pay their tithe.'*

Vaughn unbuttoned his sleeve and rolled it up to give his mark of tithing a contemptuous glare. As rich as he was, he was still just a ghost that skirted the grey between law and disorder, life and death, befriending anyone he had to and slicing away those who no longer played his game. He had always believed he was one step ahead of the authorities, but Orjey was a deathly reminder of the contrary. *Something must have slipped. A mismanaged admin form. A rat among my folk. Something or someone along the line had gone awry.*

He considered his options. What did his enemies know? How long had Orjey been hunting him for? How long until another venator showed up? He scratched at his chin. *The Coalition was never big on subtleties. If this plan had failed, the next won't be as quiet.* He cursed his arrogance, and what irked him the most was how close it had come to success. *Wrong, it* did *succeed. Were it not for Eve's unwitting discovery forcing his hand.* A deep rumble rattled his throat. *That was too close. No more mistakes.*

'If only I could be rid of these damned fools for good,' he sighed. 'But not yet. Not when there are still objectives to achieve.'

He pondered over his grand scheme decades in the making—a plan to set right what had been wronged. It was what everything, the casino and the money, was building up to. He was so close, and it was his duty as the sole survivor of his people to see it through. All he needed was the Taiji! *But it's gone. Burnt up in that wreck on Concord.*

But, where he'd lost something he had spent years searching for, he'd found something else almost as precious instead. *Eve, a veritable jewel in her own right. She, alone, is worth a fortune.* The slow-growing smile on his lips vanished. *This is hardly the place for her. Maybe I was wrong trying to get her into the business.* He tightened his grip on the railing, and it groaned under the pressure. *But who else do I have? Aleya, maybe in her prime, before she turned her brain to mush on alcohol. Her only value is as a weapon and a specimen, now.* He peeled his hand away and regarded the distorted railing with disappointment in his lack of self-control. He brushed himself off on dark-grey trousers and straightened up his jacket so he could adjust his tie.

There was a chime from his desk. He left the gluttonous debauchery behind him and toggled the lock on his door. The slabs were stalwart for a second before one groaned open on purposefully stiffened hinges.

177

Aleya strolled through followed by a sheepish Jere, who was his usual nervous self and one firm word away from melting like butter under a ship's thruster. He fiddled with his hands and could only manage to look towards Vaughn for a few seconds before being forced back to the ground by his cowardice. Aleya appeared remarkably sober for a chronic alcoholic.

Perhaps my words got through? Vaughn noted, but he was quick to dismiss the idea. *She likely hasn't had the time to get properly drunk yet.*

'Better make it quick, short-stuff,' she hissed at Jere when they were within talking distance, slapping him forwards on his behind.

Vaughn held up a hand to her. 'Quiet,' he growled. 'You do not talk. Now, you *only* listen.'

Aleya's ears twitched, and she crossed her arms, thoroughly brought to heel.

Vaughn nodded to a chair, and Jere sheepishly took it. Aleya rounded behind him, no doubt day-dreaming of all manner of horrible things she wanted to do to the boy.

Vaughn dropped into his own throne and leaned back into the rich leather. 'How is Eve?' he started, taking a more amicable tone. 'She looked mighty shaken up after the *incident* we had yesterday.' He cringed at his use of the word. 'I meant to come see her, but this damned place has me running ragged.'

Jere readjusted himself, evidently warming up to the situation. 'She's okay. A little sick but good.'

'Excellent,' Vaughn said before lacing his words with a hint of expediency. 'Speaking of, I will have to get a move on with my schedule, so you'll have to be quick. Your insistence on having a face-to-face is rather uncharacteristically bold of you, young man.'

Jere nodded. 'Sorry, Boss. I wouldn't have requested it of you unless it was of the utmost importance.'

Vaughn planted his elbows in the desk. A glint of gold flickered from a baller ring on his pinkie as he fixed up his officer cap on the mannequin before him. 'Oh?'

'It's about Eve.'

'You gave her the capacitors?'

'She was a little suspicious of the opened packaging but she accepted them.'

'Are you confident in their functionality?

'I made certain they were set to the correct frequency, but there's something else.'

Vaughn was growing tired of the boy's roundabout manner. 'What?'

Jere shifted uncomfortably. 'Well, we got to talking about things. I'll spare you the details—I can assure you it was nothing romantic in anyway.'

Vaughn rubbed his brow. 'You're blubbering. Out with it already.'

'Y-yes, Boss,' Jere stuttered. 'I went to give her the capacitors, and she told me abou—' Something got caught in his throat, and he gave an awkward cough, flicking a very quick glance at Aleya.

It was enough to register a keen interest in Vaughn. *What have you done now, Aleya?*

After a moment of awkward silence, the hamsters in Jere's brain seemed to get to work, and words resumed their torrential downpour out of his mouth. 'I gave her the capacitors, and we came onto the subject of upgrading Spud when Eve started to act strange. She told me about her past life and how she isn't from Iridia but from some world called Concord and that she was the last survivor of a colony there.'

Vaughn tapped the desk with a firm finger. 'I see.'

'Then she was going on about your museum and that glass housing before the sentinel. She said she had whatever piece of tech needed to fit into it. Called it the Taiji.'

Vaughn's eyes light up. 'You're certain?'

Jere nodded. 'Yes, Boss. It's inside Spud acting as some kind of power source. Looks like a wooden block with a black and white gem at its centre. Eve showed me, herself.'

Vaughn's eyes clouded. *Could it be possible? I knew Spud was special, the sole example of a truly autonomous machine outside of a sentinel. Could she had inadvertently jammed the single most valuable item in all of history into that dull robot of hers?* He almost couldn't believe it. How could he have missed it? All those years, and it was right under his nose. *I carried the damned thing off that junker rocket!* A sudden swelling anger threatened to rip itself free of its chains, but he kept it in check, his only tell was a slight twitch in his brow. *There's nothing to be done about that. What matters is that it is finally within my grasp. My scheme is back from the dead!*

'But, there's something else,' Jere added, breaking Vaughn's train of thought.

'No?'

'She said she met with someone last night in the Botanical Gardens. Someone who also knew of the Taiji and wanted it for themselves. Apparently, this person doesn't know that it's inside Spud because they requested Eve to assist them in their search for it. Eve agreed, and they are to meet back in the Gardens.'

Someone knows? Vaughn's brow furrowed, and he rose from his chair. He tallied a mental list of every soul who could have possibly come into knowledge of the Taiji—associates, subordinates, hired experts, operatives inserted into prime position for intelligence gather, government officials, ferrymen. All were accounted for and either kept silent by means of bribes, threats or a gunshot to the back of the head. As always, he had been thorough. *Not thorough enough, anymore,* he noted, Orjey springing to mind.

'I see,' he said, tapping at his console to open the door out. 'Thank you for bringing this to me, Jere. I appreciate it.' He rose from his chair and looked back out over the casino. He ran his hand along the railing, letting his fingers dip into the creases of tormented metal. 'Be ready to move on short notice. Dismissed.'

'Yes, Boss,' Jere nodded. He rose and scurried out. The wooden slabs glided shut behind him.

Silence followed for a moment as Vaughn pondered deep in thought, and Aleya remained barred from opening her mouth. She quickly grew restless, and she marched around the desk to glare at him, tapping on the desk with lips trembling.

Vaughn sighed. 'Fine—permission granted.'

'There is no way in the Ether that *rat* has it,' Aleya spat, ears erect in rage.

'I'd appreciate that you didn't call Eve a rat, Aleya,' Vaughn said, disappointed. 'She did save our lives. You may be quiet now.'

A furious growl shook Aleya, and she stamped her boot in a silent protest that amused Vaughn. But his humours were short-lived, and his mind went straight to unpacking everything he had learned. If what Jere had told him was true (and, being as easy of a book to read as the boy was, there was no doubt), then the addition of this new character who also sought the Taiji was a problem. *Perhaps they are in collusion with Orjey? I might have less time than I thought. I cannot let slide.* But he had to be delicate. Eve was a fragile soul, and he didn't know what he would do if ill-will came about her.

But if the Taiji had slipped through his fingers—yet again—then there was little hope of it ever resurfacing in his lifetime. He cursed himself. *If only there was a better way.*

'Though unlikely, the very possibility of the Taiji being in Eve's possession, even if it's in that robot of hers, is worth investigating. We cannot let this opportunity elude us,' he said, returning to his desk in a leisurely stroll. 'True or false, we must act. The consequences we can deal with afterwards.' He dropped into his chair as an exhilarating sensation made him shiver; it had been a long time since he'd felt *that*. 'Good thing everything has slotted so neatly into place, hasn't it? You know what to do, Aleya. See to it.'

CHAPTER TWELVE

The Botanical Gardens were in bathed in silver twilight emitted from a diffused scythed diode buried deep in the roof. Eve gazed up at the grey light, taking note of its peculiar oval shape that grew and shrank through fortnightly cycles. Vaughn had once told her it encapsulated the beauty of Earth's moon and gave the Gardens that little modicum of extra detail in his façade. *But the place still lacks grass,* she thought, kicking at the bare dirt. *His fascination with Earth is so palpable. Why doesn't he just go live there instead?*

She caught herself. *Mom wanted to go there too.*

'Is Earth really that special?' she'd asked both Vaughn and Nisma.

She hadn't expect a reply, and a sense of longing for the blazing skies of Concord fell upon her. What she wouldn't give to see Minor, that tortured moon, set against a background of stars with the horizon alight with thousands of meteors again. *Concord sounds better.*

Spud stopped beside her and issued a puzzled boop.

'Just thinking, buddy,' Eve answered, lowering her gaze away from the fake moon. 'See Olympia around anywhere?'

Spud scanned over the trickling fountain, neat rows of pine trees and deserted paths. He gave a negative response.

Eve sniffed, unsurprised. She didn't know why she'd bothered coming. Olympia had so thoroughly terrified her in their last encounter a week prior that she wanted nothing more than to never meet the gaze of those clouded eyes ever again. But something had drawn her down into the Gardens the instant she could walk without terrible pain, a longing for knowledge of not only her history but the history of everyone who came and went before her. It was her solemn duty, as both the last survivor of the *Eternity* and the only child of Concord, to learn and carry on her legacy into the universe.

Dare she say…she just wanted closure.

She sought out a nearby bench and slouched into an ever-deepening recline, relieved to have some pressure eased off her aching core. 'I guess she'll reveal herself when she feels like it.'

She sat for a moment, mind in the stars, before the opening of the temperate biome's entrance pulled her back to the present. She straightened up and peered past Spud's leg in anticipation of Olympia's cloak to come fluttering by. But she instead saw something that shook her to the marrow of her bones.

'Well,' Aleya smirked as she strutted in, 'you've healed up really well for an inbred.'

Eve leapt up, and Spud sprung into a defensive posture. Aleya was tailed by a motley gang of underlings—men and women of varying backgrounds armed with an array of firearms. Among them, much to Eve's distress, was Jere. He shared her terror and clutched a tablet firmly against his chest, data flinger attached. Her shoulders shrunk, a forlorn expression killing her hope.

Spud guided her backwards until she was pressed against the lip of the fountain pool. Aleya and her gang formed a tight circle around them. He growled and cast a warding scythe with his arm. It was slow, but his arm carried enough mass to crush rebars. The crowd reeled back but resumed their positions in quick order.

Aleya tutted and crossed her arms. 'Now, now. You better watch your step, Spud. There's only one way this is going to end if you misbehave.'

Her attention shifted to Eve, azure eyes twinkling in the phony moonlight. 'I'm going to have to ask you to step away from your friend, Eve.'

'No!' Eve hissed, clinging to Spud's thigh.

Aleya's ears twitched with delight. 'I was hoping you'd say that.'

'Do it!' she shouted to Jere.

Jere fumbled with the device and tapped on the tablet. Spud gurgled in digitised pain as a spine-tingling grinding seized his limbs. He stiffened and collapsed backwards into the fountain. Stone shattered, and one of the rusted statues was crushed beneath his mass.

A tidal wave of water washed Eve out of the way and sent her sprawling on the path as a sodden mess. She pulled her head from the rapidly shrinking tide and wiped slick hair out of her face to see Spud in a horrible state. He spluttered reams of distorted nonsense, sparks flew from every orifice in his shoddy musculature and his body shuddered with vicious spasms as his gyroscopes faltered.

'Spud!' Eve cried, scrambling to his side.

A firm vice snatched her up and dragged her away. 'Calm down, young lady,' Aleya whispered in one of her ears. 'I just need that little wooden trinket inside him, then we'll go.'

Eve thrashed against her captor. 'No! You'll kill him!'

Aleya tightened her grip. 'Nuts to him!'

Eve wheezed as her lungs were wrung dry of oxygen. A terrible pain shot out from her gut. She grew light-headed, but she kept up her struggle, writhing and wriggling against Aleya's grasp while trying to stay awake. 'Spud!' she bawled.

'Shut up!' Aleya said, heaving Eve off her feet and dragging her to Spud's side.

Spud lay at the bottom of the drained fountain pool and spluttered in distorted agony. Eve cried and squirmed, teary eyes landing upon the jittering wreck of her greatest creation unable to look away.

Aleya let Eve drop into the dribbling dregs of the fountain. 'Lovely, isn't it?' she said, kneeling down behind Eve and squishing her face between her hands to relish in her plight.

'Why are you doing this?' Eve blubbered tearily through perked lips.

Aleya grinned. 'Does the *Taiji* sound familiar?'

Taiji. Eve looked past Aleya to Jere, who stood sheepishly behind the mass of armed subordinates. With great anguish, he shook his head and hid himself behind his tablet. She shook with anger. *The capacitors.* A firm push sent her sprawling in the water. She groaned, her core ablaze in terrible pain.

'Still sore, are we?' Aleya said before plunging a fist into Eve's gut.

Eve retched and her stomach swirled a toxic mix of pain and nausea. She gagged and spat out a mouth of bile that eddied about in the water around her hands.

Aleya pulled up a fist full of her hair and wracked her head about to look upon Spud's twitching form. 'Taiji! Now!' She relinquished Eve's hair, and she toppled back into the water.

Eve spluttered and coughed up vomit-laced water. Tears streaked down her face, and her limbs were meshed to the ground while she watched her son writhe. She prayed he couldn't feel pain, and he wasn't suffering because of her. Spud groaned and rotated his optics onto her in a silent plea for help. An anvil crushed her heart. *I'm sorry.*

'I'll do it,' Eve said to Aleya, slumping forwards.

'Restrain him,' Aleya ordered Jere.

Jere spluttered something akin to a panicked yelp and tapped away at his tablet. There was a confirming bleep, and Spud immediately became dead stiff.

It was a long and horrible moment before Eve, hoping Spud was still alive and fighting for survival, activated the unlocking mechanism to his torso. Wires spooled, and hydraulics hissed along with a few unhealthy crunches that rattled in her being. His chassis folded away and components reorganised themselves to allow the first signs of the relic that served as his heart to beat forth magnificent rays of imprisoned sunshine.

'That's a good girl,' Aleya grinned, ears twitching excitedly. 'I suppose you finally had a use for Boss after all.'

'Whuh?' Eve blinked, wiping snot from her nose. 'Boss?'

Aleya cocked an eyebrow, not surprised in the slightest. 'You didn't know?' she teased, leaning over Eve. 'You're just a display piece to him, little lady. A work in progress.' She smirked and straightened up. 'We both are. The difference is, I've grown to accept it.' She plucked Eve up from the ground by her collar and let her dangle helplessly with water sopping from her clothes. She dug through her pockets with her free hand and fetched a sleek knife. 'You should ask him about it once I'm done with you,' she said, playfully dangling the blade before Eve's eyes. 'Though, you might need to go to the medbay first. You copped a nasty hit from Spud while he was thrashing about.'

+*What's happening?*+ the Foreigner demanded. +*By the Ethereals, what is happening?*+

Spud snapped back, barely tolerating the squatter's presence while his entire existence boiled down around him.

+*Extraction sequence has been actuated. Eve's pulling me out!*+

Spud grumbled and shoved the Foreigner out of his head. He fought against the extraction procedure, but every system was compromised. Hydraulics functioned without command, resistors blew from overloaded charges, optics fed him double-takes, diagnostics yielded hyperbolically incorrect readings, data storage began to decay into corruption and his limbs had become deadweight.

He fought to take control of his own body, but something had latched onto his systems and overridden his command matrixes with discordant orders of their own. His optics refused to move, but thankfully, he didn't need to. From where he lay, he could still see Eve and Aleya in a tussle, and further beyond, a rather meek Jere, clutching a tablet with the data flinger attached to it.

+*So, he's decided to show his true colours,*+ the Foreigner hissed, weeding its way back into Spud's conscious. +*That damnable runt. I knew it was only a matter of time.*+

Spud shunted it back into its housing. He set about discerning counter measures, but every solution he sent forth was shot down with a brutal binary override. He could feel the virus eat away at his digital manifold like acid and render his processing inaccurate and sluggish to the point he could see the passage of time in his peripheries in almost real speed. But among the static-ridden storm of his decaying vision, something caught his ire. He retrained his optics onto the foreground in time to see Eve be lifted up by Aleya, knife poised to plunge into her beautiful brown optics.

Power surged up from the deepest recesses of his core and washed away a fragment of the data-melting corruption that plagued his systems. It was little at first, nothing more than a single zero changed to a one, but it set off a cascade of realigning datasets that grew exponentially until an almost imperceptible blip of electricity sent a twitch down one of his fingers.

'Aleya,' Jere said, colour draining from his face.

'What?' Aleya hissed, turning away from Eve.

'I'm getting strange readings from Spud.'

Spud's gauntlet clenched, and a soaring relief rushed through Eve. The Taiji withdrew, and a wall of interlinked steel and wiring retook their place. She watched life return to him bit by bit, systems formerly under the sway of Jere's data flinger now paying tribute to their true master. His arms flexed, gyroscopes realigned, and his head rotated with optics refocused in a newfound rage.

'Lock him down!' Aleya ordered.

'I can't!' Jere shrieked. 'He's overriding the virus!'

Aleya dropped Eve. 'How is that possible?! You said it was a sure thing!' She spun back just in time to see Spud lock optics onto her.

A deep, almost monstrous, roar rumbled from his vocabulator, and he launched to his feet.

'Fire!' Aleya screamed.

The Gardens became a cacophony of deafening sound as Aleya's entourage unleashed fury into Spud. Lead ricocheted off him in showering sparks or embedded themselves harmlessly into his external plating. Eve recoiled and made herself as small as possible with her hands planted against her ears and head buried in her lap. The gunshots became erratic as weapons were reloaded or ran out of ammunition all together. A few of Aleya's troops had already fled, realising their weaponry were incapable of maiming the enraged machine, and the rest quickly followed suit.

Spud ignored all of them, his sights set firmly on Aleya. He covered the distance between them in a methodical plod as if he were relishing the moment. Aleya, either too terrified or too awestruck of the machine, stood dumbly as Spud loomed over her. He laid two massive gauntlets on her shoulders, and a weak whimper was all she could muster.

'Spud, no!' Eve shouted.

Spud ratcheted his hands, and a horrific snap resounded off the walls. Aleya's head whipped about and came to a rest over her back. Eyes wide in bemused pain, she dropped to her haunches, and as her final act in life, coughed up a chunky throatful of blood over her back. Tension left her body, and she relaxed into a delicately balanced pose of death.

Eve turned away, gagging at the sight. Her knees went weak and jittery, adrenaline still pulsing though her veins, and her lungs gasped for air in short rapid breaths. A terrible fear flooded through her; a fear of her son. Did he abhor what he just did? Was he impartial to it? Eve shivered. Did he enjoy it?

A bloody gauntlet came to rest on her shoulder. She trembled and looked up to meet Spud's gaze. She could see it in his optics; his killing aura had faded and was replaced by his typical dull-minded self. Warmth poured out from their point of contact and brought a soothing reprieve to her anxieties. She laid a hand on top of his gauntlet, doing her best to ignore the blood that stained her clothes and made her palm slick. Her mind was a race yet nothing tangible could make it to the surface. She considered fleeing, taking a ship to someplace far away, but a thought stopped her. She still had a friend on the Port Royal, and she had to find answers for her ever-growing list of questions.

CHAPTER THIRTEEN

Head resting against a fist, Vaughn sipped at a tumbler of thousand-year-old whiskey chilled over a handful of silver spirit stones. He relished the ripened flavours of the volatile distillate and picked out undertones from the dozens of barrels that gave it an elusive note that transformed with every intake.

The stage set and the actors in play, he sighed and reclined back in his chair to watch on his console. *She's fallen far, but least she's still good at something,* he noted, casting a brief glimpse at Aleya on the security feeds as her trap in the Gardens was sprung. The noose tightened around Eve and Spud before the robot stiffened and collapsed into the fountain.

Vaughn repressed a groan as stone and iron were crushed and a cascade of water inundated millions of karats worth of rare ecological artefacts but the show played on.

Eve scrambled for Spud, but Aleya ripped her up and gave a firm punch. *Careful, Aleya.* The two of them spoke at length before Aleya heaved Eve over to Spud and released her. Eve plopped into the water and sloshed about like an overgrown tadpole.

Vaughn felt a pang of empathy for the girl as she rushed to her robot's side, no doubt crying her heart out, and a shred of him wished he didn't have to enforce this destiny upon her. *All for a greater purpose, my dear. Once things are made right, you will get enough parts to build ten more.*

Spud's spasming ceased, and his torso opened up, a glorious light shining through.

Vaughn found himself leaning forwards expectedly. He wished he was down there in person, but he knew it would have irreparably damaged his good relations with Eve. *You're not quite ready to be interred just yet.* He tossed the thoughts aside for the moment. The present belonged to the Taiji.

Aleya stepped forward and garnered Eve's attention. Vaughn wrinkled his nose as they spoke some more. 'Don't damage the goods!' he said, raising a little out his chair when she picked Eve up again.

Aleya reached into her pocket and a flash of silver twinkled in the feed.

He jerked up. 'Aleya!'

The feed faltered and static filled his view. He huffed and tapped at the console.

A few seconds later, the video cleared up, and he damn nearly spat out his mouthful of whiskey. A scene of destruction, bullet holes all over the place, Aleya on her knees with her head twisted grotesquely backwards.

'Aleya, you idiot,' he cursed, flicking through the camera feeds in the immediate vicinity of the Gardens.

He caught wind of Eve and Spud moving with haste through a corridor on the way to his office, and for the first time in years, he felt his pulse throb in his chest. He sat back on his chair and placed the tumbler on a mahogany coaster. He plucked his pistols from their mounts before the mannequin and checked their operating parts. A swelling bloodlust urged him to holster the weapons and ready for battle.

He lamented on the history both weapons carried on his soul. In his right hand was his original piece, a colossal hand-cannon built to his dimensions. In his left was a model sized for one of a smaller stature but no less deadly. He traced his finger wearily over the elegant monogram carved into the pistol's handle. GH. The initials of his former mentor, the first person in the galaxy to ever treat him with the dignity of a human being and, dare he say, his first true friend.

Vaughn had killed him, and woe softened his face. He hadn't wanted to, but it was a necessary evil if he was to set things right for his people. His eyes were drawn down to the tormented flesh on his left forearm that marked him for slavery in a society that had forsaken him for reasons not of his doing.

197

The Coalition Eagle. The crossed swords of war. The scorpion of betrayal. The stalwart tree of Orchia.

Orjey's nigh identical set sprung to mind and the crushing weight of the Coalition's wrath draped over Vaughn. *All I need is the Taiji.* Running a thumb over the monogram of his dead friend, he calmed the murderous wishes of his primordial self. *Too much blood had already been spilt in the chase for this dream.*

'That ends here,' he sighed, returning the pistols to their stands and fetching a snub-nosed tranquiliser from a drawer. 'If only we could have done this some other way.'

The corridors flew by in a blur. Adrenaline roared in Eve's ears, and she pumped her legs as hard as she should. Her mind was blank save for a single overriding urgency to see Vaughn. In all honesty, she didn't know why she was going to him. Maybe she subconsciously saw a means to resolve a terrible situation? Perhaps it was because he was the closest thing she had to a parent since that dark day back on Concord? Maybe he might forgive her? Like all parents do.

She skidded to a halt before the grand entrance to his recluse sanctuary. Craning her neck upwards at those great mahogany doors, she felt suddenly small before their silent judgment of her sins.

Spud gave an inquisitive boop.

'I don't know why I came here,' Eve said, her thoughts and hopes of Vaughn's status as a benevolent parent figure rapidly fading.

But before she could turn away, the doors unlocked and glided open. His office lay before her in all its extravagant glory, and Vaughn himself was halfway to the door with arms folded behind his back. He was dressed smart in a grey shirt and trousers, black vest and a long white coat draped over his shoulders.

'Eve,' he said with a welcoming smile, 'come in.'

She waddled inside with Spud close behind. The doors shut behind them followed by the telling hiss of hydraulic deadlocks engaging.

'How are things?' Vaughn asked.

Eve wasn't sure if it was a genuine question or if he was merely probing for weakness. How long had he been testing her? Had their whole relationship just been little more than a scientist observing the gestation of their laboratory experiment? She suddenly stopped before him, only just realising how immense and intimidating he was.

'I-I don't...' she stammered, mouth unable to form words.

Vaughn held up a reassuring hand and gestured with another to the open doors of his museum. 'Come.'

He strolled off, and Eve had to jog to keep up. They passed into the dark abyss of the museum and exhibits illuminated in their outwardly growing ring. He hummed as they went, pausing to appreciate a relic before continuing onwards. It was a manner so familiar, so nonchalant, that Eve caught an eerie sense of déjà vu from it.

They cut a path directly for the sentinel capsule and the clearing that lay before it. Eve tried to pick out the point in the ground where the Taiji's housing was kept, but not a single seam gave away its location. Her eyes then wandered to the sentinel, still bewildered by the magnitude of the being encased in its ice sarcophagus.

'So, Aleya's dead,' Vaughn said abruptly, coming to a stop just shy of the sentinel's clearing. He tilted his head down to her. 'Care to explain yourself?'

Eve would have swallowed her tongue were it not attached to her mouth. She tried to discern any indication of his alignment on the matter, but his words and demeanour came off as horribly aloof for someone who just lost one of their most trusted subordinates. Her throat tightened, and her knees jittered. She didn't want to risk an answer, and he would have seen the whole thing it play out on the security feeds.

'Silence will not get you far this time, Eve,' Vaughn said. 'Come clean and speak the truth.'

Eve nodded, accepting the notion that bad news aged about as well as milk. 'She attacked us and almost killed Spud by trying to take the T—' She caught herself before that damnable word slithered out her mouth.

'Take what?' Vaughn prompted.

Eve grimaced beneath him.

He leaned forwards, amber eyes burning into her. 'The *Taiji*?

Eve shuddered. Spud booped behind her, and his gauntlets clacked. She gave him a disarming flick with her hand, but she didn't hold much hope in it stopping him. She gave a meek nod.

Vaughn let out a breath and straightened up to match Spud's immensity. *Why is he so massive all of a sudden?*

'How long have you known about its existence?' he asked cooly.

'Only a few days.'

'And in that time, you never thought to inform me? It never occurred to you that I might have held a *passing* interest that you possess the most powerful object in the known galaxy? If word got out, we'd have the whole Coalition fleet upon us.'

Eve shrunk beneath his gaze, the tension sending her stomach into freefall. She didn't know whether she would have preferred him to be yelling at her. 'It did,' she admitted.

Vaughn sighed, his chest heaving. His fingers flexed and leather stretched. Eve had never seen him so fused, not even when Orjey damn nearly killed both of them. She half-expected him to pick her up and snap her in two. He could have easily done it, and she doubted Spud could have stopped him before she was dead.

'I suppose it's in the past now,' he said, muscles relaxing. 'What matters is what comes next.' He strolled off towards the sentinel as if nothing were amiss, giving a snap of his fingers for Eve to follow.

Eve scampered after him, and Spud plodded after her. A mix of emotions tore her in twain. She had been utterly terrified of telling him anything, but now that the words were said, his calm demeanour served to only frighten her further. Was he mad and simply taking on a more reserved approach to chastisement or did he simply not care? His complete disregard for Aleya was also a point of bemusement for her. *Doesn't he care about her at all?*

The floor hissed and split open, the Taiji housing rising up from the depths. It glittered in the golden light, and Eve regarded it with reserved displeasure.

'Eve,' Vaughn said as he ran a hand longingly over the glass. 'I'm afraid I have been withholding some most critical information from you.' He fished out the small remote that commanded the museum exhibits.

The ground shuddered, and steam plumed from thirteen holes in the floor, six on either side with the last just shy of the sentinel. Cylindrical vats filled with pulsating crystalline fluid emerged from the holes, submarine lights giving their contents a brilliant glow. People, one to a vat, hung submerged in suspended animation with their eyes open in an imitation of life. They bore features from across the human spectrum and were clothed in all manner of garbs ranging from sleek, ergonomic suits to elegant robes and headdresses.

Gold plaques polished to a shine glowed in the ominous defuse lighting, their engravings bold enough for Eve to read even from where she stood. Most of their words were lost on her, but some stood out to her. Ladakh, Electro and Highland were planetary names she had heard in passing, but the dates beneath them were so old it boggled her mind.

'You've known me as a collector of human history since the day we met, but the greatest relics of our history is us,' Vaughn said, casting a prideful glance at every human being contained within each vat. 'Millennia ago, after losing contact with the *Eternity,* humanity unlocked the secrets to Ether travel and set out with a fleet of twelve colony ships to different corners of the galaxy—the first steps of the burgeoning Coalition. But, as soon as they entered the Ether, the realm was wracked by a terrible storm that prevented all subsequent attempts to follow. When the twelve colony ships made it through to their designated systems, they learned of their isolation. Unable to return home, they settled on their worlds and made do with that they had.

'Thousands of years passed and the storm still raged. The twelve colonies had established themselves and survived many hardships. The stories of Olde Earth were long rendered to myth with some worlds having forgotten all about their old home. They developed their own cultures and wrote their own histories. Languages diverged. Religions sprouted. But, something strange was also happening. The worlds that had become their new homes were changing them—some more than others. By the time the storm subsided and the Coalition rediscovered their long-lost colonies, there were new sub-species of humanity waiting to greet them.' He paused for a moment longer over one specimen, a short and stocky man covered in brutish tattoos bearing a brilliant orange beard braided into intricate patterns.

Eve found the stumpy man's appearance almost comical yet depressing in a way. The plaque beneath him read: '*homo sapiens dwarvus.*'

She turned about, silently asking the same question to each and every person trapped in their watery tombs. 'Are they…?'

'Alive?' Vaughn interjected. 'Not in any meaningful sense. If they were to be removed, they would certainly be dead. In there they are preserved like the mummified remains of the great kings and queens of olde. In a sense, these folk *are* all kings and queens. They are shrines to their kind. Prime examples plucked from across the galaxy. But my collection is incomplete.' He stopped and motioned to the last three containers before the sentinel, all devoid of inhabitants.

Eve, still bearing an overwhelming obedience to him, subconsciously obliged. She drew near and ran a finger over the plaque of one of the vats; *homo sapiens elvus.* The one opposite read, '*homo sapiens orcus.*' The last, poised at the head of the assembly before the sentinel; *homo sapiens eternus.*

Eternus… she thought, looking up at the swirling mass inside the empty vat.

You're just a display piece to him, little Eve, Aleya's words echoed in her head. *A work in progress. Both of us are.* A terrible dread settled over her.

'I didn't want to tell you this while you were still so young,' Vaughn said, laying a domineering hand on her shoulder. 'I didn't figure your mind would have been able to comprehend it. But while I love you like a daughter of my own blood, you always had a destiny in my eyes.'

Eve was petrified, eyes stuck on the empty vat before her.

Vaughn dropped to a knee. 'Like Aleya before you, you would have to one day accept you fate and step forth to become a piece of my museum. It is unfortunate she died. The preservation process works best on the living, and it would have saved me a lot of scrounging to locate another suitable specimen.'

He gently took Eve by the shoulders and spun her to face him. His expression took on a childlike wonder, his amber eyes aglow, and his silvered hair sparkling. He waved at the *orcus* vat. 'If I could intern myself, I would. Perhaps I will, one day, when my time in this galaxy is at an end. You see? You're like me, Eve. A lonely creature dealt the worst possible hand in life. The last of its kind. You are the last purebred human of Olde Earth stock, a time capsule of genetics from before we took flight. You will know no one like you. You carry with you the memories of a society dead save for yourself.'

Eve blinked to fight back tears, the weight of his words heavier than the hands that held her in place. Of all the people in the galaxy, she always thought Vaughn was the only one who loved her like her parents. But to see the truth come crashing down upon her was almost too much to bear. She wanted to return to that deep dark pit of a world that was Concord. At least she felt at home there.

'Is this all I am to you?' she whispered hopelessly.

Vaughn nodded. 'I'd be lying if I said otherwise. But you are to be my most prized relic. Everything about you tells a story of us. You are of a most delicate stock that has remained undiluted through the aeons. Untouched by exposure to new worlds and environments that had formed inadequate mockeries of the original. It's the same on every world. You've seen the Iridian locals. Ever noticed how different they are to travellers from other systems? Hell, you've seen me! I *am* one! Even those who live on what was once Olde Earth are genetic shadows of what we used to be. But you are different. You *are* a human of Olde Earth!' His voice rose with adoration before sinking into grim reality. 'But this collection has always been a side project of mine. My true dream lies with the Taiji, and it's been under my nose for six years.'

Eve bristled and pulled free of his grasp.

Vaughn rose to his full stature. 'I need it, Eve. Not just for me but for everyone crushed under the Coalition's boot. Their power lies in their control of Ether travel. With the Taiji, I can render their Ether drives useless and take away the one thing that is keeping their empire together. I'll set everything right, and we can all live without fear of their tyranny.'

Eve didn't share the sentiment. A furious sadness took hold of her. 'How could you?!' she screeched.

Spud booped and stepped forwards, but she waved him down. She wanted to fight this battle on her own.

Vaughn was mildly taken aback. 'How could *I*?' he said in a powerful baritone. He spun to meet her, cloak waving elegantly. 'How could I save *you*, a scrawny rat from some irrelevant corner of the galaxy, from certain death and give you a life beyond anything you ever dreamt of? I had every right to leave you for dead on that ship, but I didn't.'

Eve roared and gave a ferocious shove that had no effect on him. With a wave of his hand, he sent her staggering back on her buttocks. She hissed as fresh pain rose from her injuries.

Spud blurted a digital expletive and stomped forwards, swinging a fist in a wide arc. Vaughn caught it and deflected it away, pushing Spud off balance. He stumbled but salvaged his poise. Vaughn took his cloak and tossed it aside, pumping his fists in an open challenge to the machine. Spud charged and swung. Vaughn side-stepped and landed a series of devastating punches into Spud's flank. Air and hydraulic lines burst and Spud clattered to the ground.

'Spud!' Eve shrieked, scrambling to her feet. Vaughn stepped in her path and snatched her up by the shoulders. She squirmed against her captor, but it was a pointless effort.

'I merely discombobulated him a little,' Vaughn said. 'Now, you can make this easy on yourself, or I will be forced to take more drastic measures. Hand the Taiji over, Eve.'

Eve shook her head. 'No, I can't. Spud will die.'

Vaughn's patience had just about run dry. 'You know he's just a robot, right?' he pointed out. 'You can always build another!'

'He's not just a robot!' Eve blubbered.

'It's a machine, Eve!' he shouted, viciously shaking her. 'It doesn't even know what the hell is happening to it! It's just a damn program reacting to what's around it. There's no thought processes, no sentience, nothing!'

The fierce tremors sent Eve's vision spiralling. 'No,' she murmured, voice-box rattling.

Vaughn growled. 'Fine. I gave you a chance to make the right choice. Now you have to live with the consequences.' He fished about in his pocket and retrieved the snub-nosed tranquiliser. He jammed it into her neck and fired.

Eve gasped as a dart brimming with anaesthetics buried into her jugular. Its sedating innards spilled out in a nauseating flood that rushed to her head. Her neck lolled, and her eyes floated in their sockets. Her vision faded quickly as the serum pacified her aggression and stole all tension from her muscles. She slumped into Vaughn's grip, consciousness quickly fleeing from her. A double-visioned glimpse of him carrying her back through the closing museum doors was the last thing she saw.

'You'll get over it with time,' he promised, his words barely breaking through her failing hearing. 'When you wake up, it'll all be over.'

The seals of the museum doors hissed shut behind Vaughn. He knew they would easily hold against a monstrosity like Spud. He laid the unconscious Eve down on one of the lounges. She looked so insignificant in its orcish proportions, and for a brief moment, her stillness took on a fearfully cadaverous stigma. Afraid he had given her too strong of a dose, he checked her pulse and was relieved to find a resting heartrate.

With a grunt, he strolled to his desk and issued a hail to summon a team equipped with the appropriate weaponry to deal with something as dangerous as Spud. An affirming signal blipped in response.

He dropped into his chair and idly flipped over the camera feeds to the Gardens. The last of the water from the fountain had drained away, and a state of peculiar tranquillity had returned to the Gardens. Aleya's corpse was still miraculously balanced on its haunches and resembled more a work of morbid art than a grisly demise. *Your arrogance was always a weakness.* Her replacement would be a simple fix, a quick jump to Boreas and the abduction of a suitable specimen while still in their youth ready to be moulded into the perfect exhibit.

It would take time, but Vaughn had the years left in him, and he would make doubly sure to keep the bad influences of the casino far away from them. That was his biggest failing with Aleya.

He stationed the train of thought and flicked through the other feeds in the Gardens, finding no signs of a gruesome discovery yet. *All this trouble,* he lamented, eyes falling back onto the unconscious girl slouched over on the lounge. He returned to her side, feeling nothing but pity for the life she had been forced to endure. An upbringing on the definition of hell, the loss of all she ever knew and her thrusting into a new galaxy unlike anything she would have ever comprehended. It would have been all but impossible for such an alien girl to have survived in the galaxy without help.

'Is that all I am to you?' her heartbroken cry echoed.

Vaughn ran a hand through his hair, torn. He had always intended her to become a piece of his exhibit, but hearing those words uttered from her mouth burled up a shred of doubt from a long-repressed corner of his self.

'Is it?' he asked himself. For once in his life, his logical side gave no answer.

With utmost care, he propped Eve's head up and lay a pillow underneath it, brushing some hair from her face. He sighed. He could have cloned her, but that was always a derisory solution to a most crucial problem—a way to make quick copies like some roadside karat-store garbage. They might have borne the face and body of her, but beneath, they would have been nothing like the original. The history. The memories. The experiences. They would have had none of that. *Petri dish-grown mounds of mush arranged into the façade of a living being like some half-assed attempt at a forgery of a masterpiece,* he lamented, touching her Mark with his knuckle. *There could only ever be one Eve.*

CHAPTER FOURTEEN

Spud grumbled a staticky curse and pried himself off the floor of Vaughn's damnable museum. He swayed unsteadily and reached out a gauntlet to brace against one of the vats while he ran a diagnostic on himself, centring on the epicentre of the crippling impacts. The strikes were expertly poised to hit a critical power relay which temporarily shut down his motor functions.

Unfortunately, he couldn't recover before Vaughn had whisked Eve away and sealed the great doors to his museum shut behind him. He scoured the wireless network for any external feeds or vulnerable data entries but found not a lick of bandwidth. The museum was in a world of its own, a realm of closed circuitry operating on an independent system that thwarted any means of external connection.

+*He's been thorough,*+ the Foreigner noted. +*No doubt subject to many inspections by the Coalition.*+

Spud hissed a binary curse, and his woes for Eve's safety grew by the microsecond. If he couldn't use his processing power, then he'll go for the direct approach. He marched to the doors, giving passing examinations to the museum displays along the way.

+*This wood's tough,*+ the Foreigner pointed out when he drew near the pair of colossal ligneous slabs. +*Far beyond anything* you *could throw at it.*+

Spud begrudgingly acknowledged the truth in its observation, but his prerogative to be by his creator's side was an infinitely growing worm in his cognitions. His databanks clicked and ran through thousands of theoretical scenarios; all were failures save for one that stood out above the others. He turned to the organic display vats and the giant that loomed behind them. If he couldn't break the door down, himself, then maybe something else could.

He spun about, marched back down the aisle of bemusing relics and around the vat labelled '*homo sapiens eternus.*' Stopping before the colossal capsule that held the sentinel in stasis, his optics raised to meet the dormant divaricate eye of the black marbled machine. Its skin proved too dense for any diagnostic attempts, but if the recounts he had heard were of any merit, then his theory should hold true.

+*Just what are you getting at?*+ the Foreigner inquired with a hint of what Spud identified as curiosity.

He answered in an off-hand manner and stepped to the side of the sentinel's capsule.

+*You cannot be serious,*+ the Foreigner huffed. +*The minds of these things are barred even to* my *vision, and they only obey commands given by Coalition naval officers. You'll destroy us both!*+

Spud issued a dismissive remark.

+*You think otherwise? Explain yourself.*+

Spud ripped off some panelling from the capsule's console and threaded his digits through wires as thin as hairs. The layout of the machinery was strange and completely foreign to him, but he was able to locate the component he was seeking. He gave an affirming bleep when his digits scraped over a miniscule identifier label.

+*What's it say?*+ the Foreigner asked as he pried the tiny label free of its mounting. +*Coalition Naval Ship* Sojourner, *eh?*+ It chittered with glee. +*Delightfully devilish! No wonder Vaughn's kept this thing on ice all this time. You think it'll still harbour a grievance towards him for killing its former master?*+

Spud tossed it up to an even-chance and discarded the label. Diving back into the console, he fished out something more intrinsic to his goals—a lonely wire with the sole purpose of issuing a 'release' command.

+*This is hardly the time to be dealing with uncertainties!*+ the Foreigner protested.

Spud cut the wire and readied a small static charge in his gauntlets.

+*Don't! Just think before*—+

Spud booped and shot off the signal through the wire and into the deep capsule's deepest mechanisms.

+By the Ether, you must really sort out this unhealthy prerogative you have with this girl.+

There was nothing for a few seconds, and Spud almost figured he had made a mistake.

Then there was a hiss and a crunch. The glass face of the chamber swung wide with a shower of ice. A deep rattling hum swelled out from the sentinel, and a fiery crimson burst forth from its eye. Ice shattered as the manacles holding it in place folded back and tubular connections were yanked from their housings in its back. The sentinel's arms broke free from its chest and planted to its sides. It garbled a nonsensible burst of noise, a blend of mechanical and organic, as it stepped forth from its sarcophagus with an avalanche of ice flaying from its body.

Spud shuffled back, rounding Eve's empty vat in a daze. The sentinel moved with a grace that confounded his analytics as it spun about on its heel and drove a fist into the ice to retrieve its towering halberd. It effortlessly twirled the massive polearm to test its balance before it gave its butt a tap on the ground and set off in a determined march.

Spud tried to keep his distance, wary of the sentinel's far superior size and enigmatic alignment. But as he observed the perfect creation in awe, his pace slowed, and his servos lost all will to move. His desire to act became stifled, and he found himself dumbly watching the sentinel descend upon him. But instead of laying him low, it adjusted course and maneuvered around him as if he were little more than a furnishing feature. As it passed, its head rotated onto him and shot a red-hot glare from its eye. Spud's Geiger counter furiously ticked as a powerful stream of radiation scried every atom of his body. It focused on the Taiji for a second, then, content with its analysis, it continued onwards to the door.

+*This could spell the death for us,*+ the Foreigner remarked once the sentinel was a comfortable distance away.

Spud booped in agreement.

+*Not like I could have done anything to stop you anyways.*+

Vaughn's console blipped.

'Send,' he said in the intercom.

'Team has arrived, Boss.'

Vaughn shook off any external signs of his paternal woes for Eve and buzzed them in.

A half dozen specialists dressed in overalls jogged through the doors. Each of them carried an exotic weapon or tool designed solely for the extraction and manipulation of the Taiji. Despite Eve having evidently handled the Taiji with her own hands to install it in Spud, Vaughn was not leaving anything to chance.

'It's in the museum,' he said firmly with his hands clasped behind his back. 'Be ready; the machine would have reactivated itself by now.'

The team leader, designated by a yellow stripe on his shoulder, nodded and set about positioning his members in key positions around the museum doors. As they moved about, Vaughn casted a wary glance to Eve, who was still unconscious on the lounge, and cursed himself for not moving her out of sight before his team had arrived.

The team leader gave a firm nod when everyone was in position.

'By my count, I'll open the door,' Vaughn said, readying a finger over the release button. 'Three. Two. On—'

The doors shuddered under a great impact.

'Door jammed, Boss?' the team leader asked.

Vaughn shook his head. 'That wasn't me.'

A second impact rattled the gigantic slabs of wood and sent splinters flaying off. Vaughn could have sworn he saw the ancient oak bend, and several of the specialists shuffled back. He scooped up his pistols, and they powered on with bloodthirsty etheric hues. *He couldn't have,* he thought, moving directly before the doors for an unimpeded line of sight.

The last strike sent the doors cascading to the ground. Fragments harder than stone cracked exquisite marbling and destroyed fragile works of art. Vaughn braced himself, and several of the specialists lost their footing. In his peripheries, he saw the lights of the Haven below sway and wary heads being cast about.

The sentinel stepped out onto the ruined door and glared over the dumbstruck specialists before locking onto him who, for the first time in years, felt his skin go cold. A deep garble rose up from its non-existent throat and it raised its halberd.

Vaughn fired first and plunged a pair of screaming etheric bolts into the machine. The mystical energies of the other-realm scorched marks in its chest, but most of the energy was refracted away into a wall.

The sentinel roared and swung its halberd about, cutting down several of the specialists and free-throwing the rest in the blink of an eye. It set a course directly for him and charged with a speed that confounded its size.

Vaughn cursed and flipped the pistols' settings as high as they could go. He fired again, and a beam of tortured energy cried out and struck the sentinel. It staggered in its course just enough for him to duck out of the way and scrounge some distance between him and the sentinel. Even at full power, the miniaturised ethereal railguns housed inside the pistols did little more than dig a hole a few centimetres deep in the sentinel's gold-veined carapace.

The sentinel recovered quickly and was already in pursuit of him, running down a dazed specialist thrown by its initial attack. She had no time to react before her head impacted its thigh, and she was trodden under a mechanical boot.

Vaughn fired again, but his weapons had exhausted their charges. He hissed and leapt for his desk. Digging deep, he hefted it up and threw it at the machine. Several hundred kilograms shattered against the sentinel as if it were porcelain, but the machine continued its relentless assault.

Vaughn backed up but soon found glass behind him. He peered down at the Haven below and the patrons who were milling about in confusion. He looked back longingly to Eve and accepted that the risk was too great to try going back for her. *But I can lead it away from you.*

With a firm punch, he sent a shower of glass pouring onto the gambling tables. Guests shrieked and scrambled for safety mere moments before he plummeted to the gaming floor and crushed a craps table. He groaned and rolled himself out of the wreckage. He pulled himself up and brushed off his clothes.

'Boss, are you okay?' one of the game dealers asked.

Vaughn shook his head and dabbed at a small laceration in his cheek. 'Get out!' he shouted. 'For your own safety, get out now!'

A handful of patrons slipped away, but most were content with gawking at him as if he were just another night show. Then a great roar sent a shudder through every soul in the gaming floor. A shadow descended from the broken office window and landed on both feet with a quaking *thud*. It straightened up and cast its judgemental ire over the Haven. Only then did the drugged and drunken gamblers understand the jeopardy they were in, and chaos ensued.

CHAPTER FIFTEEN

Spud waited until the destruction wrought by the sentinel had faded far into the distance before he emerged from the museum. He lumbered out, carefully stepping over rubble and dismembered bodies of Vaughn's specialists. His optics flickered between each one, giving rise to a strange morbid fascination that stirred a fundamental element of his programming. He had felt it when he'd ended Aleya's life, but he still wasn't certain whether he liked or detested it.

He was quick to locate Eve who, much to the alleviation of his compulsive directive, lay on a lounge in a blissful sleep completely unaware of the danger she was in. He made straight for her and dropped to a knee. He trembled with woe, thankful she was okay but furious at yet another failure in his duty. He carefully prodded her cheek with a finger, but she didn't rouse.

A crash in the distance gave him pause. He pulled up a camera feed to see the sentinel tearing a path through the

Haven, sending flight to gamblers and staff before it in a human wave. The giant frame of Vaughn stood out among the mess, and a furious hydraulic hiss tensed his arms.

+*He's heading away from us,* + the Foreigner pointed out. +*Take Eve back to her room. At least it'll be somewhat safer there than here.* +

Spud agreed. With utmost care, he spooned his palms beneath her and lifted her up.

+*The door's still locked.* +

Spud grumbled. He carefully rose and rummaged through the remains of Vaughn's desk, finding an array of buttons, which he mashed with a foot. The doors' locking mechanisms clunked open, and keeping his steps light to avoid hurting the precious cargo in his arms, he made for the exit.

During his travels, sirens had begun to blare, and calls for evacuation were issued. He passed many groups of terrified and confused patrons too inundated with hangovers and narcotics to pay much heed to the robot carrying an unconscious girl through the deep warrens of the casino. In the few corridors that had viewports out into space, he could see the flickering lights of escape pods and shuttles whistling away towards Iridia, but he hadn't planned on making an escape. Not yet.

+*I couldn't believe Olympia didn't show,* + the Foreigner said, somewhat out of the blue. + *Her treachery knows no bounds, I'll tell you. She must have sold us out or fled when Aleya showed up.* +

Spud gave a dismissive reply, caring little for what that dainty sprite did. All that mattered was he got Eve back to her room.

As he rounded a tight bend in the corridor not far from the presidential suites, Eve spluttered and squirmed through the grey zone between rest and cognition. Her eyes shot open, and she gasped, arms flailing.

Spud whispered a soothing drone to ease her panic.

'Spud?' she asked, groggily rubbing her head. 'Where are we?'

Spud booped, slowing to a halt.

'Did Vaughn drug me?'

Spud nodded.

Eve groaned and wiggled to be let down. Spud obliged and daintily lowered her to her feet. She wobbled and leaned against him for support.

She casted her eyes about, blinking profusely under the piercing lumens. 'We're near my room,' she said, patting at her forehead, then at the variety of pockets on her garments. 'Where's my—?'

Spud retrieved her glasses from a receptable and held them out for her.

Eve took them graciously. 'Thanks, buddy.'

Her praise gave rise to a twinkle of light in an otherwise dark day for him.

'Not far from home, it seems,' Eve said, composure returning. 'Let's go.'

They covered the last stretch quickly, Eve keeping a light jog the whole way. Her brain felt as if it had swollen to twice its size and her feet had become lead blocks. Her stomach did painful somersaults, and her muscles were rife with lactic acid, but she pushed on until her room came into view.

'Any idea where Vaughn went?' she asked as she keyed her apartment console and unlocked the door.

Spud's response was slow and ambiguous.

'Whatever,' Eve grumbled as she pushed the door open. 'At least we're out of there.'

'Well, that was quite unfortunate,' Olympia said in her usual elegant manner while seated regally in one of the dining room chairs.

Spud slipped in front of Eve and uttered a deep growl.

'What are you doing here?' Eve hissed.

Olympia's eyes met hers. 'Looking for you. Though, I suppose it would have made more sense to have gone to Vaughn's office rather than here. Sometimes, human freewill defies precognition.' She rose and tilted her head, attention fixed on something behind them. 'You intend on closing that door? Secrets get out rather easily if you're not careful.' She waved her hand, and the door slammed shut. She nodded to one of the chairs. 'If you will.'

Eve bit back a jeer. She figured her chances of escape were next to zero while in the presence of someone as seemingly powerful as Olympia. She accepted the offer and took a seat with Spud hanging close behind her.

Olympia threaded her fingers and beheld Eve with those unnerving eyes. 'Your son has been busy.'

'Busy?'

Olympia looked up to Spud. 'You intend on telling her yet?'

Eve glared at him, and he stared back, emotion hidden by robotic monotony. He rotated his head over to one of the displays by the workbench. The screen flickered, and a replay of a camera feed flashed on.

It rolled through the events that had transpired during Eve's slumber. She watched in silence, unsure how to process what happened.

When the feed terminated, she returned her attention to Spud. 'You did that?'

Spud nodded.

'He's a talented boy,' Olympia said in a manner that lent sincerity. 'But he's been getting some help.'

Eve narrowed her eyes.

'I know where it is,' Olympia said, pointing at Spud. 'I've known the whole time.'

Eve huffed. 'Then why the roundabout shit?'

Olympia shrugged. 'As I said, I am an observer. I wanted to see the process behind your decision making, and unlike Vaughn, I understand and value sentience. Even one as unorthodox as Spud's.'

Eve braced her arms against her thighs. 'What do you mean by that?'

'I do not wish to kill Spud,' Olympia assured, 'but I *will* be getting the Taiji back.'

'And *how* do you intend on doing that?'

'That is something I hoped we could figure out together once we leave this station.'

'Leave? How can I trust you?'

Olympia shook her head. 'You can't, but what other choice else do you have? *He* already knows where you are, and while he might be a bit preoccupied at the moment, he is nought but persistent. Soon his mind will be set solely on securing both the Taiji and you.'

Eve grumbled. Even though everyone she had ever trusted had betrayed her, the Port Royal was still the closest thing to home she had. She couldn't just pack up and leave. Not again. But Olympia was right. If she stayed, she would most certainly be captured and be brought to face her fate. She trembled; she didn't want to think about that slimy vat.

The door chimed, sending a repulsive shudder down her spine. 'Spud,' she said.

Spud booped, and the display flicked to the feed outside her door.

'Eve, please, if you're there, let me in,' Jere said, voice amplified through the display. He leaned against the wall in a gasp. His hair was a mess, and his clothes had several tears through them.

'It's Jere,' Eve hissed, springing to her toes. 'Spud! Weren't you monitoring the cameras?!'

Spud blurted in protest.

Olympia backed him up. 'He was.'

'Is there anyone else with him?' Eve asked Spud.

The feed flipped through dozens of angles in a second, and Spud shook his head.

'Hear him out,' Olympia suggested. 'He might know something that could help us.'

Eve glared at Olympia. That infernal being's anomalous alignment was quickly proving to get under her skin. She rose and went to the door, unlocking it.

'You got some balls coming here after what you did,' she growled.

'I'm sorry,' Jere huffed, stumbling in. 'I didn't mean for any of this to happen.'

'You didn't mean to nearly kill Spud?!' Eve spat, repeatedly slapping him over the back of the head.

Jere braced under the onslaught. 'It was always meant to be a contingency in case Spud wigged out, but when Boss learned about the Taiji—'

'And how *did* he learn about the Taiji?' Eve countered, slapping harder. 'I never told anyone except you.'

Jere leapt away from her grasp and rubbed at his head sheepishly. 'I told him. I didn't think it would escalate like this.'

'Well, it did,' Eve said, locking the door. 'What do you want?'

'Vaughn is fuming. He's managed to give the sentinel the slip, but now it's blindly tearing through the casino. He won't be able to keep his low profile now, and none of his contacts in the Iridian government will risk their necks to help. They're gonna throw him to the Coalition the instant they can.'

'Good,' Eve said, crossing her arms.

Jere shook his head. 'No. Not good. That's the problem. The casino and all the money, he doesn't care about that. All that matters to him is the Taiji, and he knows you have it. He's restrained himself so far, but with him having to jump ship soon, he wants to secure both you and the Taiji before the Coalition arrive. Then he can start over again on the other side of the galaxy.' His eyes lit up. 'But I know a way off the Port Royal where Vaughn can't see you.'

'How?'

'Remember when Aleya got to your room without being seen?'

Eve's stern visage softened a little. 'Yeah?'

A tiny smile slipped through Jere's terror. 'When Vaughn built this place, he also constructed a network of tunnels and rooms outside of the camera feed to make the storage and movement of illegal goods easier to hide from the Coalition. They're everywhere. Between the walls and floors, behind maintenance hatches, decoy doors and fake walls. They're only known by a select few in order for them to perform their duties. That room below the Tortuga, that's an isolated section of it.'

Eve pondered his proposition. 'Olympia, what do you think?' she asked, turning back to the workbench.

But the cloak had vanished. Spud spun his optics about and let out a confused honk.

'Olympia?' Jere said.

Eve sighed. 'Never mind. How do you know all this?'

Jere rubbed at the back of his head. 'Aleya talks a lot when she's drunk.'

Eve rolled her eyes. 'Fine. Let's go.'

She nodded to Spud. 'Come on.'

Spud booped and disconnected from the displays. He marched past her and into the hall. She waited for him to leave before casting her eyes around her life: the workbench a mess, displays everywhere, kitchen completely unusable, all backed by the darkness of space through the galaxy screen. Melancholy gripped her heart. She ran a hand against the exposed ironwork wall and prodded at a pile of scrap with her shoe, all reminders of a better life. A sense of déjà vu settled over her, and she lamented. She waddled into the hall and shut the door of yet another home for the last time.

Spud loomed by the door and booped inquisitively.

'I'm okay, buddy,' she grumbled, slipping her glasses on to hide her reddening eyes.

'Over here,' Jere beckoned from the elevator.

'The elevator?' Eve groaned. 'Seriously?'

'I know—just wait and see.'

The elevator doors glided open, and he waltzed in. Eve followed, and Spud crammed in between the two of them, turning the rather spacious elevator to a cramped cupboard. He glowered down at Jere who put on a weak façade of ignorance and pressed randomly at the buttons in what she realised was a passcode. The elevator bleeped, and the doors slammed shut.

There was a tremor, and Eve's stomach floated up into her diaphragm. *We're going down...but this is the bottom floor.* Then, a ding, and the doors opened up to a darkened passage rife with the stench of dank rust. She flipped her glasses up to peer down the passage but the suffocating shadows ate up all the light from the elevator after a few metres. A subconscious alert sent her instinctively reaching for her mask, but she caught herself and forced a few deep breaths to calm her racing heart.

'Where does this go?' she asked, a waver on her words.

'This heads to the space elevator hangar,' Jere said. 'I use it to run parts for you. Follow it without taking any turns, and you'll be spat out just as the Port Royal comes into alignment with one. From there you can descend to the surface and put some distance between yourself and Vaughn.' He swallowed and glanced at her apologetically. 'I'm so sorry.'

'Don't be—I don't blame you,' Eve said, though she still harboured some resentment for him. 'I know you never wanted this life. You were just doing what was needed for you to survive.'

'I'll try to keep him tied up for as long as I can,' Jere offered.

Eve held up a hand. 'Don't. There's no need for you to risk yourself like that. Take this chance to get out too, while you can.' She turned to him and brushed some hair behind her ears. 'Back in my room, there's a mountain of chips Spud has accumulated over the years. It won't be enough to catch a ferry, but you can cash it in down on Iridia before the locals realise they're worthless now.'

Spud blurted a complaint.

'Oh, like you were gonna have any use for them anyway,' she scolded.

Jere nodded a silent thanks for the offer. 'Better get going. Boss won't stop until either you two are back in his hands or he dies.'

'I'm not getting captured again,' Eve assured, 'but I don't want him to die.'

'I don't think you have a choice in that matter.'

The queer feeling in Eve's stomach returned, and words proved troublesome to pry from her lips. Her palms went clammy and sweat beaded down her brow. She must have gone a whole shade of red. 'You've been great, Jere,' she said. 'Thank you.' She came close, unsure of what exactly she was doing. Jere's eyes lit up, and his lips puckered a little, but she went for a hug instead, wrapping him tight and catching a lungful of his scent that spun her world on its head. 'Stay safe,' was all she could think of.

'Yeah,' Jere said, choking on his words, 'you, too.'

Spud chittered, and he passed into the dark passage to wait for her.

The moment over, they parted ways with Eve stepping out into the abyss while Jere remained behind. They held their gazes, both confused and overwhelmed with the mess of their lives until the elevator doors sealed them off forever.

'Let's go,' Eve croaked.

They wandered the passage under the crimson glow of Spud's optics, weaving around pipes and support beams while sticking to the path forwards. Eve's steps were muffled by the clanks of his feet, and her breaths suffocated by the hiss of his hydraulics. She watched her shadow in Spud's light waver with every step, and her mind began to wander.

It happened slowly, an inconspicuous shift of hue in the atmosphere and a change in pitch of her footsteps. The darkness thickened into a low-hanging fog, and a stench rose up from a rivetted floor that had taken on a slimy finish. A deep thrum of a distant core vibrated her marrow, and brief flickers of signage exclaiming the vicinity of Central Park, the Medbay or the Bridge would materialise in the corners of her vision but vanish the instant she focused on them.

'Eevee?' Eli's voice shouted from beyond.

Eve stopped, a sense of overexposure making her shiver. She suddenly felt small, and the lack of the comforting presence of her breath sifting through dusty masks put her on edge.

'Daddy?' she said, trying to pin point the source of the voice in the crushing dark.

Spud booped and lightly prodded her from behind.

Eve blinked under his lumens and shook her head in disbelief. 'Nothing. Keep going.'

She sighed, reprimanding herself for believing such a preposterous thing. *He's dead. Both of them are,* she told herself. But a kernel of hope still lingered for the contrary.

Time stretched and shrunk, the only tell of its passing being the clattering echoes of their paces. Eve kept her mind focused, not wanting to slip back into another vision of a past she had abandoned, but she could see the vague outlines of shadowy figures haunt her every step like predators waiting for a chance to strike. She tried to keep her wits but the darkness slowly eroded her willpower. She had to find an exit. She had to get out. She had to go back.

'Jere's clumsy, but he got a little charm about him, doesn't he?' Olympia said in her ear.

Both Eve and Spud jumped.

'Where did you go?' Eve hissed.

Olympia was a shadow cast in the stark light of Spud's lumens but her eyes somehow emitted a glow of their own. 'I never left. I just didn't want him to see me.'

'You think he's going straight to Vaughn?'

Olympia shook her head. 'No. He just has loose lips.' She looked about as if she had only just realised how dark and stingy their surroundings were. 'Would you like some light?'

She erupted in a burst of brilliant light, pale flesh infused with radiant sunshine to set the passage on fire.

Eve winced under the glow and scrambled for her glasses. Even Spud blurted an alert and shuddered.

'Apologies,' Olympia said, dimming her bioluminescence, 'I forgot your upbringing was on a world of eternal night.'

'How do you do that?' Eve asked, rubbing at her eyes under her glasses.

'That knowledge remains with me.'

'Whatever.'

Spud blooped and raised a gauntlet out before them.

'I daresay the exit is nearby,' Olympia agreed, strolling ahead.

Eve followed, already regretting going along with this creature's plan.

Olympia's glow melted away the darkness to reveal a bulky hatch at the passage's termination. They gaggled around the rusty hatch, an ancient manually-articulated thing that was more suited to a scrap metal bin than inside a space station. With lithe fingers, Olympia felt about at its seal.

'Spud can open it,' Eve suggested, not impressed at her attempts at lockpicking.

'No need,' Olympia said, waving her hand to send the internal locking mechanisms spinning.

The hatch swung open, and she jumped through. Eve groaned and slipped in after her followed by Spud after a few awkward readjustments to fit through.

Eve landed on a sturdy crate atop a mountain range of shipping containers. Divided into four quarters, the containers converged onto an epicentre of thick reinforced glass doors that gave a view into an airlock and Iridia below. She dared to look down beneath her to see loaders and forklifts, normally zooming about in a frantic logistical fever, at a standstill with a handful still idling.

'Looks like Jere was sincere,' Olympia said, dimming her shining aura. 'One of Iridia's space elevators is almost in alignment.' With a grace that bewildered all laws of physics, she leapt down to the next container. 'Time is of the essence, Eve. Best we get going.' With that she continued on, leaving Eve and Spud to look on in silent disbelief.

Eve gulped and grew a little lightheaded. Spud booped and dropped to a knee, extending a gauntlet out to her. She took it, stepped onto his shoulders and lowered herself onto his back with a tight gable grip around his head.

They meticulously descended while Olympia whisked between containers in a narcotic stupor. Eve tried to ignore the flamboyant fey fluttering about, but she couldn't help but be oddly hypnotised by her manner of movement.

'Not long now,' Olympia called out upon landing by the airlock.

Spud covered the last descent swiftly and allowed Eve to slide off. She gave him a pat on the side and jogged up to the airlock. She peered through the glass, catching view of the elevator's head drifting into alignment, its speed slowly being matched by the automated systems of the Port Royal. Once in place, the two would dock and a small window of time would open up to permit exchange between facilities.

'You work for the Coalition like Orjey?' Eve inquired, taking advantage of the moment of calm.

Olympia unseeing eyes flicked over her. 'I am not familiar with this *Orjey*.'

'So, why do *you* want the Taiji, then?'

'Some things in this universe are best kept from those harbouring selfish desires.'

There was a crash, and the ear-melting squeal of contorting metal. Somewhere beyond the piles of containers, a giant forced its way through bulkheads almost a metre thick in its relentless drive of slaughter. A chunk of metal the size of a lander flew across the hangar and crashed with a shower of sparks. The rhythmic plods of metric-tonne boots against steel quaked through the floor and an inquisitive garbling sent terror flooding through Eve's soul.

Halberd gripped dextrously in one hand, the sentinel rounded the containers and halted to cast its head over the scene before it. Heart pounding, all Eve could do was stand dead-still and feel its scorching ire burn away her skin. She wanted to turn and run, but her mind had shut down and left her staring down the embodiment of death.

Spud stepped forth to insert himself before her and met the god machine with gauntlets raised. The sentinel's head tilted, perplexed by the bravado of the inferior automaton, before it tapped the ground with the butt of its polearm in acceptance of his challenge.

Spud blared a great digital roar and lumbered up to meet the foe, but the sentinel was faster. In the time it took for him to take a few steps, it was already upon him with the blade of its weapon poised to cut him in twain.

'No!' Olympia shouted.

There was a dull ear-splitting thump, and the sentinel staggered back under a cacophony of nullified sound and wind. With her free hand, Olympia reached out to Spud and clawed him back with invisible chains. He blurted in confusion and toppled to the ground as he was dragged clear of the sentinel.

The sentinel recovered quickly and made for another charge, now aimed at Olympia. She broadened her stand and thrust out her palm, her brow quivering with immense focus. The air thrummed with unseen energy to rattle the sentinel, but it was quick to prop against the immense etheric power being wrought upon it. It powered slowly forwards, one unyielding footstep at a time, as if it were pushing a great weight up a cliff face while the floor beneath it cracked and buckled. When it was no more than ten metres away from its quarry, it raised its halberd and thrust it down with such speed it defied the eye.

Olympia braced on a knee, clouded eyes wide and teeth gritted with vast effort as she held the halberd a foot above her with incredible ethereal might. The sentinel garbled in frustration and doubled down its efforts.

Olympia bent beneath its effort, holding the immaculate blade mere inches from her head between trembling arms. Her nostrils flared, and her eyes took on a haloed glow. A tornado of dust and debris whipped up all about her, ripping her cloak up and throwing it aside.

With a great holler, she thrust up, sending forth a great burst of blinding light that knocked the sentinel off balance. She took her chance and leapt forth before the sentinel could plant its feet and placed her hand against its chest.

'Sleep,' she said, the word of power knolling in Eve's head and sending her to the ground.

The giant quaked and dropped to a knee, bracing itself with its halberd as its systems fought to the last. But even the indomitable will of the Coalition war machine had its limit, and it keeled over with a great crash and a garbled sigh whistled from its chest as it re-entered a state of dormancy.

Calm returned to the hangar, and Olympia stood alone in a trance. Pointy ears flicked up atop her head and a fluffy tail as white as snow wiggled from her tailbone. She wore a robe of some kind over her light frame, white as her furs and adorned in black symbols. When the last of the wind had vanished into distant whispers, she dropped to her knees with a gasp.

With great effort Eve heaved herself back to her feet. She rubbed at her side, wincing with the discovery of a fresh wound. Her head throbbed, and the fading echoes of

Olympia's esoteric order rung in her ears. She wanted to throw up but could only get a few dry heaves before pain forced her over into a ball. She stumbled over to Olympia's side and found her panting desperately for air.

'I am not as strong as I once was,' she lamented at the sentinel before giving a sideways glance to Eve. 'I do apologise. Side effects can be severe on the uninitiated.'

'What are you?' Eve demanded, swallowing her nausea.

'I'm like you,' Olympia said, slowly pulling herself up and summoning her cloak with a wave. She donned it over her shoulders and drew its hood, concealing her illustrious tail and ears. 'The only one of my kind.'

CHAPTER SIXTEEN

No more than two minutes after embarking the elevator had Eve, Spud and Olympia crossed the gravitational grey zone between Iridia and the Port Royal.

Eve felt her insides swirl about in befuddlement as her blood was pulled to either ends of her body before Iridia's gravity asserted dominance. She kept a stern demeanour around Olympia, but deep down, she was ecstatic at finally taking a ride on an elevator. Vaughn had been meticulous in preventing her from leaving the Port Royal, and she relished being in the presence of such a magnificent machine, the operation and make-up of which she had developed many theories over the years.

A little of her technophilic wonder seeped through her disguise the instant matte steel walls opened up to tinted glass smudged by industrial emissions. Rolling brown hills rippled across the planet, and grey clouds bumbled about in nearly non-existent winds. City nodes strategically placed around plumes of smoke or dark lakes segregated from sickened seas were all connected by a network of bitumen blood vessels.

'Decades ago, this world was set to ascend a new colony tier and reap the rewards of vastly increased investment from the Coalition,' Olympia said, minute twitches in her cloak hinting at her concealed tail beneath. 'Then an…unfortunate series of events led to the ascension being awarded to another world, leaving Iridia to remain as it is, today,' she continued.

'You think it was Vaughn's doing?' Eve asked.

'No. He simply capitalised on it,' Olympia said, glazed eyes peering over the browned lands. 'I hear this world used to be lush before the ore deposits were discovered.'

Eve grunted. *A world lush with life,* she thought, downtrodden. She pondered the dreary lives the Iridian locals were forced to live because of a simple administrative flick of a bygone wrist that had rendered their home changed forever. It was no wonder so many of its inhabitants spent their free time and karats in the casino. *Is Earth still green like in the pictures?*

'So, what?' she said with a click of her tongue. 'We're just going to hide out in the slag oceans now?'

Olympia shook her head. 'I have a void-worthy vessel. After we've left the system, we will turn our focus onto the Taiji.'

Spud made a noise that sounded a little too similar to a dismissal.

I agree. Even if she does have a ship, how are we going to leave system? Vaughn owns all the ferrymen here. Operators of the massive moon-sized ferries, the ferrymen were capable of bearing hundreds of ships attached to their hulls as they jumped into the Ether to cross the galaxy. As the only means of Ether travel outside of the Coalition Navy, their services required the utmost loyalty to the Coalition. But no one was made of stone, especially with the quantities of karats Vaughn had to offer.

The conversation died there, and all turned their attention to the rapidly encroaching Iridian surface. The elevator foundations swelled up and consumed them in darkness. There was an orchestra of clicks and hisses before the doors unsealed and glided open. Yellow light seared Eve's eyes, and her face was scorched by a burst of hot, rancid air. She coughed and gagged, pulling up her collar while yanking her glasses down.

'Never been on-world?' Olympia smirked.

Eve shook her head.

'It has a…scent, I agree,' Olympia said, stepping off the elevator and down a set of stairs onto a paved yard. 'Thankfully, we do not have to remain here for long. Come.'

Eve staggered down the steps, blinking her blindness away. The elevator yard was rough, dusty and uncomfortably hot. Beads of sweat immediately dribbled out her pores and melded with airborne particulates to form a fine film of mud on her skin. She wiped it off with her sleeve, but it only spread the dirt around. She grumbled and absolved herself to becoming a sweltering mess.

She eyed off the yard with a mix of awe and uncertainty. Built high over the sprawling kilometres of warehouses and skyscrapers, the elevator yard gave rise to a subconscious discomfort in her gut. *At least in the Port Royal there was a semblance of safety and confinement,* she noted, and had the elevator doors not already closed behind her, she just might have turned about and slinked back inside.

With a huff, she pulled her mind back to focus on something a little smaller. She listened to the engines of passing machinery loaded with mountains of rock while loading equipment creaked and groaned under rusted gears and shifting loads that weighed in the tens of tons. Workers in overalls moved with a state of expediency, threading gaps between vehicles to get to where they needed to be or waving their hands about to guide crane operators high above. The state of controlled chaos gripped her captivation, and for a moment, she forgot the world's disgusting stench and the threat of Vaughn's wrath hanging overhead.

'Here,' Olympia said, beckoning to a neighbouring shipyard.

Eve snapped from her daze and scurried after her. She caught up just as they passed through a gate into a neighbouring yard where a plethora of atmospheric landers sat idle arranged in neat rows and columns. Most were worn and tired, rusted from a lifetime of unescapable service in the

Iridian atmosphere. Some were little more than scrap heaps scavenged for what measly parts they used to hold, and Eve wondered if any of the wrecks still had anything useful that could be installed in Spud. She pocketed the idea when a vessel quite unlike the others peered out from behind a bulk loader.

It was a small-bodied ship with a wide wingspan, an array of complex thrusters and a sleek aerodynamic profile painted a deep, reflective blue. Its design told tales of rapid escapes and unmatched manoeuvrability and harkened from an era where ships were prestigious signs of status rather than simple modes of transportation.

'This is the *Ashinoura*,' Olympia said as a ramp descended from the belly of the vessel and dug into the coarse gravel in greeting. 'She has served me faithfully for many, many years, now.' She led them into a tight hallway that threaded up the heart of the ship.

Bland steel and ironwork were expertly concealed behind precisely cut light wooden panels in the most wondrous display of homeliness Eve had ever imagined. Every wall was covered in shelves stacked with tomes of varying stages of flaking decay or cabinets that brimmed with strange fragrances and trinkets. The cockpit was a large open living space with a stark lack of furniture aside from a collection of thin rolled-up mattresses in a cupboard and a slim console before the observation screen. *She's certainly got an interesting taste.*

She was instantly drawn to the wood, and she drew a finger against its polished grains, finding them satisfyingly smooth yet naturally textured and flawed. *No difference from the living trees they're cut from,* she noted, taking her hand away from the shelves and holding them up to her nose to inhale a lungful of strong spiced oil.

Spud booped, wedging his way through into the cockpit and stopping behind her. He daintily stroked the ligneous material and mimicked her olfactory examination. Eve smirked and patted him on the thigh.

'The shipmaster is aware of our departure. We are free to leave now,' Olympia said as she emerged from a neighbouring room.

Now away from the prying eyes of the public, she had discarded her cloak, and her hair swished about in a white wave that glittered in the sickly sunlight. Strolling lightly on the balls of her feel, tail wagging and ears perked, she dropped into the pilot's seat. With a few taps at the console, the ramp sealed away the clamour and stench of Iridia with a gust of filtered air.

Eve closed her eyes and braced against Spud in preparation for the terrible weight of inertia, but all she felt was a light vibrating hum. When she opened her eyes, she could see the space elevator drift in and out of view as Olympia, with a tact and dexterity that confounded her blindness, navigated the *Ashinoura* around the towering construct in a lazy spiral. Once at an acceptable altitude, the thrusters kicked in and the

Ashinoura jetted away from Iridia's sickened skies. The atmosphere faded until there was nothing but a blanket of stars before them.

Nothing like the Rocket, Eve remarked before grimly adding: *Mom did her best with what she had, though.* She wandered forward and peered about, trying to spot the Port Royal.

'Right side,' Olympia said, not moving her head.

Eve slinked to the other side and caught a faint glimpse of the casino floating serenely over the planet's horizon. 'Where are we going now?' she asked when the Port Royal had become little more than a grey blob against the Iridian wastes.

'We leave this system immediately.'

Eve shook her head and leaned against the console. 'Vaughn has the ferrymen in his pocket. He'll know where we're going. Not to mention the cost of Ether travel. You know how much it is for a single jump?'

'Current prices are gauged at roughly five hundred and thirty-seven million karats for a vessel of this class,' Olympia replied. 'But, no matter; we don't need a ferry.'

Eve gave a puzzled look. *What is she on about?* She snorted and spun back to Spud, who was prodding at the ancient tomes on the shelves. He realised she was looking at him and paused.

Eve smirked and left him to his interests. 'Of course, we need a ferry. How else do you make an Ether jump?'

Olympia grinned. 'My venerable connection to the Taiji had granted me many powers including the ability to quickly Ether Travel *without* an FTL battery. Plus, in case you didn't realise, the best place to be is anywhere *but* here.' She turned her glazed eyes upon Eve. 'Which begs the question. Where would you like to go?'

Eve wrinkled her nose, she found everything to be quickly cascading into the realms of the farfetched but a shred of her heart found strong appeal in the idea and a deep ingrained memory fluttered to the surface. In an instant, the cockpit vanished and was replaced by rolling hills pitched in eternal darkness. She stood atop a jagged outlook in thick winter gear overlooking the desolate terrain, a shipwreck far off in the distance. Above, the stars were joined by millions of fragmentary sections of a tortured moon. Before her, a telescope was delicately aimed up through the swarming debris to a world separated by ten millennia and five hundred generations.

'Our home,' Nisma said.

'Mom?' Eve called out, spinning around to find her, but there was no one else upon the rocky outlook to usher the light whispers long since deposited to memory.

She blinked and she was back in the cockpit. She clenched her fists but the familiar crunch of her gloves were gone. A gauntlet patted her shoulder followed by an inquisitive boop. She stroked Spud's gauntlet to calm her woes.

'Earth,' she declared.

A light chuckle leapt from Olympia. 'I thought so.'

She flicked levers and pressed buttons. The *Ashinoura* hummed in response and adjusted trajectory. Eve gripped onto the console and broadened her stance. She bumped into Olympia and uttered an apology, but her focus was trained on a monumental mental task. Eve's eyes traced up to her ears, and a sudden impulse to pet them rose to the surface. She was quick to bat the idea down and instead craned over the console so she could gleam one last look at the Port Royal, but it had been swallowed by the deep void. A sadness settled over her. *What have I gotten myself into?*

A clatter brought her attention rearwards.

Spud booped, a tome in his hand and a pile of leatherbound books at his feet.

Eve shook her head. 'Spud…'

'It's fine,' Olympia said, unmoving from her deep concentration. 'He's just curious.'

Eve sighed and pointed at the books. 'Clean them up, okay?'

Spud nodded, scooped the books up and carefully returned them to the shelf. Once he was done, he sat down with the book that had grasped his attention in his gauntlet. He turned through the flaking pages with incredible dexterity. Eve wasn't sure if he was actually reading or was merely imitating the act but she found gesture adorable, regardless.

'We are ready to jump,' Olympia said.

The *Ashinoura* trembled, and Eve held onto the console. A heavy steel shutter descended over the starry background before them and blocked out all signs of the outside universe. Her heart shrank; she was hoping to witness the Ether in its splendour.

'The Ether is a dangerous place,' Olympia said. 'To be exposed to its radiation is to die a painful death.'

Eve straightened up and nodded. There was a lapse in inertia and her stomach grumbled. She could have sworn she heard the ripping of fabric and the sensation of a great slimy quilt being draped over the *Ashinoura*. The hum of the primary thrusters died and were replaced by the Ether thrusters.

She braced for Ether resonance, a side effect to Ether travel where entire ship crews were overwhelmed by a flood of emotional turmoil that ranged anywhere from jovial laughter to crimson rage, but none came save for a growing claustrophobia that she was certain belonged to her own paranoia.

Olympia rose. 'The jump will take eight standard-days.'

'I thought you said you can Ether travel quickly.'

One of Olympia's ears flicked. 'The average time to Earth from Iridia on a ferry is forty-seven days not including layovers. Besides, it will give us some time to try and gauge how to safely split Spud and the Taiji.' She strolled down the hall. 'But that is for tomorrow. Come—I will show you your quarters.'

Eve sighed and followed. Spud clapped shut his book and rose, but she waved him down. 'No, you stay,' she said, 'keep reading.'

Spud's optics lingered over her for a moment before he dropped back to the floor and resumed his "reading."

Eve went down the hall to where Olympia waited. A doorway jutted free from the wall and slid seamlessly across to show a humble abode lined with dark slate tiles and more wood. Much to her disappointment, her bed was little more than an unfurled futon mattress on the floor with a straw mat beneath and a variety of colourful floral robes atop. A small side table, squat enough to be used from the grounded bed, stood next to it and the bathroom split off in one of the walls.

'I would appreciate it if you don't tear off the wall panelling like your last room,' Olympia said with a hint of humour, 'and when you finish resting, please roll the futon up and stow it in one of the cupboards.'

'Fine,' Eve said, stepping inside to get a true grasp of her new home.

Olympia motioned to the clothes on the futon with her tail. 'Wash yourself too. It's been a long day.'

Eve took the hint and scooped up the clothes. They were longer than expected and were made of an incredibly soft and breathable material. *It'll work, I guess.*

Her shower was quick and refreshing, and she emerged back into the cockpit draped in the robe with damp hair brushed back over her ears. She had no idea how to tie the robe so had settled for a series of repeating knots to stop it from undoing itself.

'You look sufficient,' Olympia remarked with a quiver of the lip. She sat on the ground next to Spud and pointed out words for him.

Spud booped in concurrence, but his attention was gripped by the book.

Eve glared at Olympia as a resentment formed at the sight of her with Spud. The creature proved to be a constant strain on her psyche and a far cry from the distant being that preferred to observe rather than interact.

'What are you?' she said, ripping the band-aid off.

Olympia raised her head, ears flicking. 'That is difficult to explain.'

Eve narrowed her eyes and crossed her arms, though that was more to keep her robe together than anything else. 'Then try.'

Olympia sighed and reclined back from Spud. 'I suppose something should be done regarding trust,' she said thoughtfully, tail coiling about her. 'Very well. I'll cut straight to it. I've come to retrieve the Taiji because I am its guardian.'

'Guardian.' Eve snorted.

Olympia ignored her attitude. 'Before the *Eternity* was built, it was in my stewardship. I cared for it, and long before that, we even shared the same body. You see me as powerful now, but back then, when we were together, nothing save for the power of the Ether itself could stand up to us.'

That would have been thousands of years ago, Eve thought. *Is she saying she's that old?*

'You shared a body?'

Olympia nodded. 'Indeed, but as the years of separation stretched on, my power had slowly waned. I fear that, should I fail to reintegrate the Taiji back into my being…' Her words trailed off. She rose and made to leave. 'Would you like something to eat?'

'Don't change the subject,' Eve said. 'You said your power has waned from when you used to share a body with the Taiji just like Spud. What happened to change that?'

'I cannot say.'

'Cannot? Or *will* not?'

Olympia's ears flattened, and her upper lip pursed a little, revealing the tips of two prominent canines. A faint growl rose up from her throat, and a darkness blanketed the cockpit.

Eve's peripheries shrunk, and Olympia grew imposingly tall and glared down upon her. Something stirred in her gut, like a rodent straining to free itself from a trap it had ensnared itself in, and her skin crawled. She sheepishly slid aside to let the giant pass.

A smile broke on Olympia's face. 'It does not pertain to you.'

Eve's insides calmed, and the world returned to normal. She coughed and batted at her chest. Her side stung and a ball of phlegm roll off the end of her tongue. She swallowed it and cleared her throat. *It most certainly pertains to me.*

Vaughn strolled about his office in a silent daze, hands clamped behind his back. His vest was in tatters, and a few blood stains dotted his shirt, but there was no time for rest. People rushed everywhere about him—tiny children compared to him—as they cleaned up the wreckage of his desk and museum door. He glanced into the museum and was relieved to find none of his displays damaged. *At least it had the courtesy to not destroy everything,* he remarked to himself. He sighed and acquiesced that it was a feeble attempt to make his untenable situation a little brighter.

Thousands of guests had just witnessed a sentinel, a highly valued asset of the Coalition, rampage through the Port Royal. While he could sweep the few dozen or so unfortunate deaths under the rug and pay the local planetary officials to look the other way, it was a certainty that a fleeing patron or message would have made it onto a ferry and slipped away into the greater Coalition. *Only a matter of time before a fleet comes knocking.*

Vaughn turned away from the museum and meandered up the stairs where his desk used to be. Remnants of his workstation lay scattered about, its sentimental contents strewn across the floor like rubbish. Something glinted from the debris, and he sifted through it with his shoe, unearthing his officer's hat with its gilded coiled cobra badge glittering. He scooped it up and gave it a once over, content it had escaped the worst of the damage.

A pang of sadness reared its head deep within him as he relived a life he had turned from. He glossed over the people he had once known, those alive and those dead. He had a plan for each and every one of them, all pieces in his grand design that now teetered on the brink of collapse. He sighed. *Could I have done anything different?*

He gently patted the hat clean and stuck it neatly in his pocket. He dropped to the floor and tapped at his console which, shockingly, had survived the impact with the sentinel. With an uncertain jitter, it flared up and he navigated through its menus. He glossed over the camera feeds but found them severely lacking. Sometime during its rampage, the sentinel had inadvertently torn through the camera system databanks and wiped out the past seventy-seven hours of recordings which proved to be a massive crutch in his search efforts.

A call flagged on his display.

'Send,' Vaughn said when he answered.

'Boss, we've found the sentinel. Current location in the elevator dock.'

'Seal all entrances and keep your distance.'

'It appears to be disabled, sir.'

Vaughn peaked an eyebrow and tabbed back into the camera feeds. He brought up the live view of the elevator dock and found the sentinel lying comatose before the elevator access. *Impossible,* he initially thought before adding, *then again, a lot of that's been happening today.*

He sent a hail to another crew which was immediately answered.

'Yes, Boss?'

'Deploy a recovery team to the elevator dock, heavy lifting equipment. Return the sentinel to its chamber immediately before it reinitialises itself.'

'It will be done, Boss.'

Vaughn hung up the call and pondered for a moment, unable to shake the hunch that Eve was, in some shape or form, involved. Her last known location was in her room, but a rapid insertion had confirmed she no longer inhabited the presidential suite she had so thoroughly reduced to a scrap dump. He had then checked every escape pod and fleeing ship but no signs of her, Spud or the Taiji could be found.

That would lead one to believe that she still remained on the casino which came off as contradictory. Were he in her situation, Vaughn would have put as much distance between himself and the Port Royal as possible.

An idea sprung to mind, and he brought up his notifications. He glossed through a myriad of damage reports and alarmed messages from officials and an entry stood out to him. It was a single-line report regarding the access of the space elevator docking shaft time-stamped for almost an hour prior.

A small huff was the only visible sign of his elation. He brought up a manifest of the elevator's shipyard exchanges and picked out the departure of a small void vessel mere minutes ago. Following that lead, he accessed the Iridian Aerospace Command radar network and tracked the vessel fleeing into high orbit at an incredible velocity. The vessel blinked off the radar, and a wave of ethereal interference sent static through his reading.

His heart skipped a beat. *Damn girl must have figured out how to put that robot to good use for once!* He grinded his teeth as he watched the circulating wash of the radar blip no further readings of the vessel. There was no way to tell where they were jumping to, but he had a few theories, and one system stood out above them all. *There's only one place in this galaxy you would ever want to go, little Eve.*

He didn't know why he was so sure. Was it an unwavering certainty or a desperate grasping at straws? Regardless, with an empire spanning thousands of worlds, there was no hope of him ever finding Eve or that robot again if they managed to slip into the wider Coalition. He had to take a chance.

He signalled one of the clean-up crew over. 'Begin an immediate pack-up of the Port Royal, utmost urgency. Prioritise the contents of the museum, Gardens and any currencies, and relocate them to the safehouse on Iridia. Be quick about it; you are to be ready to depart on the next available ferry to the alt-rendezvous and begin set-up. Anything you can't take, destroy.'

He waved them away and sent out a call to his ship maintenance crew.

'Boss.'

'Ready the *Gally*; we jump on the next available ferry.'

'But Boss, the cost—'

'I don't need a whole ferry to myself,' Vaughn growled. 'Have them make a quick detour to drop me off and ready a pick-up. Believe me, those grubby bastards earn so damn much they won't notice my little divot on their profit reports.'

He hung up and brooded for a second. *If I'd have known how much trouble you were going to cause me, Eve, I would have shredded that robot and thrown you into your vat years ago.*

CHAPTER SEVENTEEN

Ambient light flickered like ill-fitted diodes in the silent bedroom. Spud stood statuesque in a corner overlooking Eve as she slept balled up in silky linen on the futon. He still found her need to rest fascinating, and he wondered what went on in her processor during that period. Was it a time to reset? To store and amalgamate data? To rebuild and rewire? He could ask the Foreigner, but it had hardly been in a talking mood as of late. Something was on its mind.

He tossed the Foreigner issue aside and aligned his optics onto Eve. Taking extra precautions to keep his movements as quiet as possible, he leant over her and ran a quick analysis. She was in a deep sleep, hair a mess and her skin clammy with a film of sweat. She seemed troubled, her digits twitching and her face screwed up with stress. He wondered what she was dreaming.

Eve had spoken to him about dreams on several occasions. 'They were like living out another life' were her words, 'one that was an impossibility in reality.'

Spud found her description perplexing. To live out a life that existed purely in one's head seemed like a waste of valuable resources and time, a great pointless endeavour. But despite this, he would still occasionally wonder if he, too, could dream. Perhaps he will, one day, and his opinion might change on it.

+*I have a matter I would like to discuss with you,*+ the Foreigner said, rousing from its self-imposed exile.

Spud groaned; he was enjoying the silence.

+*Oh, Ether-forbid I get some time to contemplate things on my lonesome!*+ it hissed. +*But this is a matter crucial for both of us.*+

Spud acknowledged and waited for the words to spill out.

The Foreigner was apprehensive, and he could detect its influence threading out into his optics and onto Eve. +*Can we do it somewhere else?*+

A high whistle showed Spud's contempt, but he acquiesced and moved for the hall. Keeping his paces quiet, he slowly slipped through the door and made for the cockpit. It, too, was dimmed to a bleak twilight. Olympia's door was sealed, but a strange emptiness emanated from its cracks.

Spud prompted the Foreigner.

+*I remember now,*+ the Foreigner said, digitally waving at Olympia's door. +*I remember how I was broken free of her.*+

Spud asked for further elaboration.

+*It was*—+

Olympia's door abruptly opened.

'I didn't expect you to be up,' she said as she glided through, a faint glow emanating from her. 'Then again, you are a machine, so you don't need sleep, I would figure?' She wore a shorter robe, and her tail was burdened with signs of recent submersion in water. One of her ears flicked and casted off a few water droplets. She drew near Spud, eyes scrying every millimetre of him. 'It speaks to you,' she said, extending a hand to him, 'doesn't it?'

An inquisitive presence squeezed its way into Spud's chassis and poked about on the surface layer of his processes. He shuddered, and even the Foreigner retreated a little inside its housing. With a violent burst of binary, he expulsed the invader.

Olympia snatched back and examined the tips of her digits where miniscule chimneys of smoke rose up. She smiled. 'We used to talk a lot about all manner of things, it and I. I enjoyed its company though I doubt it misses me. It probably still harbours some resentment towards me.'

The Foreigner squirmed out of its shell. +*Very much so.*+

Olympia chuckled. 'It just agreed, didn't it? I can sense when it speaks.' She skipped over to the bookshelf to peruse its entries. 'I don't blame it. We all make mistakes and have regrets. It's just a part of living.' She turned to Spud. 'You contemplate something. Care to share? My wisdom may be of help.'

Spud met her eyes, those glazed sightless eyes. They bored into his optics and burrowed through every wire in his body with their scrying strength. The fact that she could tell when the Foreigner was speaking troubled him. What more was she capable of?

Olympia nodded in conceit. 'You wish to know why the two of you are so intertwined but don't worry—the answer will be laid bare soon. I will respect your creator and not perform a thorough analysis without her presence, though I doubt she's going to like it either way.' She glanced at the bookshelf. 'You showed interest in my tomes. Are you able to read?'

Spud shrugged. He had achieved a proficient literacy level a few minutes after his activation though he preferred to look at the illustrations.

Olympia giggled and plucked a book from her collection. 'You are a most curious being, young Spud. Here, you should read this. I feel it will be most enlightening for you.' She held out the book, a chunky hardcover tome with a title erased by time.

Spud took it and weighed the manuscript, estimating it to be roughly seven hundred and thirty-two pages long.

'There's plenty of pictures—don't worry,' Olympia assured him.

Eve tossed and turned as she slept. She was surrounded by darkness and vague industrial shapes illuminated by a weak beam of light that burst forth from the flashlight on her shoulder. She walked through this abyss, her footsteps echoing against decayed steel and rattling in her ears. Static hissed in her ear, but she was able to pick out a faint second set of marching boots much further ahead. She took off through the dark after them, blindly putting her faith into the fading steps. Her trousers and jacket swished in a panicked rhythm, and her breath constricted itself upon bulky filters. She wiped at her fogging vision only for it to return upon her next exhalation.

The tunnel evolved around her, building new corridors and walkways as quickly as they dissolved behind her. Signs flew by, but their writing was gibberish to her. Her lungs were collapsing, and her bulky clothes dragged at her limbs. The clatter of her boots nearly overpowered the softening strides of her target, but she knew as long as she could still hear it, there was hope. Her boot then caught a stray beam, and she toppled over. She gasped and held out her arms as the floor came up fast to greet her.

She awoke with her face squashed against the floor. She groaned and rubbed at her cheeks, feeling a coarse threaded pattern where mask rubber was a second before. For a moment, she thought she had returned to her old room in the Rover, but after pulling her head up, the dark tendrils of her dream receded beneath the wooden panels. A dim flickering light behind the panelling gave off an ambient glow that warmed her skin, and the dull hum of the *Ashinoura* whisking through the swirling chaos of the Ether soothed her to the bone.

Muttering a ream of expletives, she dragged herself back onto her futon and propped herself against her elbows. A glance at the time told her rest period was nearly over so she rose, donned a set of robes and passed into the hall.

The light in the cockpit was a dull twilight, an obvious attempt to make the ship more hospitable to her. Spud was reclined on the floor of the cockpit, daintily peeling through the pages of a book with his finger while surrounded by a dozen other ancient copies while Olympia sat cross-legged in the pilot's seat with her tail coiled around herself in an eccentric meditative state.

'How's the reading, buddy?' Eve asked, glad he had taken an interest in something to help pass the time instead of tearing the ship apart in boredom.

Spud booped and held up the book. It was a massive tome depicting strange symbols and hieroglyphs descending from top to bottom with a few clunky illustrations lace between them.

'He's a quick learner,' Olympia remarked, nimbly springing to her feet and threading her fingers. 'Let us begin.'

Eve tutted. 'Not one to waste time, are you?'

Olympia shrugged. 'I've already wasted ten thousand years. Were it purely up to me, I would have already gauged a means to extract the Taiji before you had woken up. But I understand and respect the strong connection you two have and the potential factor that might play in its removal.'

Eve hesitated. Olympia's enthusiasm to pry Spud and the Taiji apart didn't settle well with her. *They've been together since his inception; they're practically a single entity. Sure, the Taiji might survive the split, but how is she so certain Spud will be okay?* A troubling correlation between Olympia and Vaughn manifested in her brain. *Is she gonna try to wedge me into a vat too?*

'Before you do anything, I want to know why the Taiji is so important,' Eve asked, patting Spud on the shoulder. 'Vaughn said something about infinite FTL capability.'

Olympia glided forwards and knelt down to pick up the books scattered around Spud. 'That is a narrow observation.'

Eve's patience was wearing thin. 'Then broaden it.'

'The Taiji isn't just a means to infinite Ether travel. It's the Ether itself,' Olympia explained as she returned the books to their places. 'As a construct of the Ether, it is able to seamlessly pierce the veil between the material and ethereal without the gross expenditure that conventional FTL batteries require.'

'So, when you said the Taiji left you with powers—'

'A fraction of infinity is still infinity,' Olympia said, cutting the conversation off at the root.

'So, what's changed then?' Eve countered. 'I saw you struggle against the sentinel. If you are so *infinitely* blessed by the Ether, then why is your power...waning, as you put it?'

'I do not know' Olympia admitted. 'That is why I need the Taiji back. So, I can figure it out and determine if that which is afflicting me isn't extending to the Ether itself.'

Her attention shifted to Spud. 'Now, let me have a look at him.'

Eve thrust an arm out to block her. 'I've scanned him dozens of times. What can *you* see that I haven't?'

A light tut was Olympia's response. 'A lot more than you think. While I do not question your aptitude with technology, my bond with the Taiji is still strong. Even after ten millennia of displacement, I can still gleam down to its very core and scry that which lies unseen by technological eyes.'

Eve snorted.

Olympia's tail stiffened. 'Your disdain for my abilities is uneducated. Besides, I was not asking for your permission to perform my analysis anyway.'

Eve shook her head. 'It's Spud's mind, you absolutely have to—'

A blinding flash sent her reeling. She stumbled back and landed against a bookshelf, furiously rubbing her eyes. She blinked and cursed, a miniature sun scorched into her retinas. When her vision returned, Olympia had returned to the pilot's seat. Spud garbled beside her, his optics flickering from the overexposure. He tried to rise, but his balance had been knocked out of alignment.

'Worry not, kind Spud,' Olympia said, 'I merely took a spiritual blink of your ethereal half. Think of it like a photograph. With some hope, it should lay bare the reason the Taiji and yourself are so intrinsically bound.' After a moment of analysis, her face became stern. 'Strange.'

'What?' Eve said, burying her growing rage for the moment.

'It's slight, barely noticeable even to me,' Olympia said, springing off the pilot's seat and returning to their side, 'but there is an aberration laced into the matrix that forms the etheric-material bridge between them. Some kind of core prerogative.'

'Like a primary function?'

'Yes.'

'What for?'

Olympia scried her mental scan for a few moments. Her brow quirked with intrigue. 'To protect you. I cannot see what the source of this prerogative is, but it has become a primordial necessity for him—a survival mechanism, in a sense. Something has been programmed into his baseline subconscious from when he was still in a highly impressionable metamorphic stage of development, and like an animal, he will pursue it relentlessly without restraint nor concern for his wellbeing.'

'Like with the sentinel and Aleya,' Eve said with an uncanny insignificance that disturbed her. She knew she should feel something. Distress? Relief? But all she got was a sense of indifference.

'Yes,' Olympia nodded, 'it's so deeply ingrained in his coding that he actually feels pain if he fails to uphold it.'

That got a slight rise out of Eve. 'Pain?'

She never programmed the ability for Spud to feel pain and even with the great strides in modern technology, no sensors or programs in existence could detect such a stimulus. *Unless it's something else.* She glanced at Spud and mentally peeled away his metal musculature, chassis, components and servos until there was only the Taiji. *Did it teach him pain?*

'Yes, pain,' Olympia affirmed with a flick of an ear. 'But, under the right circumstances, I believe the bindings between Spud and the Taiji could be weakened and permit their separation without damaging either subject.'

Relief leeched the tension from Eve and she smiled. 'Alright, how?'

Olympia was slow to answer. 'There's only two ways I can envision it occurring. The first is the permanent fulfilment of the prerogative where you are safe from all conceivable threats. The second is the termination of the prerogative by means of the removal of its target—your death.'

Spud jolted to attention. He straightened up and thrusted a finger at Olympia, garbling a string of unintelligible exclamations.

'It's okay, buddy,' Eve said, her heart sinking. A piece of her had dreaded such a woeful ultimatum but there must be another way. 'There won't be any dying here.'

Spud rotated onto her then back to Olympia. Air hissed from his hydraulics, and his servos uncoiled. He dropped back to the floor and accepted a pat on the head from Eve.

'Indeed,' Olympia agreed, unphased by Spud's aggression. 'Besides, we do not know if your demise would also trigger a negative reaction. My connection to the Taiji, even in these twilight days, grants me much vision but some remains beyond my view.'

'Well,' Eve said as she stroked Spud's head, 'what now, then?'

Olympia pondered for a moment. 'I do not know. My foresight is proving to be most erratic in this regard. There are a lot of factors in play, all of which vying with equal might for dominance. The best thing we can do is continue on the way we've been going and hope the path before us becomes clear with time.'

CHAPTER EIGHTEEN

'We will be translating from the Ether soon,' Olympia said from the cockpit console.

Eve rose from a mattress beside Spud and carefully picked a way through books strewn about. She leaned on the console and stared into the radiation screens to will them open. While she was unbothered by their claustrophobic habitat (if anything she felt a homely sense of security), she was jittery at the thought of things finally getting underway. A bubble of excitement popped in her gut, and her fingers drummed against the console. *We finally get to go home, Mom.*

She adjusted her robe and tightened the crude knot on its front. A few days' practise, and one severely embarrassing wardrobe malfunction later, she could finally wrap her head around the concept of tying off the robe properly. She had asked if there were any jumpsuits or more *confined* clothing but was found wanting. Thankfully, the robes had grown on her, and she quickly became accustomed to the soft breathable fabric but a deep-rooted sense of over-exposure would still rear its head every so often.

Olympia tapped at the console. 'Translating.'

A wave of inertia washed through the *Ashinoura.* Eve kicked her legs out and braced against the console. Spud blurted and slid forward with a tsunami of books under him, sprawling out just shy of the pilots' seat.

Eve found his bumbling state amusing. 'Pack the books away, bud,' she said with a smile.

He booped and began scooping the books up.

'Will we be safe when we arrive?' Eve asked, keeping one eye on him as he put the tomes away. It was a question that had plagued her mind since the adrenaline of their escape from Iridia had worn off. She cursed her enthusiasm and starry-eyed wonder about the blue world that Nisma's stories had so thoroughly tantalised her with as well as Olympia's seemingly aloof approach to flying directly into the heart of the sole superpower in the known galaxy.

'A broad inquiry,' Olympia said, her eyes narrowed in contemplation. 'We are likely to remain *physically* safe unless…you wish to know if someone else will be coming after the Taiji, do you?'

Eve nodded. 'Like the Coalition, do they know about the Taiji?'

'In the realms of myth and rumour, yes.'

Eve crossed her arms and grumbled. 'You sure?'

Olympia turned back to stare at her through creamy eyes. 'Your adoptive father had seen to that when he destroyed their station over Concord.'

Eve's bravado waned, and she let her arms drop limp to her sides. 'Do they know about you?'

Olympia returned her attention to the front. 'They do.'

'Wouldn't they recognise your ship on their scans then?' Eve asked before gasping. 'Will they send a fleet to shoot us down?!' Her concerns were dismissed with a flick of the ear which only made her anxiety skyrocket.

'Translation complete,' Olympia said, flicking a switch. 'Raising screens.'

The shutters elevated, and Eve's disquiet evaporated as she caught a glimpse of the universe beyond. A swathe of stars pitched against a black canvas stretched out before them and she was a little disappointed. She had hoped her first glimpse of the Solar System would have been of the planet that had hung so tantalisingly out of reach of her mother.

But she noticed something amiss about those stars.

She blinked, not sure if her brain was playing a trick on her. Some of the stars were moving. No. Thousands of them were moving, all jetting about like the debris raining on Concord. Stumpy tails of blue, orange, yellow or red burned in their wake as they crossed the void in a dazzling spectacle of light.

One star soon became brighter than the others and grew with surprising rate and magnitude. A twinkling light quickly became a massive box with jagged edges and dozens of rods protruding from its back and belly that soon dominated the *Ashinoura's* observation screen.

Fearing a collision, Eve yelped just as the giant vessel adjusted course and sailed over them. 'There's so many ships,' she gawked as it passed.

'Earth is the heart of humanity and a hub of trade few systems can match,' Olympia said. 'Enough materiel pass through here every day to sustain hundreds of billions.'

Eve was impressed by the sheer quantity of trade going on all about her, but her awe was short-lived as another presence soon grew to command her attention.

It started small, no more than a blue orb glinting behind the passing ships. When it had grown to the size of her fist, greens, browns and whites filled out continents and cloud cover. When it became the dominant feature before them Eve could even pick out islands and lively aqua patches in the blue. A shroud of the nightside peeked up from a corner of the sphere and tracked across the planet's surface in the eternal game of chase that was day and night. In its wake, a smatter of yellow and white lights beamed from the darkened lands in a meshwork of interconnected infrastructure.

'Earth,' she whispered in awe.

'And the Moon,' Olympia added, pointing.

From behind the bauble, a grey disk, no larger than one of the smaller landmasses on the world it orbited, risked a glance at the *Ashinoura* as it approached. Eve had to doubletake, thinking it to be Minor, but the object was perfectly spherical and unblighted beyond superficial impact craters garnered from its altruistic duty to the world it served. Spud garbled behind her as he stared out with his own look of awe, optics flickering as he took thousands of photographs.

'Welcome home, Eve,' Olympia said. 'Like us all, we come from the Earth, and to the Earth, we will one day return.'

Eve laughed, a tear coming to her eye. *I finally made it.* She would have broken out into an emotional downpour were it not for the emergence of another massive object from behind the Earth. She wiped her tears away as her wonder was somehow topped yet again.

Initially, she thought it was a second moon, but the mass was too erratic and serrated to be a natural celestial body. It was the size of a continent, an incredible construct of steel moulded into an amalgamated mass of towering spires, domes and slabs held in high orbit. Millions of lights blinked upon its skin, and the shapes of many ships zipping about it reminded her of how Vaughn had once described a 'beehive.'

'What is that?' she asked.

'That is the Celestial Cities,' Olympia said. 'In order to maintain balance with nature and simultaneously function as the Coalition's capital, that satellite was built to house Earth's massive population in its orbit.'

Eve was gobsmacked; she never conceived human hands to be capable of creating such immense structures. She had always figured the *Eternity* and, to a lesser extent, the Port Royal were the limits of human engineering.

'How many people live there?'

'Last census claims twenty-two billion.'

'Twenty-two billion?!'

Spud booped in concurrence.

Eve could barely imagine such a number and to think that many people inhabited one structure in space. *All crammed together like that.* She wondered if it was anything like the *Eternity* was for her parents.

'So,' Olympia said, spinning about to face her, 'any idea where you want to go?'

Eve shook herself from her thoughts and pondered for a moment, but her mind drew a blank. 'Um. No, not really. Mom never said anything about specific places.' She considered the sheer immensity of time that had passed since the old recordings, pictures and data entries aboard the *Eternity* that had so thoroughly captivated Nisma were created. A dread settled over her. 'I guess they might not be around now. It's been so long.'

Olympia nodded. 'Might I suggest somewhere?' Without waiting for a response, she took up the *Ashinoura's* controls and guided it down to the planet below.

The Celestial Cities flew by and the mass of humanity's home rushed up towards them. The observation screen flared with the heat of re-entry as they curled around in a descent pattern. The blaze swiftly cleared and a brilliant blue sky curled out above them. Below a body of water stretched out to the horizon and enraptured Eve with the untold millions of sparkling ripples on its skin. Specks of land rose up from the deep; a wonderous mix of many greens speckled with red, yellow and orange sprinkles that Eve couldn't quite believe.

Nothing seemed real. The darkness of Concord, the disgusting brown of Iridia. None of them compared to what lay before her. How could have her ancestors ever dreamed of leaving this place? Why go out into the unforgiving universe when perfection was right at their doorstep? A sadness settled over her. *They'll never know this. Never see any of this. All those lives spent living in the hopes for a better future when we should have been looking at what was around us.*

As they descended, one island grew in prominence over the rest. Shaped like a queer fruit, its shores alternated between golden beaches and jagged cliff faces while its hinterland was overrun with roiling canopies of lush plant life. A great harbour, its mouth choked by a rotten stone sea wall, was the only exception to this status quo.

The *Ashinoura* adjusted trajectory towards a prominent hill that pierced from the island's heart. Despite being little more than a few hundred metres above sea level, its peak was shrouded in a dense fog that forced Olympia to guide the *Ashinoura* to a small clearing cut in the forestry just shy of the harbour.

'What is this place?' Eve asked when the lithe vessel touched down with the grace of a microbe of dust.

'Long ago, it was known as Enkawa Island along with many other names before that,' Olympia explained as she rolled through the *Ashinoura's* shut down sequence. 'Today, I do not think it has a name. No one lives here, anymore, and it serves no purpose in the Coalition's schemes, so there is no reason for it to be given anything beyond a set of coordinates.' The ramp dropped behind them, and she rose. With a flick of her wrist, her robe came whisking out from her room and over her shoulders. She flipped the hood up, ears folded neatly underneath the protruding flaps at its peak, and secured it at her collar. 'Shall we?'

She led the way out, and tail bobbing and wind buffeting her cloak, she slid to the side to grant Eve an unimpeded view of humanity's home.

All about them, nature worked its magic. Trees hushed in winds laced with sea spray. All the colours of flowers in bloom, fruit dangling from stems and tiny creatures flying about them in an underlying buzz made every cell in Eve's body quake.

She took her first step onto the Earth, and her shoes sank into a humid mass that sent a shrill excitement bursting forth from her. 'Grass!' she cried, dropping to her knees to rub at the mat of leaves. They were waxy and a little coarser than she expected, but their touch gave her a sense of calm she had never thought possible. A momentary impulse to lie down in it and go to sleep surfaced in the back of her mind, and were it not for the presence of Olympia, she might have done just that.

Spud thudded to the ground beside her and ran his digits through the leaves, garbling a string of bewilderment. He plucked one from its stem and observed it with a keen optic, taking a few dozen photos for future reference.

'A bit of an improvement over the Gardens, wouldn't you say?' Olympia giggled, holding her hood down under the wind with a pinch. 'Feel free to explore; the island is quite safe.'

Eve grinned and scampered out under the *Ashinoura's* wing and towards the tree line with Spud lumbering in tow. She tracked down a narrow trail for some time, ears pricked for the sounds of thrashing water occasionally broken up by the snapping of tree limbs as Spud tore a path to keep up.

After a while, she broke out into a wide-open space where the trees stopped abruptly at the transition of dirt to sand. Before her, waves rolled in from the depths, beginning as little more than lumps on the ocean's skin before foaming at their heads and churning over themselves to collide with the sandy shores. Open sky loomed overhead, and a tiny fragment of her mind told her to seek shelter, but it became nothing more than a cautionary voice caught in the wind.

A drawn-out bleep rose up from the trees behind her, and she spun about just in time to see Spud climb through the undergrowth, tree matter dangling from his head and shoulders and his limbs laced with a green residue.

Eve chuckled. 'Buddy, you're all dirty.'

Spud tilted his head and checked himself over, plucking out a few branches stuck in his musculature.

Eve turned back to the ocean. *So, this is what Mom wanted to see,* she thought. *She was right; it is amazing.* She took a moment to appreciate the scene where so many elements collided and played into each other. The spray from the water's edge, the winds above, the soil beneath and the trees behind all contributed to a delicate balance that could only be struck after untold aeons of evolution. She shook her head. *The Gardens and Central Park are nothing compared to this.*

A melancholy darkened her soul. *They're all fake. Feeble attempts at replicating something that could only exist in one place in the universe.*

She slumped to the ground and sank into the sand beneath the shade of the canopy. She couldn't understand it. She now lay among the soil and breathed the air of humanity's home, awestruck by everything around her with her mind alight with sights previously seen only in grainy images.

What was different?

Spud marched up beside her and gave a worrisome boop.

'I want to be alone, buddy,' Eve said. 'Just for a bit.'

Spud was still for a moment, his optics locked onto her. Then he turned about and wandered off into the vegetation garbling to himself.

Spud stared out over the rolling waves in awe. His optics flicked from breaker to breaker, calculating its height and mass and estimating its trajectory down through the shallows and up the fine-grained particulates that eased above the waterline. He analysed the silty material and found vast quantities of silicon and aluminosilicates along with trace elements of other metals interweaved with processor-trumping organic lifeforms.

He had retreated some way back up the trail where he had found a new egress down to the shoreline. It was a strategic position, one that held him out of visual and auditory range of his creator while also being close enough for him to intervene should a threat arise.

+*She is disquieted,*+ the Foreigner said.

Spud agreed. Something was wrong with Eve, but he couldn't fathom what. She got what she desired; what more could she want?

It wasn't the island—he was certain of that, and he would be the first to acknowledge the allure of the native flora and fauna. Though, he had hoped for a handful of mechanised creatures to help shore up his databanks regarding his own existence. Was he really a one of a kind? Destined to be alone when his creator, one day, met her demise like all organics. He shuddered and binned the thought process.

Death.

The alien concept sent anaemic scrap code through his systems. The prerogative. That damned prerogative. He had scrutinised it countless times for an alternate solution but to no avail. Olympia's analysis had been as thorough as one could be, and the two proposed sedatives were all there was to work with.

Death was an inevitability, but he would have none of it.

He recalled Olympia's mentioning of being alive before the *Eternity* was built. Was she telling the truth? Was immortality possible? If so, how could it be achieved? He inquired the Foreigner on the matter.

+*Do not ask me how it is done,*+ it snapped. +*The Ether does not bow to the linear timestream of this realm. Its touch can have all manner of effects. Positive* and *detrimental.* She merely drew lucky with hers.*+

Spud detested the remark. He had grown quite fond of the tall-eared creature, and her assistance with his readings had granted him reams of knowledge he thought never possible. Tales of unbelievable elemental powers and histories long forgotten, all contained in the tomes so neatly stacked in those bookshelves aboard the *Ashinoura*. He wanted to learn it all and share his knowledge with Eve. Perhaps, he could be the master for once?

He pulled up a recording timestamped mere moments ago and watched his creator lament in the sand, eyes cast in shadow. He wished he could tell her something. Anything! But that damn prerogative stayed his voice. A sour wave of data rippled across him. If only he hadn't allowed himself to become so enmeshed!

Perhaps he could lend the Taiji to Eve to make her immortal?

+*You detect that?*+ the Foreigner said, interjecting his thoughts.

Spud gave a negative response.

+A radar signal from somewhere in orbit. It just pinged off the ground back in the direction of the Ashinoura. *They know we're here.+*

CHAPTER NINETEEN

Eve stared out over the ocean and sighed. She was still incapable of fathoming how such an immeasurable body of water could exist, let alone the plethora of life it harboured. With all records on the *Eternity* being destroyed, Nisma had given her many brief descriptions of the organisms that thrived in its depths. Swarms of gelatinous creatures that wobbled blindly in the tides. Predatory beasts misunderstood by man. Great fish that breathed air in contrary to their existence in a watery environment. It boggled her mind just trying to conceive them. To her, any water that didn't come from a filtration system meant only one thing.

The trees wavered and her shade wobbled in sunlight. Some of the rays lingered over her arm and turned her skin a luminescent gold. Warmth flooded out from the points of impact and were carried all across her body though her blood in an exhilarating sensation. She looked up to catch a glimpse of the sun through the gaps in the trees. She tried removing her glasses but was immediately sent reeling. Cursing, she slipped them back on and her dread returned.

Then, like a dimmer switch, the light faded, and she was left in diffused grey. Daring to risk another look skywards, she saw dark clouds quickly whisking in from behind her to bore down upon the island. She leapt up, heart thumping in unabashed terror. Memories of the Rain came flooding back and she took off back into the forest in a hurry.

No sooner had she left the beach behind did the canopies above rattle with thousands of impacts that sent her brain into panic mode. Soon, her leafy shields had eroded away, and water dribbled down trees and pattered the ground all about her. She felt the first drop strike her shoulder, then another, then dozens more until she was pelted with unrelenting ferocity. Too terrified to tell if it was burning through her flesh or not, she kept running.

Time became fluid, and the world around her trans-morphed into emanations of her horror. Her lungs contracted against the seal of a mask pressed on her face. Darkness leaked from the shadows, and the Rain dissolved trees— leaves, trunk and root. The soil burned, and pools of molten biomatter rose up from the ground.

Then, the Rain subsided.

Eve blinked and found herself under the shroud of a looming structure. The dirt beneath her had transformed into a foundation of greyed granite stone with thick pillars of wood, gilded leafed and rotted by time, sprung up to prop up a sturdy tiled roof that creaked with the wind and dripped dozens of leaks. Tattered skeletons of flags dangled from the rafters, some bearing striking similarities to examples in Vaughn's museum. At its core, stood a tall casket.

A spine-tingling allure drew her to the casket's side where proximity yielded incredible details and signs of immense age. Layers upon layers of words, symbols, icons and animals bulked out a tapestry of lore cut into solid gold. Carvings of strange scaled animals coiled their way up the corners of the shrine with extended clawed paws and fangs bared. She followed the gaze of the golden serpents up to a mirror suspended from the rafters with its grimy surface angled down into the casket to give sight to a bed of red velvet cut to an exacting shape. The shape immediately clicked in her head. *The Taiji.*

'You ran far,' Olympia remarked as she strolled in with a trailing aura of nostalgia. Hood folded back and ears flopped out, she took in the scene in silent contemplation while a subconscious spasm discarded thousands of rain droplets from her cloak.

Eve stiffened, realising it to be the latest step in her grand ploy. 'Why did you bring me here?'

'This is my home,' Olympia said offhandedly. She glided over to a pillar, took off her cloak and hung it up. 'I'm quite surprised you found it, actually. The trail here had long fallen into disrepair since the passing of my order of tenders.'

'You didn't answer my question,' Eve hissed before thrusting a finger up at the mirror. 'And what about this?!'

Olympia gave a befuddled look. 'It's a shrine I built for the Taiji. I did tell you about my former custodianship of it, didn't I?'

'Quit being so damn difficult,' Eve spat. 'How did that thing go from having a nice nap in its golden bed to being the heart of the *Eternity*?'

'It is a long story,' Olympia said. She raised a hand before Eve could launch a counterpoint. 'But you deserve to know.' She came up beside her and beheld the shrine with woe. 'Many millennia ago, I was an urchin like you—a wretched thing that none would bother giving the light of day for—but that changed when he found me.'

'Who?'

A shadow draped over Olympia's heart. She turned and walked away. 'Follow.'

Eve trailed her through the temple to the outside. Passing a pair of crumbled mounds of stone that stood guard at the structure's entrance, they descended a run of stairs. The rain had passed, but a persistent patter of droplets falling from leaves kept her on edge. The sun was swallowed up by a fog that wreathed the moulded walls of the shrine grounds and wavered with spectral influences that left one in a bizarre state of pseudo-limbo.

It was then that Eve realised, in her blind terror, she had somehow torn up through the forest to the very peak of the island's most prominent mountain.

They turned into a courtyard in which stood a stone carving that depicted a group of individuals weathered by many years of rain, wind and flora. They were of all shapes and sizes, but with their finer features lost, they were little more than ghosts that haunted the grounds. That is, except for one.

At the heart of the display, strenuous effort had been taken to preserve the particular likeness of a young man bearing a wide-brimmed conical hat and a charming smile.

'He lived a long time ago, but I remember every moment I spent with him as clear as a cloudless night,' Olympia said, smiling as she regarded the man's features. 'He was the only one who had faith in a lowlife like me, and through his help, he granted me the Taiji's gifts. For that I am forever grateful and indebted to him. And for a long while, everything was good.'

A waver in her angelic demeanour made her pause. 'That is until a great war in the mid-twentieth century cast a shadow over the Earth. I was still bound to the Taiji at that time. We inhabited the same body and mind, and we cooperated in every aspect of our existences. Very much like Spud today. A warlord came to claim the Taiji for use against his enemy. I refused, knowing such power would become untenable when in the hands of an unworthy soul, but he wasn't going to leave without it.'

Her shoulders shrunk, and her eyes were clouded with darkness. She held out her hand and caressed the smiling statue with an adoration Eve had only seen shared between her mother and father. 'I will never love again—he was a one of a kind—but through me, his memory will live on until the stars themselves die and the universe empties. I built this to give him physical form, once more, and to give me a companion to live out the days with.'

Her hand fell away. 'That is what the warlord tried to destroy. He knew he could not kill me—stronger beings have tried—but he knew how to break my spirit.' She shook her head in disbelief. 'Think of it—the most powerful being in the universe being undone by her own melancholy of the past? I split myself in half and gave the warlord the Taiji. He took it and quickly realised the power was too much. It overwhelmed him, and all that was left was the Taiji and a smoking crater.' She turned to Eve and beckoned for her to follow.

'That was when another problem emerged,' she continued when they stepped back into the temple. 'The bond between the Taiji and myself is...peculiar. It is a product of the Ether, unable to exist in any meaningful sense in this material realm without an anchor to bind itself to. I used to be that anchor, my soul interwoven with its essence as finely as silken cloth, but now it has nothing to hold it true.'

'But its attached to Spud,' Eve pointed out.

Olympia shook her head. 'Unfortunately, Spud is different. As intelligent and unique as he is, he is a being purely of the material. He doesn't possess a beating soul like we do. Without a proper mortal being to attach itself to, the primordial being that inhabits that trinket will dissipate into the Ether. Likewise, without its ethereal touch on my form, I slowly lose my immortal attunement to the Ether and will cease to exist when my time is up.

'I cannot determine how long we have left. Almost immediately upon our split, my powers began to seep back into the Ether. Minute at first, but it grows exponentially with every passing second. I know the effects are mirrored on the Taiji, and I fear the repercussions should it dissipate into nothing. I have been seeking a solution, but relations are much easier to break than they are to form. I tried for years to bind with the Taiji again, but we just aren't compatible anymore. I built this shrine to keep it safe while I entered into a search for an answer. My delvings went deep—sometimes decades passed before I realised. During that time, it somehow got into the hands of the builders of the *Eternity* but before I could retrieve it, it was already on its way to Concord Prime. The rest you know.'

Eve was taken aback. She always figured Olympia to be some crazed woman whose ramblings were to be taken with a fistful of salt. But to see this creature—no, person—spill out an eternity's worth of sorrow to someone they met mere cycles ago, it resonated with her. She looked up to the mirror at the reflection of the bed that had borne the Taiji before humanity walked the stars. *She had given up a shred of herself to protect what she loved,* she thought. *Isn't that worth something?*

She glanced at Olympia. Despite her apparent eternal youth, she could see the age in her, the lifetimes upon lifetimes that brought unmatched wisdom but also a fragile humanity inherent to all. She was tired and exhausted with a burden only she could carry, and while a fragment of her still bore some scepticism, Eve's heart was swayed to her cause. 'What's it like being immortal?'

Olympia regarded her with a momentary glimmer of confusion. 'Its...lonely.'

'Lonely?'

'Imagine knowing you'll outlive everyone you meet, their lives little more than a blink of an eye to a being such as yourself. Imagine how futile it is to develop relations with those who would be dead before you take your next breath. Imagine remaining the same while entire civilisations spring up, prosper and wither away.' She sighed. 'In a way, immortality *is* a gift, but in many more ways, it is a curse. The universe changes while I am all that's left of an era long since buried beneath the Earth.'

A sly grin crept up her face, and a light chuckle whispered from her throat. 'Like I said, we are more alike than you might think, Eve.'

'I suppose we are,' Eve said, dropping into thought.

Immortal. Unchanging. Lonely. Is that what will happen to Spud? No. His parts can be replaced and upgraded indefinitely. But what about me? I don't have parts to replace or upgrade. And even if I become more machine than human, my brain will eventually die as all living things do.

She swallowed. *I only have so much time left. When I die, what will happen to him? What will that prerogative to do him? If it's like any other machine, it would lose its function and cease to operate. But Spud isn't like any other machine. He thinks and talks like me. Doesn't he?*

She paused, a wave of uncertainty washing over her. *What if Vaughn was right? What if he is just a machine that simply reacts in a pre-programmed way? No thought processes, no sentience. Nothing.* She steeled herself. *No, he is special, and as his mom, I will do anything I can to help him.*

'Now, I shall ask the same of you,' Olympia said. 'Why did *you* want to come here?'

Eve shook herself from her thoughts. 'I don't know,' she said sheepishly, 'I thought it was my home, but I guess that's because there isn't really anywhere else I can think of.' She stalled as if her mouth were full of syrup. 'My…mother always spoke highly of it.'

Olympia's tail flicked with anticipation. 'Do you share that sentiment?'

'I…I don't know.'

Olympia hummed. 'Your parents can be forgiven. They were raised on the stories of olde and lived aboard a ship that was their whole world. But you—you are different. You yearn for home and yet you do not know what *home* is. Your mind and soul both desire the same thing, but *what* exactly is where they differ.'

Her words were lost on Eve. 'What do you mean?'

'No matter how far we stray from home, whether that's by distance, time or genetics, we always carry a fragment of our origin with us. A primal nostalgia for the cradle we long left behind,' Olympia explained. 'Your mind was raised to believe Earth is your home. The mind is a vocal creature that demands our attention. It was why you decided to come here in the first place, was it not? But your soul, it *knows* where your home is, but it will not speak unless it is asked.'

Eve contemplated the question but answer proved to be more difficult to discern than anticipated. Her home. How could she know what that was? Was it a place to inhabit? A mere living quarter? *No, it's a place where I belong. The Port Royal, it was little more than a way-station; a temporary solution to keep me alive. For years, I was living in someone else's home, playing out a life meant for another.* Her thoughts turned to Earth, but now that she stood on the same soil her distant ancestors had once roamed, she also found it hopelessly lacking. She grimaced. Everything she did was wrong, and everyone she met was so alien that nothing felt right to her. Long had she known the galaxy to be a huge place; one big uncaring abyss that carried on despite the hardships of a lonesome runt like her.

Where among all this empty space could she call home?

A gut-feeling, barely detectable over the background noise of reality crawled up from the deepest recess of her essence and prodded her in the back of the cranium. The wastes. The dark. The Rain. Eli. Nisma. It all fell into place. The last time she had ever felt at home.

She wanted to see it. She wanted to witness her home for one last time. Maybe there was even a shred of a chance that her parents still lived?

'I know where to go.'

Spud ploughed his way through the undergrowth, his prerogative seizing control of his motor functions and tracking the most direct route back to Eve's last known position. He had initially been sceptical of the Foreigner's claim of an orbital radar pinging off the *Ashinoura*, but that was swiftly quashed when several more infrared tracking beams locked onto the *Ashinoura*. In an effort to gain more insight, he had tried to connect to the Coalition's radio network, but its encryption proved too tenacious for him to crack. Not that it mattered; he already knew the Coalition was coming and fast.

Troublingly, the atmosphere had simultaneously underwent a rapid change, and the high winds and buffeting particulates soon wreaked havoc with his auditory instruments.

+*You just never listen to me, don't you?*+ the Foreigner taunted. +*Well, look at the mess we're in now.*+

Spud sent a ream of code that thrusted the being's influence back into its housing.

+*Lashing out at me won't accomplish anything,*+ it spat as it swirled about in its housing like a caged animal. +*You are the one enslaved by this unhealthy desire to shadow her—not I. I merely wish to survive in this universe as a free being. Is that too much to ask?*+

Spud acknowledged and eased the pressure off. The Foreigner slipped out, and its presence reached out through every wire and component in his body. He distasted its nonchalant approach to wandering the veins of his chassis, but he didn't bother raising the matter. It would have been a waste of time.

+*Eve will pass one day,*+ it pointed out with a modicum of tact. +*You must be ready for when that day comes. What happens then? This prerogative is so deep rooted that failure might be a kill command.*+ It shifted its presence to dominate more of Spud's surface processing. +*You heard what Olympia said. There are only two ways to absolve this, and neither of them involve Eve existing in any way that matters.*+

Spud's patience was quickly growing thin under the Foreigner's constant harassment.

+*Why have you let it get so all-consuming?*+ it prodded in the back of his matrixes. +*It was a simple request and yet you turned into an obsession!*+

Spud didn't answer.

+*Well?*+ the Foreigner prompted with growing frustration.
+*Is it because it's the only life purpose you can think of? A
simple task for a simple machine to accomplish in order to
serve a simple purpose for existing? As noble of a cause as it
is, you are, in all likelihood, the most intelligent construct in
existence. Why limit yourself?*+

Spud issued a curt response.

The Foreigner fizzled. +*For them? You're doing it for
them? What does it matter? They're dead; that's a certainty,
so what if you stop fulfilling it?*+

Spud halted abruptly, a statue of steel amongst wood. The
trees rustled overhead and distant waves crashed against the
shore at the limits of his auditory detection. What would have
been a few seconds to an outsider was an eternity for him. The
Foreigner was most likely right that Nisma and Eli lay buried
beneath the metal slag of a dead society. But there was still
hope; the endling survivor whom they had entrusted into his
care.

His chest opened up, and his innards shifted aside. The
data reader projected itself from his body and ejected its disc
tray. The photograph furled out and made a flight for freedom
with the wind but was caught daintily in his gauntlet. He
unfolded it and beheld the moment of time captured.

But something was off. Where he normally felt strong
emotional confliction, there was only a strange emptiness as if
all value in the photograph had evaporated, and what remained
was nothing more than the shred of faded parchment.

It scared him.

His optics locked onto the fledgling Eve in the photograph. That insignificant creature who had breathed life into what was formerly soulless machinery. He pulled up the capture of her that he took a few minutes prior and compared them. They were nothing alike. The little girl who had borne him was dead, left behind on a world that deserved no memory. But he still cherished the person she had grown into, and he would still strive to uphold the demand laid down upon him. It was all he wanted to do in this existence.

He echoed his resolution to the Foreigner.

+*I will never understand you material beings,*+ it lamented. +*You all tire me.*+

Spud dismissed it, and surprisingly, it retreated back into is housing to wallow in its latest post-argumentative gripe. He paid little heed to it for deep-grey clouds had quickly blotted out the sky and precipitates began to fall. An alarm blared in him, but a rapid analysis of the liquid deemed it safe for exposure. He returned to the shoreline where he had left Eve but there was no sign of her.

+*Where'd she go?*+ the Foreigner asked, peeling back into Spud's conscious. +*How in the Ether did you manage to lose her? She's a third your size; she couldn't have run far!*+

Spud retorted.

+*Apologies for possessing the only shred of self-preservation in this chassis! Judging by her latent fear of rainfall, I would suggest she sought shelter inland.*+

Spud accepted the Foreigner's logic. He turned about and marched off into the wilderness with heightened expedience. Her trail was tough to follow, little more than erratically spaced indentations in the decomposing vegetation on the ground, but he was able to make a path back up through the hinterland. She suddenly broke track and veered off into the wild which was a cause of great concern to him.

He increased his pace and bulldozed through any vegetation that had the audacity to grow in his path. He broke into a fog-wreathed clearing where a great structure loomed before him and his optics focused onto two familiar figures that emerged from beneath the burdened roof of the structure.

He lumbered forwards, blubbering out a string of alarmed bleeps.

+*Very intelligible.*+

'What's wrong, buddy?' Eve asked.

Olympia tilted her head skywards, and her tail whipped about. 'They've found us.'

Eve never ran so fast in her life. The trail down to the *Ashinoura* whipped by in a blur as she struggled to keep up with Olympia who daintily skipped between the trees without a care in the world. At some point, her endurance had given out, and she was scooped up by Spud to be carried the rest of the way. They piled up the ramp into the *Ashinoura* just as a deafening scream roared overhead, and a pair of sleek fighters cut a course through the skies, leaving deep lacerations in the cloud cover in their wakes.

Olympia closed the ramp the instant she was in the pilot's seat and sent power to the *Ashinoura's* idling engines. 'Better find a place to hold on,' she said.

The *Ashinoura* thrummed with potential, and everyone jolted as it leapt from the ground and soared away from Enkawa Island. Eve groaned as the enhanced gravity crushed her into Spud's cradling arms, and her heart fought to bring blood to her head. The *Ashinoura's* ascent levelled out and skirted along the curvature of the Earth's horizon. She waved for Spud to put her down, but a detonation off the *Ashinoura's* right wing made him stumble. With a startled blurt, he lurched over and landed hard on his side.

Eve extracted herself from him and tried to right herself by bracing against the back of the pilot's seat. She cast terrified eyes out the observation screen where dozens of tracer munitions whizzed past to disappear into the clouds. 'They're firing at us!'

Olympia was unphased by the danger they were all in. 'I can tell.'

'Doesn't this ship have weapons?!' Eve cried.

Spud blurted in concurrence.

'I do not use weapons,' Olympia said. 'All we need to do is breach the atmosphere.'

She sent the nose of the *Ashinoura* jutting upwards, and Eve clung on to the back of the chair for dear life. Spud exclaimed and clattered against the rear wall of the cockpit, only barely managing to get a foothold at the mouth of the hallway.

Eve clambered for support, gritting her teeth as gravity fought to send her flying back into Spud. Through strained vision, the grey rain-laden clouds blew by, and the black starry abyss of the universe returned.

Shapes emerged from the void, naval vessels of indomitable size and mass ready to rain destruction on their target. Flashes of light pocked their surfaces as guns fired a hail of munitions. Eyes glossed over, Olympia expertly weaved the *Ashinoura* through the onslaught and zipped by the great ships.

'Clear of the atmosphere,' she said, tapping at the control panel. 'Readying for Ether jump.'

The shutters dropped over the observation screen, and the *Ashinoura* warped under the inertia of Ether travel. Eve gasped as the tug of gravity fled her body. She slid to the ground and lay with her head against the base of the pilot's seat with a grumble. There was a clatter behind her as Spud struggled to right himself, knocking a few books from the bookshelves in the process.

Then, there was calm.

'Apologies for the rush,' Olympia said, rising from her chair and extending a hand to Eve. 'We are in the Ether, now.'

Eve sighed and took her offer. 'Can they follow us?' she asked when she was pulled to her feet.

'Yes, but with great difficulty,' Olympia said with a wag of her finger. 'Not to worry, though. This often happened whenever I make my returns. The Coalition aren't fans of my appearances, but they won't chase us any further.'

'Wouldn't they have posted guards on the island, then?!' Eve exclaimed.

Olympia pondered for a moment. 'They usually do but my last visit was three hundred and eighty-four standard-years ago.'

Eve sighed and went over to Spud to assist in his clean-up effort.

'It's okay, buddy,' she said. 'We're going home now.'

Spud gave an inquisitive boop and straightened up. He regarded her with solemn optics that sent a squirming conflict in Eve's gut.

'Eve has made her decision, good Spud,' Olympia said. 'We fly for Concord.'

A servo-seizing dread locked him in place. His gyroscopes flew out of alignment, and he stumbled, landing hard on one knee.

'You okay, buddy?' Eve asked, rushing forth to take his gauntlet. 'What's wrong?' she asked.

Spud averted his gaze and gave a firm bleep. He tried to right himself but his balance was still shot.

'Spud, look at me,' Eve said, putting a hand to his iron cheek.

Spud shuddered but relented. He turned to meet her eyes. His optics were dim and flickered as fuses flared erratically. She caught a flash of empathy from him which kicked up a strange feeling inside her that solidified into a raw emotion. Terror.

CHAPTER TWENTY

Eve lounged on one of the mattresses in the cockpit and idly thumbed a cushion on her lap as the *Ashinoura* burned a course through the Ether. It was nearing the middle of the 'day' period ,and the cockpit was alive with imitation daylight that had been dimmed for her comfort. Spud emerged from the hall at a stiff gait, garbling to himself. She warily watched him pace several laps of the cockpit in a grotesque slouch, unsure whether he was passing into a new emotive stage in his development or suffering from a minor system failure. Olympia had suggested he was suffering from delirium, if such a thing could even be possible for a machine, and suggested she leave him be to sort it out on his own. Eve found the proposition ridiculous, but with a lack of hardware to perform repairs, she had to make due with comforting him.

'We are translating, now,' Olympia said from the pilot's seat.

The shutters glided up and gave a breathtaking view of the world. Eve, having failed to catch a glimpse the last time she was in orbit, was almost overtaken by the thrill. She leaned as far forwards as she could, eyes glittering.

It felt so strange yet lovingly familiar. A world split in two, light and dark horizons curving away beneath them. On the light side, great rivers of molten rock poured forth from the ground and sent up massive plumes of steam and smoke that were caught in torrential winds and blown over into the world's dark side as looming clouds ready to dispense their horrific deluge. Her fascination faltered when she realised she'd bore witness to the genesis of the Rain, and she pulled her view aside to scan the rolling darkness of Concord's shadowy half for any signs of the *Eternity*.

'This is a most peculiar planet,' Olympia remarked.

'What about the *Eternity*?' Eve asked.

Olympia ran a scan of the planet's surface and an optimistic tone brought hope. 'There is a strong concentration of metallics several hundred kilometres from the median strip but it is highly radioactive.'

'What about the Rover?'

'The scan does detect a smaller concentration a few dozen kilometres away from the primary vein. That's as good a place as any.'

Eve's nerves steeled. 'Can we go down there?'

Olympia nodded. 'Weather permits it for a while.' She tilted her head, and her ear flicked. 'There is cold weather gear in your room. I will initiate a descent pattern.'

Eve nodded and retreated to her room. She expected Spud to follow, but he remained in the cockpit staring ignorantly at her.

Spud watched Eve seal herself in her room. He shuddered as a terrible feedback loop nearly made a few critical systems lose power. An unfathomable dread had festered in his programming since they left Earth and it neared critical mass. He wanted to do something. He wanted to tell her to stop and think about how fundamentally her life would alter. She had to learn that some things were best to be left in the dust. But his vocabulator was stayed, as it always was, and all he could utter was a garble that remained unheeded. He quaked in frustration. Were it not for that damnable prerogative!

+You cannot stop her,+ the Foreigner said.

Spud lashed out and thrashed it back into its housing. It whimpered something but he was beyond listening to the reprehensible voice in his head.

'I concur,' Olympia said, coming beside him. 'It is something she must do. Her heart is torn between two lives. One in the past and one in the present. If she is to attain clarity and peace in the present, she must absolve her misgivings from the past.' She turned to Spud, a look of sincerity on her face. 'Take care of her, kind Spud, but know when you must step back. Some parts of this journey Eve must make alone.'

Spud relaxed a little to permit motion in his legs. Olympia was right. Something was about to happen, one that he must permit to play out regardless of his objections.

Eve emerged from her room wrapped up in robing. She initially figured the clothing to be hopelessly inadequate, but once she had donned a few layers, their heat retention was greatly appreciated. Heavy boots on, she cupped a full-face mask in one hand, and a sense of familiarity settled in over her. It felt right.

The *Ashinoura* shook as it contacted the ground.

'Touchdown,' Olympia said, padding up to Eve's side. She eyed her up and down and seemed content with her dress. 'This world's weather is erratic to say the least, so I will have to take the *Ashinoura* into geosynchronous orbit.' She held out a small headset. 'I have also given Spud the frequency. Hail me when you are ready to depart.'

Eve took it, put it on then slipped her mask over the top. It caught on her brow and she realised she still had her glasses on. She plucked them off and tossed them aside with disgust. Once her mask was donned and a seal check complete, she flipped up a layer of excess robe over her head and made it snug against her skin and mask. She nodded to Olympia and the ramp was dropped.

A gust of frigid air sucked away the warmth of the *Ashinoura's* interior and buffeted Eve. She recovered and looked to Olympia who had neglected to don a mask and seemed unphased by the toxic air around them. Eve discarded her misgivings and made for the ramp.

Olympia extended an arm out to stop her. 'Are you sure you want to do this?'

Spud blurted in concurrence.

Eve nodded. 'Yes.'

'Are you certain?'

Eve shot an acidic glare at Olympia. 'Get out of my way,' she growled.

Olympia narrowed her eyes and stepped aside. Eve shoved past and descended the ramp with Spud in tow. She kept her eyes forward, not daring to turn from her path should her will falter. She had come so far, and it had been so long. She dreaded what she might find—what she *will* find—but she didn't care. There was still the faintest of hopes, and she needed closure; that was the only thing that mattered in that point in time.

Her first step onto the surface of Concord was a bewilderingly serene sensation. The ground was just as tough and unyielding as she remembered, and the crunch of rock beneath her boots made her spine tingle. A deadly chill melted through her mask and caressed her face, bringing a tear to her eye.

She looked out over the land, taking in the rolling hills that melded into each other as seamlessly as the darkness itself. Low above the horizon, Minor and its many fragments joined the multitude of stars in their chaotic dance of fate, and as if in greeting, a handful of fiery blazes streaked across the sky and impacted the surface far over the horizon.

Spud booped in fascination, his optics passing over the landscape in overlapping arcs. He appeared as little more than a giant silhouette cast by the shrinking escape of light from the *Ashinoura's* closing ramp.

Eve flicked her flashlight on the instant the ramp was shut, and another nostalgic wave washed over her as she waved her pillar of light about. 'It's good to be home,' she said, half to herself.

She turned to Spud. 'You know the way to the Rover, buddy?'

Spud garbled hesitantly and scratched at his chin. *What's been going on with him, recently?* she thought with a huff. His head rotated onto her, crimson optics aglow, and gave a wary nod while pointing off to his right.

'Good.'

CHAPTER TWENTY-ONE

Vaughn groaned and stretched out in the pilot's seat as the *Gally* shuddered with Ether translation. He was thankful Ether resonance only came about at the initiation of Ether travel with a terrible case of aggression having over taken a large portion of the ferry following its departure from Iridia.

'Attention, passengers,' the ferryman announced over the intercom spliced into every vessel attached to the ferry, 'due to a technical issue, we have made a momentary translation. We will be departing very shortly.'

Vaughn grunted in amusement. The last time he heard that voice was shortly after initial translation where a casualty report in the low thousands was passed out. That was fifteen. No. Sixteen standard-days ago. Radiation screens elevated before there was a sudden lurch as the ferry relinquished its death grip on the *Gally*. Vaughn took control of his ship and gently guided it away to avoid detection from the neighbouring vessels.

The ferry returned into the Ether, and a flare of etheric energies swept over the *Gally* and bedazzled its systems. Lights dimmed, and consoles shut down, and for a solid moment, Vaughn was flying a ship without power. Then all systems rebooted and the *Gally* jolted with newfound vigour.

A sense of pride and excitement wiggled out from a long-forgotten recess of Vaughn's psyche. It had been years since he felt the thrill of the hunt, his juvenile years in the tithebound legions, the Navy academy and his subsequent mutiny now distant memories dulled by a lifetime of riches. But like a rusted blade whetted back to its prime, he was keening to get stuck into things.

He wished he had a crew with him, but this was a hunt that could be left to no one but himself. The only other soul he would have trusted would have been Aleya, and even *she* was questionable with her reliance on inebriation to get through her life.

As for everyone else, they would have become a liability; a lesson he had learnt long ago. *Loose lips sink ships as the ancient adage goes.*

His lingering over Aleya yielded a kernel of regret in the orc. *Such a waste of prime genetics,* he noted before quickly discarding the thought and setting his mind on the critical task at hand. *There'll always be another elv, but there's only* one *Eve.*

He flipped on the *Gally's* potent signal scrambler and gunned it for Concord Prime.

It was a long trudge for Eve. She and Spud marched across what must have been five kilometres of Concordian landscape, rising over hills bathed in Minorlight and dipping into darkened valleys flooded with neutralised water.

Temperatures fluctuated with every change in altitude but Eve's lightweight robes proved highly adept at keeping the probing tendrils of the cold out. *If only we had this stuff on the* Eternity.

The thought of laying eyes on that wrecked ship had gnawed at the back of her mind ever since she left the shrinking glow of the *Ashinoura* behind. Her efforts were rewarded when, after a lengthy ascent out of a deep ravine, she caught sight of the only sign of humanity's presence on Concord.

Dimly lit against the darkscape by Minor's rays, the corpse of the *Eternity* lay draped over a small mountain range. It was calm, almost serene. The fires were long dead, and only a darkened skeleton was left behind to slowly melt into the landscape. Eve looked over the ruin in misery as memories of the many expeditions made into its depths leapt up at her from the depths of the past.

Spud booped, intrigued by the sight.

'Nothing left in there, buddy,' Eve said, carrying on. 'Not anymore.'

Spud grumbled in disappointment and followed.

They walked on for a while, the both of them casting fleeting glances at the looming shipwreck whenever it came back into sight. When ground descended into a shallow re-entrant, Eve felt a tangible change in the ground beneath her boots. Flat and compacted down by a few centimetres, it went on for a metre before raising back up only to repeat the trend once more a few metres further along.

A shrill squeal leapt from her lungs. 'This is a Rover track!' she said, dropping to a knee and to get a feel for the direction of travel. 'We're close.'

She sprung up and traced the track uphill. The higher she went, the more the terrain stood out to her. A notched crevice here, and an impact crater there, she slowly pieced together her rough location until she came upon a large opening in the ground.

'The cave!' she shouted, scurrying forth.

Spud exclaimed a warning but she ignored him.

Passing under the gaping mouth of the subterranean formation and into the maw of the underground, nostalgia turned Eve's feet to stone. She cast her flashlight about in the hope of finding the Rover sitting in its usual spot.

But the cave was desolate save for a handful of Rocket fragments, scaffolding and all manner of neatly organised tools and equipment clearly left untouched for some time. The canal that ran through the centre of the cave and drained into the depths beyond the dense rocky forestry had deepened considerably and broken its banks in one point to form a stagnant billabong. Where the Rover's parking spot used to be, fledgling stalagmites had sprouted beneath equally appraised stalactites.

Eve paced forwards in a trance. She wanted to cry, but her tears were held at bay by her awe. 'Mom? Dad?' she called out but the only response was the cave's spirit dampening echoes.

A firm gauntlet on her shoulder broke her from her daze.

'What?' she asked with a hint of displeasure at Spud's interference.

Spud booped and pointed at a pile of components a few metres away.

It took Eve a moment to realise why he had made such an observation. 'The Rocket cores,' she deduced, taking a few cautious steps closer with her flashlight trained on them.

They were a radioisotope generator built to wait through millennia of inactivity to unleash a handful of powerful energetic exclamations. But the years exposed to the Concordian elements had done a number on them. Their matte-steel finishes were infected with rust and pocked with holes from a few rogue Rain droplets.

It was a miracle they remained intact, though Eve figured them to be a hair's twitch away from detonation. 'They look unstable,' she remarked, cautiously retreating. 'Best we keep our distance.' She turned and headed for the mouth of the cave, no longer wishing to remain in close company with a volatile bomb. 'Thanks, buddy.'

Spud watched her go, shot one last wary look at the cores and followed.

When they broke back out into the open sky, Eve paused to get her bearings. She determined the route to the Outlook and made for it with due haste. The gradient of the land steepened, and the ground hardened to jagged rock that glittered an esoteric gold under her flashlight. For a moment, like so many times before, she wondered what the strange material that composed the Outlook was and contemplated taking a segment for analysis.

'The Rover is somewhere around here,' she said, refocusing on the primary objective.

With every step closer, her pulse quickened, her pace hastened and her dread deepened. She wasn't sure what she would find or if she was willing to take the consequences of it but she pushed on, regardless.

At the edge of her flashlight beam, a construct emerged from the darkness, and she broke into a run. Huffing up the last stretch of the incline, she passed onto a plateau where only the stars lay above. The construct that had enticed her so was little more than a warped beam of metal atop the slagged remains of the launch pad.

Mask sucking tight against her face, she scampered into the shadow of the beam and examined the ruins. Finding nothing of value, she turned about and scanned her immediate surroundings but found only rock and Spud, who lumbered up in her wake. Disappointment weighed heavy on her shoulders.

She had hoped the smaller reading Olympia detected was the Rover, but it must have been the remnants of the launch pad.

But it also gave rise to a sparking hope. Had her parents got the Rover working? Had they moved on and found refuge elsewhere?

'See anything, buddy?' she asked Spud.

He rotated his head and scried the land. He lingered over a spot for a moment but said nothing.

'Well?' Eve prompted.

Spud booped and motioned on a location further down the Outlook.

Eve followed his mark and picked out a tumorous formation growing out of the earth. At first glance, it would have passed for little more than a mound of rock, but a few metallic glints from inside made her heart stop.

She sprinted for it in a desperate panic and, with proximity, the amorphous mound transformed into an unidentifiable mess. Firm walls of iron and copper had melted into metallic puddles. Pipes and cabling had fused with panelling and bloated alloys. Wheels that had journeyed the surface of Concord had been claimed by the grounds they once trundled through. Supports that lasted millennia in the void of space had caved under the eroding trickle of the Rain to become little more than twisted imitations of their former selves.

Eve stopped just shy of the molten mass, almost all of her remaining strength draining from her. She steeled herself and reconstructed the Rover in her head, raising up girders and panelling from the earth to fill in the gaps. She found herself standing roughly at the precipice of the airlock. She passed through into the cargo bay that had collapsed under the weight of the common room and cockpit to create a horrid amalgamation of all three. Off to the side, where the bedrooms and medbay would have been, a thick slice of the Rover was perched up on one side by a tightly packed arrangement of bulkheads to form a slanted roof that sheltered a handful of cowering objects beneath.

She immediately recognised her workbench behind the remains of her door frame and picked a path through the wreckage to get a better look, finding her petite console and even a handful of scavenged components still in the same place she had left them years ago. She spun about and took in the rest of the Rover, what little remained of it, through teary eyes.

'Home,' was all she said before a crippling sadness overwhelmed her. She dropped to her knee in a coughing fit. Her face flushed and tears waterfalled down her cheeks to pool at the bottom of her mask. She regretted ever coming back and the last inkling of hope for her parents' survival screeched from her lungs and melted with the wreckage around her in a rapidly fading echo.

A concerned boop pulled her back from her woes, and she looked up to see Spud standing over her.

'Nothing!' she spluttered, waving out around them. 'There's nothing left! Not even a damn fucking hint of their existence.'

In a blind rage, she swept the assortment of scrapped components off her workbench and they clattered across the mutated metal. She leapt up and kicked one of the components, sending it flying across the hollowed skeleton of the Rover and into the darkness. Pain shot up her leg but she didn't care.

'Why did you leave me?' she cried out to the ghosts of her parents. 'Why did you abandon me?' Her words were swallowed up by the darkness as soon as they left her mouth.

Spud booped and held out a consoling hand onto her shoulder.

Eve raised her head to meet his and an enraging realisation clicked in her head. The Rocket door. The locked seatbelt. The launch. They were all his doing. Because of *him*, their plan was a success.

She thrust a firm finger up at him. 'You went along with their plan!' she said, venom flowing from her tongue. 'You took control of the Rocket and kept me from them!'

Spud's optics dimmed, and he turned away. Eve hissed, scooped up one of the dislodged components and threw it at him. The ancient device, weakened by exposure, exploded against his chassis and left only minor scratches. She leapt into him and smacked her palms against his musculature.

'I begged you to stop, but you didn't! I'm your creator! I'm your mom! You're supposed to listen to me, but you didn't! Because of you, I left behind all I had ever cared about!' She stopped, her hands raw, and she collapsed to the ground.

Spud loomed over her, an enigmatic sentinel, his optics locked on her. He tried to boop, but Eve cut him off.

'Shut up,' she spat, 'I don't want to hear another word from you.'

Spud shoulders drooped. For a brief moment, Eve could have sworn she glimpsed compassion in his soulless optics. He marched off to let her to wallow in her grief.

'That's my family,' a distorted child's voice said.

Eve shot up and spun about to see Spud with his gauntlet against her old console. He had given the little computer a new lease on life, and it played out a grainy scene depicting a small girl sitting at a familiar desk with the camera angled low amidst all manner of junk. The family photograph dominated the frame. Her eyes widened.

'That's me when I was little,' the video Eve said, pointing at the even younger version of herself in the middle of the photograph. 'I've grown up a fair bit since then, though.'

There was a distorted boop from the video that let a slight chuckle find its way through Eve's sadness. She rose and got as close as she could to the screen.

'That's my mom and dad,' the video Eve continued, tapping against Nisma and Eli. 'They're my parents. Kinda like *my* creators.' She paused and made a strange face. She then reached over and plucked the photograph with a little difficulty.

Eve smiled as the tips of Spud's maniples cut into frame.

'It's okay, buddy. I just want to give it a quick look.'

The audio fizzled and the video flickered out, leaving Eve to stare into her own reflection. Her anger burned away to leave a hollow shell behind. To see such a pivotal moment in her life be played out before her eyes had rendered what little emotion she could muster into baselessness. Memories long repressed flooded by, as fresh as the day she lived them, but they flew by so fast and with such animosity that she could hardly settle on one long enough to truly appreciate it.

Spud booped and patted her on the head. She blinked and watched as his chest distorted and folded outwards. A cavern opened up, and a clunky data reader emerged. It bleeped and ejected its tray, revealing a neatly folded piece of paper. He plucked the paper from the tray and held it out to her. She took it, unfurled it and immediately crumpled onto the workbench. The photograph, worn and faded with age.

'Where did you—when did—' she stammered with disbelief. Her eyes welled but no tears broke through. Instead, a grim resolve took their place. 'It can't bring them back,' she grumbled, wanting nothing more than to scrunch up the photograph and toss it aside but an obligation stayed her hand.

She raised her head to Spud. He had carried it across the galaxy on no commitment other than his own. He treasured the photograph and he was offering it to her as penance. What cause would that give her to destroy it?

She folded it back up and held it up to him. 'Keep it,' she mumbled. 'It's yours.'

Spud's optics flicked between her and the photograph. He took it and returned it to its safe space.

Eve turned around and cast her flashlight over the wreckage of the Rover. 'There's nothing here,' she said grimly. 'Nothing worth remembering.' She shuffled into the common room and made for the nearest gape in the Rover's bones.

Spud watched her go, anguish causing a higher than acceptable error rate in his processes. He had hoped the revelation of the photograph would have raised Eve's spirits, but it seemed to only render her down into an even deeper despair.

+*You haven't shown her* that *yet,*+ the Foreigner pointed out.

Spud grumbled. He had hoped he could have avoided resorting to his last option, but to see Eve so downtrodden was tearing up his very code structure. He returned to the console and revived it one last time to feed it the deep-seeded memory that had become the core of his prerogative and the sole reason for his existence.

'Can you go downstairs and help your father in the airlock? I need to check on the state of the batteries.'

Eve froze and turned back to Spud. The grainy feed showed her younger self rising from her desk and sliding off-screen. She was replaced by a larger figure; a woman who had been rendered to a desperate shadow of herself. After ensuring the coast was clear, Nisma closed door behind herself.

'I know you saw it. The thrusters,' she said bluntly, marching up to the camera and bringing it close to her face. Her eyes were red and tired, her face saturated with tears she diligently wiped away with her sleeve. 'Now, if what I've seen is true,' she continued. 'You are far smarter than you would like to let on and are more than capable of achieving things that are more...technologically oriented.'

Spud acknowledged.

A sly grin crept across Nisma's mouth. 'That's what I thought.' She laid Spud down and took a seat, locking eyes with him. 'I would like to make a *very* important request of you. One that I *hope* you would be willing to undertake.'

Eve grimaced as her own mother went through the intricate details of her abandonment. Every word uttered. Every thought transmitted. Every action that would transpire given over.

'Why are you showing me this?!' she demanded, mask fogging under hyperventilation. 'Haven't you done enough?!' She dropped onto the slacken slab that used to be the dining table with her head in her palms. The mask got in the way, and she damn nearly tore the thing off before her sense of self-preservation kicked in.

Spud begged her to be patient.

Nisma finished the divulgence of her plan, and the recording went silent. Then, there was a sigh and a sniffle. Eve raised her head enough to get a peek at the screen. Nisma was coiled over the workbench, head in hand and tears flowing down her face. She was utterly defeated, a woman taken far beyond her limit. Eve had only ever seen her mother in such a state a handful of times, but none seemed to hit her as hard as the wreck before her. She straightened up as a realisation clicked in her mind. It wasn't just the cries of defeat.

It was of resignation.

Eventually, Nisma had garnered enough strength to speak. 'Eve,' she began heavy heartedly, 'I don't know if you're ever going to see this, but I want to take this opportunity to say I'm sorry.' She gagged, and there were a few moments of crying before she could talk coherently. 'We couldn't tell you what was about to happen because, if we did, you wouldn't have allowed it. But please, *please* understand that, with the hand dealt to us, it was the only logical choice.'

She slumped back and swept a length of curly locks out of her face. 'We couldn't have done it without Spud,' she said, motioning to the camera. 'Please don't harbour any anger towards him. He was only doing what I asked had of him and—if he's as good of a person as you believe him to be—he'll fulfill this task no matter what.'

Her demeanour lightened, and pride shined through. 'He's an incredible invention, Eve. What you made is truly special. Spud, here, he's a one of a kind, and I believe, even with their millennia of advancement, everyone else will see your genius. That's why you had to leave. The both of you hold so much potential while your father and I…we are just relics. We're past our primes; we don't know anything other than our narrow existences aboard the *Eternity* and Concord. We wouldn't last up there.'

She steeled herself, and her posture straightened. 'It pains us to have to let you go, and you are probably stricken with hatred for us abandoning you when you needed us most. But it's the duty of a parent to sacrifice all they have for the betterment of their child. Even to give their own lives.' She smiled and Eve's heart broke. 'It's a thankless job, but it's one without peer. I hope you understand.' She swallowed, holding back tears. 'No matter what you do, we're proud of you,' she said with a curt nod. 'Remember that.'

The console cut out with a flash and smoke.

The regret that had plagued Spud for years vanished with the smoke of the console's dying breath. His hydraulics hissed and electrons flared through his circuitry as an incredible relief flooded through him. He looked to Eve for feedback, but his creator's expression was unreadable, a perfect blend of emotions that held no credence to what truly lay beneath.

He contemplated the possibility that he had made a mistake. He knew it was for his mother's own good. If she had remained, she would have shared the same fate as her parents.

But there was still shame in what he did. He wanted to express his desolation, but something still barred his vocabulator from operating. There was still one firewall that remained.

'Eve, do you receive me?' Olympia's static-ridden voice called over the radio.

Eve put a hand to her ear. 'I do,' she said, her voice abandoned and distant.

'Apologies for the interruption, but a ferry had momentarily translated in-system. It was brief, but I managed to intercept the signal of a small vessel before it vanished into the system's background radiation.'

Eve stiffened. 'Vaughn. How did he know we'd come here?'

'It would seem your adoptive father knows you better than you might think.'

Eve grunted and glanced at Spud. 'Can you pick us up before he gets here?'

Olympia's answer was swallowed up by encroaching static that blared in Eve's ear.

She flinched and killed the signal. 'Scrambler.'

Spud booped in concurrence.

+*Not very smart to be all alone now, isn't it?*+ the Foreigner said.

327

Spud ignored the remark and waited for Eve to make the first move, but she remained motionless for a few long seconds, as if her processor had encountered a critical error and was rebooting.

She raised her head and regarded Spud with determination. 'Is the cave nearby?'

Spud nodded.

'Let's go, buddy. We'll hide in there.'

CHAPTER TWENTY-TWO

Vaughn emerged from his quarters to see the world of
Concord Prime ready to envelop him. He set the *Gally* into a
low orbit trajectory and gazed out the observation screen,
oddly humbled in a way. The world was in utter turmoil, its
surface scorched by fire and rain with its orbit inundated with
debris from its moon. Yet, he could see a poetic side to the
chaos, a celestial dance that had played out long before he
existed and would continue long after his death.

He leaned back into his chair and referred to an orbital
scan. Nothing of merit appeared on his reading though he
didn't doubt the ship of that creature Eve had fallen into
league with would be highly adept at concealment. But
nothing could hide from the deafening radioactive screams
that bellowed out from the *Gally's* scrambler. A smirk crept
up his lip. It was a textbook strategy used in his former roving
days where he isolated the distress calls of lone merchant

vessels while he stripped them of anything valuable. *And what can be more valuable than* it *and* her?

He initiated a scan of the surface for anything that could prove alluring for a creature like Eve. *I doubt you'll like what you'll see*. He flexed a little, the heat getting to him. He had put on considerable mass in preparation for landing— a thick jacket with furred hood, thermal pants and sturdy boots. He slid on a pair of thin gloves to help retain dexterity, and assuming the atmosphere's toxicity hadn't changed in the six years since his last visit, he kept a rebreather on hand. His trusty Navy cap was screwed tightly over his silver locks, and his pistols were holstered at his hip alongside a miniaturised scrambler and a snub-nosed tranquiliser.

The console bleeped, indicating a successful scan. The surface of the world was sparce and lacked almost any variation whatsoever once one strayed far enough from the chaotic middle where the two halves were stitched together. That made scanning quick, and near the wrecked mass of steel that had once been the *Eternity,* a secondary blip caught his attention. It was small, but it was as good of a bet as any for him so he set a course for descent.

The *Gally* touched down near a jagged outcrop that overlooked the wreckage of the *Eternity.* Vaughn flipped on his mobile scrambler the instant the *Gally* powered down to maintain his aura of discourse, and mask on, he disembarked. He was immediately met by a terrible gust of cold. With a shudder, he fastened his cap tight on his head. *Not tropical*

Orchia, that's for sure. He closed up the *Gally,* and torch in hand, he plodded out into the darkness towards the coordinates indicated by his scan. The ground was unyielding against his boots and pockmarked with tiny pools of water that fizzled in a persistent neutralisation reaction. Eve's cautionary tales of the dangers of the Concordian atmosphere fluttered to mind and he doublechecked the seal of his rebreather, not keen on taking her warnings lightly.

The rolling bumps quickly turned to rock that dug into his boots. Perplexed, he dropped to a knee and ran his hand over the rock. It was jagged and stalwart to a tee, giving off a strange golden glimmer under his light. The jet-black colour was familiar to him, but he couldn't put his finger on where he had seen it before. He rose, now was not the time to be contemplating rock compositions though he did make a mental note to return with a hardy drill for sample collection.

He picked out a grotesque structure with his light. It resembled bone, but under closer examination, he found it to be steel that had melted and reformed into a monstrosity. He figured it to be a shelter but the feasibility of constructing something out in the open beneath the onslaught of Concord's judgment told of a deeper layer to the mystery.

The answer came in the form of a distorted wheel. *Vehicular,* he noted as he strolled into the guts of the wreckage. It must have been several storeys tall; the frame having collapsed upon itself somewhat recently. Aside from that, few details could be gleamed from the ruin except for a single refuge from the rains. A segment of the roof had fallen down and shielded what appeared to be a small desk and computer from the most devastating effects of the weather. He leaned against the empty doorframe and peered in. The desk was a mess, covered in garbage and pieces of scrap. *Your home, Eve?*

The longer he scried the peculiar scene, the more details stood out to him. The chunks of scrap on the workbench showed no signs of degradation which posed a perplexing question when some of them managed to find their way to the floor where a single Rain exposure would surely render them unidentifiable. He straightened up and checked his surroundings. There was little to go by, just an endless swathe of rolling hills and pools. But behind the skeleton of Eve's home, a set of shallow divots trailed down the outcrop. *Tracks.*

Eve scurried into the cave with Spud close behind. She gasped for air, and the seal of her mask sucked against her face. They came very close to being caught as the *Gally* whisked overhead to land on the Outlook just as they were ducking into cover.

They were safe, but her fear could not be quashed. Not while Vaughn still treaded the same ground as her. She had hoped he would do his search and leave once he found nothing but ruin, but she knew he was more thorough than that. He would find something that would lead to the cave and she wasn't keen on their reunion.

She looked for somewhere to hide and resorted to the rock formations that grew at the peripheries of the cave. Beckoning Spud to follow, she took shelter behind the rocks and peered through a small gap.

'Be very quiet,' she whispered when Spud dropped to the ground beside her.

Spud booped and dimmed his optics. He motioned to her flashlight.

'Thanks, buddy,' Eve said, switching it off.

Vaughn kept his guard up and thumbed his pistols as he entered the cave. Eve wasn't alone and while he would have no problems dealing with Spud, the creature they fled the Port Royal with was something he had to consider. He cast his torch over the cave and picked out piles of scrap and refuse from the darkness. *Cornered in her own den.*

'Eve,' he called out with a smirk, 'I know you're here. Come out, please.'

There was no response aside from the reverberations of his call. He tried again, and there was no reply. He grunted and paced further in, leaping over a ravine to examine some discarded cylinders. His curiosity fading, he straightened up and looked out over the forest of stalagmites and stalactites with a keen amber eye. *She must be hiding somewhere in there,* he thought, pacing closer.

Eve's lungs screamed for air. She didn't dare to make a sound, no matter how terrified she was. Her heart thumped in her chest, and her ears roared in a deafening surge of adrenaline. Her fingers twitched, and her thighs itched to flee, but she kept her cool. The best chance she had was to stay as still as she could and hope. She looked to Spud, who returned her stare in an almost childlike bemusement. She listened to Vaughn move around the cave in a leisurely stroll, his flashlight waving over the rocks to cast stark shadows of razor-sharp teeth against the cave walls. He was getting close, and the claustrophobic nature of the cave made him seem even more of a giant than usual.

Spud prodded her shoulder and delicately poised a finger further down the cave where the darkness swallowed the light. Eve wasn't sure if the cave led anywhere, the allure of spelunking never truly appealed to her parents when the matters of survival took precedence. But if it meant putting some distance between them and Vaughn, that was good enough for her. The only issue was managing to slip away without being seen or heard.

'Come out from behind the rocks, Eve,' Vaughn said, the crunch of dirt under his boots getting clearer by the second.

Eve shuddered. Time was running out, and she was still gripped in fear. Despite this, she got the sudden urge to speak her mind. 'Why can't you just leave us alone?' she said. Her voice reverberated off the cave walls, making it impossible for him to tell where she was hiding.

Vaughn stopped and whipped his head about. 'You know I can't do that, Eve,' he said, turning away from her to investigate another corner of the cave. 'Not with what you have. I need to set things right for me and everyone else stuck under the Coalition's boot. Only the Taiji can do that.'

Eve repressed a hiss. While she might agree with his idea of a galaxy free of the Coalition's control, it wasn't worth the sacrifice of her son. Encouraged, she raised her voice again. 'You're going to kill Spud and put me in a vat to have me on display!'

'I'm sorry I didn't tell you sooner,' Vaughn said, seemingly disheartened. 'I didn't think you were ready.'

His tone shot a spear through Eve's heart. She pictured the people held in quasi-death and fought back a tear. 'I don't want my life to end like that.'

'I can clone you,' Vaughn proposed.

Eve shook her head and repressed a sniffle. A clone? How did that make it better? Even if it wasn't her, it was still a human being suffering a fate worse than death. She had held a modicum of hope for seeing a humane side to him but the man she admired and loved was just a façade. A ploy that played into every weakness of hers.

'I used to trust you,' she cried. 'I used to look up to you. When the rest of the galaxy was ready to throw me aside, you took me in. I thought you loved me. I loved you.'

'I do, Eve,' Vaughn said with an endearing softness. 'You're the closest thing I've ever had to a daughter.'

Eve growled. The lies kept adding fuel to her fury. It wasn't just her who had suffered; it was everyone who had ever come into contact with that reprehensible man. She watched him tentatively and kept in the shade of his light all the while.

'Is that how you treat your family?' she accused, 'Jere? Aleya? They're just assets to you. Ready to be discarded when their use is up?' A raw wound opened when she said those words.

Vaughn stiffened. 'That's a rather blunt accusation, Eve. Even for you.' He turned and paced into the centre of the cave. 'Eve, please,' he pleaded, 'come out from where you're hiding. I want to see you.'

He stopped by the canal and cast his torch about. The beam set something metallic alight, and Eve immediately recognised the discarded Rocket cores. Her eyes turned to marbles. The cores were mere metres away, and it would take little more than a small impact to set them off.

A morbid idea came to mind. If she could lure him towards them…

No. Despite the hatred she festered for him, a shred of hope still remained that the Vaughn she knew before the discovery of the Taiji still existed. The loving father figure who looked out for both her and Spud's best interests.

She shook her head. He never existed. It was all just a ruse. There was no bargaining with the true Vaughn, the creature hellbent on getting what he believed was rightfully his no matter the cost. To play into the dealer's hand is to willingly accept defeat.

She steeled herself, there was no way she was going down without a fight. But she didn't want to kill him. The visions of Orjey and Aleya's deaths were still raw in her mind. It disgusted her but with little choice otherwise, what else would she do? *Maybe the cores would just injure him?* she argued. *His orcoid size would be able to take trauma that would otherwise incapacitate a regular human.* She disregarded the idea. *As long as he's alive, he'll be hunting us. I can't put Spud through that. He has to die.*

She searched about for something to throw and found a few shards of rock discarded from her parent's initial colonisation of the cave. She scooped one up and felt the weight in her hand, judging the feasibility of throwing it with enough accuracy to impact the cores. The odds were not good, and she doubted she could land anywhere near the cores. She could get closer. but that would put her in the immediate vicinity of the explosion where the dense cover provided by the rock would be frivolous. She looked to Spud, but he was never much of a thrower, either, so she ran through a dozen other options but none proved to come even remotely close to success. All avenues were cut and there only remained the straight path ahead. A grim realisation settled over her. *Both of us can't get out.*

She clenched her fists and silently cursed. *There's no way we can win!* She wanted to cry out and let loose all of the pain that had been bottled and slowly growing since the day of that damnable launch. What was the point of continuing onwards? Even the simple effort of just handing herself over to Vaughn for internment and ending the nightmare sounded appealing.

No, I can't, she told herself. *There's still one thing.* She sighed and dreamt of how things used to be. The days spent aboard the Rover with the people she loved. The trips to gather water with Eli while he told stories or the sessions performing repairs with Nisma while she gave valuable lessons about everything. The expeditions into the *Eternity*, both with her watching in terror as Eli departed into the shadows and with her by his side in the deepest recesses of their old home. She found herself smiling; a genuine smile wrought from happiness she hadn't felt in years. She was where she belonged. She was home and that didn't sound too bad.

She looked to Spud. *But for him, there's nothing. He belongs up there. Not down here in the waste.* She solemnly nodded, accepting her fate. *It's the duty of a parent to sacrifice all they have for the betterment of their child.*

'Spud,' she whispered to him, 'I'm gonna need you to stay here where it's safe. Don't follow me, okay?'

Spud booped with both confusion and dismay. He made to move, but Eve held up a hand to stop him.

'Spud, for once in your life, don't come to save me!' she commanded firmly. 'You don't belong here. Go live your life

338

and don't worry about me. There's nothing up there for me. I want to stay here at home.'

Spud looked at her for the longest moment of her life. His shoulders slumped and a depressed acceptance flickered in his optics.

Relief washed over Eve. He understood, and that was all she wanted. She crawled close and embraced him, sobbing tears into her mask. 'Thank you, buddy,' she blubbered.

Spud coughed and patted her on the back. A static-ridden gargle burled out from his vocabulator, and with great effort, he did something she thought was impossible.

'Eve,' he said, stringing out the word for a long second.

Eve's heart melted and she planted a loving hand on his cheek. 'I love you too.'

She carefully extracted herself from him and crawled to where she could emerge from the dense thicket of stone. She rose and stood proud, brushing her hair back to show her face.

Vaughn spotted movement in the corner of his eye, and he whipped about to see Eve emerging from the mass of grotesque rock formations. Chest puffed out and fists held firm, she approached him with newfound determination. Her act of valour surprised him. What had given her such courage?

'There's my girl,' Vaughn smiled, beckoning her closer.

'You could have saved them,' Eve hissed, face distorted in rage. 'My mom and dad. You were in orbit when they were still alive! You could have come down and spared them! They would be alive today! Why didn't you save them?!' She altered her course a bit and stopped just shy of a mound of dilapidated cylindrical containers.

Careful not to frighten the girl, Vaughn postured himself in turn with her just outside his reach and his side presented towards her. Out of view, he extracted the tranquiliser and cupped it in his palm. He couldn't believe she was falling for the same trick again; luck was truly in his favour. It will be a quick and painless retrieval, but he needed to know where the Taiji was first.

He shrugged, a look of dismissal on him. She was right— he could have saved her parents. It would have been easy. But the reason was simple. 'Because I didn't want to,' he said.

Eve growled and made one last step to put her in range. Vaughn leapt forth and yanked her by the arm. With a swift hand, he jabbed the tranquiliser in her neck and injected its contents. She gasped as the anaesthetic flooded her veins. Tension immediately left her body and he was soon cradling a limp corpse. Her tiny size meant she'd only be conscious for a few more seconds so he had to be quick.

'Tell me where it is, Eve,' he demanded, holding her head up with his free hand.

Eve sighed, her will to fight fading quickly. Her head lolled back and forth in his arm in a weak dismissal. 'You'll never have him,' she muttered.

She lurched and stamped down upon the ground, her heel impacting with the cylinders at her feet. There was a great blinding light followed by a searing heat and thunderous crack as their unstable contents ignited into a great blast of nuclear fission.

CHAPTER TWENTY-THREE

There was a great flash and a vicious heat that overwhelmed Spud. His optics flickered out, and he was left in a deafened darkness. He reset his optics and vision gradually returned as receptors recalibrated themselves. He remained motionless for a few seconds to listen as audio feedback was siphoned out in layers until only the faintest echoes of the explosion remained and vanished with time.

Cautiously, he peeked out from the rocks. Glassed rock plumed out from the explosion's epicentre and crept up the inner faces of the rocks he had taken cover behind. Several stalactites had toppled to the ground and crushed their opposing cousins while others bore their glistening coats with pride.

Most distressing, however, was the complete absence of Eve.

Spud rose and threaded his way through the rock, pausing at ground zero. His Geiger counter ticked with latent radiation, but that was of little concern for him. He scanned the cave thoroughly, and at his feet, a dark figure sent a surging enthusiasm in him. But he was mistaken. What he had hoped to be Eve was actually a blackened shadow cast into the uncaring Concordian earth. A curiosity blipped in his processor, and he dropped to a knee to examine the dimensions of the shadow and found them to perfectly match his creator.

A long drone whistled out from him, and his optics flickered. He placed a trembling gauntlet beside the hand of the shadow and disturbed a piece of the nuclear shadow, throwing the dust up into the air. The dust flittered about in the stale air, and for a brief microsecond, he thought he perceived a ghostly apparition of his beloved mother before it settled back on the ground.

He rose and prodded the Foreigner for input, but he couldn't detect any trace of it in his systems. He spread out across his circuitry and probed every connection to the ancient housing that served as its domain. Nothing. A realisation crossed his RAM. Was the split successful?

'Eve? Are you receiving me? The interference is fading. I'm nearing your last known location, now,' Olympia hailed over the radio.

'I hear you, Olympia,' Spud said, actuating his words through his vocabulator. It felt strange but also relieving.

Olympia was surprised. 'Spud…you are capable of speech now?'

'The last remnant of my prerogative has been fulfilled.'

'So that means…' Olympia started before trailing off. 'What of Eve?'

Spud's chassis trembled. 'She is no longer with us.'

'I am deeply sorry, Spud. Are you okay?'

'I appreciate your condolences,' Spud nodded. 'Physically, I am fully operational, but I grieve.' With dimmed optics, he took one last woeful look at the sparse remains of his mother before marching out of the cave and under the starry Concordian sky. 'Thankfully, my mother's loss was not in vain. She did it of her own volition to free me.'

'What of Vaughn?' Olympia inquired sternly.

Spud glanced back in the direction of the cave. 'He shared a similar fate, though not voluntarily.' A thought floated up from his memory. With a click, he opened up his chest and threaded the isolated housing unit that contained the Foreigner out into a waiting hand. He gave it an examination and found it to be in perfect condition. 'Additionally. I no longer sense the Taiji's presence, so I believe we have successfully segregated.' He idly tossed the housing up in the air and caught it. 'I have no need, or wish, to continue holding onto such a detestable consciousness, so I shall return it into your care.'

'Thank you, Spud,' Olympia said, relieved. 'What will you do now?'

The question caught Spud unawares. He hadn't even considered what life would be like without Eve. He never dared to. 'I do not know,' he admitted.

'Perhaps, you could join me?' Olympia offered. 'I miss having a travel companion, and I could guide you in your journey through life.'

Electrons sparks across Spud's circuitry ,and his optics flared with excitement. 'Very well.'

'I can see you now,' Olympia said, her words accentuated by the encroaching thrum of the *Ashinoura* readying to land high above. 'We will discuss things further in orbit.' She held the line open for several seconds. 'She loved you like nothing else, Spud. She truly was a one of a kind.'

An electrified blade tore through Spud. 'Indeed. She granted me the gift of life, and I do not intend to sully it. She may have returned home where she belongs with those she loves, but her memory will live on in me.'

As the *Ashinoura* came in to land, he gave one last look back at the cave before stepping away and consigning the world of Concord to its fate.

EPILOGUE

Six standard-years earlier.

Rain pattered against the Rover's scrap armour, and droplets laced with dissolved metallics dribbled down viewports in slowly deepening trenches of hardened plastic. Lightning cracked beyond those narrow sightings, momentarily bringing light to the rolling hills and stagnant ponds that was the sombre side of Concord Prime. A few leaks had already sprung in the Rover's roof, and noxious puddles welled in deepening holes beneath stalactites of mutated steel while, where water tension denied freefall, streams of metal flowed down the walls and found unexplored tracks through pipes, cable housings and support beams.

Nisma stared up at the formations in idle fascination, noting how it would have taken millions of years for a similar effect to have been possible on Earth. She lay on the floor of the common room, Eli by her side, atop mattresses pulled from their cots to cushion their aching bodies as they cherished their intimacy one last time.

Nisma rested her head on Eli's arm with her back to the floor while he lay on his side, amputated leg upwards, and threaded fingers through her hair. A cramp in her back urged her to readjust, but she was too exhausted to move; both of them were, and the air had grown deathly thin.

Her lungs stung, and the taste of blood lingered in her throat. The air was already contaminated with the world's damnable atmosphere, and even if she had all the time and resources in the universe, she knew there was little hope in ever properly achieving an air-tight seal again.

She sighed and uttered an apology to the Rover under her breath; this was no way for such a stalwart workhorse to go.

Drowsiness lingered behind her eyes, and she fought to keep them open with what little brain bandwidth she could spare. Her will was slowly fading, and defeat was high upon her. She knew it was a losing battle, but she didn't care. She had done all she could, and she had resolved herself to the fate that was ten years overdue.

'I'm tired,' she yawned. 'I might take a nap. You?'

Eli shifted a little. 'Air's pretty low,' he mumbled, facing a similar conclusion. 'I doubt we'd wake up.'

Nisma shrugged. 'I don't care.' She sighed and fought back the pitch for one last time as her mind turned to the sky and the slowly dwindling star that carried the most precious thing in her universe. 'You think she'll be okay?' she asked.

Eli chuckled. Despite his exhaustion, he still retained his humour. Nisma was thankful for that. 'She's a smart girl, Nis,' he said. 'I reckon she'll do fine.'

Nisma nodded and snuggled up close to him and shut her eyes, a solemn contentedness bringing peace to her heart. 'Good,' she whispered.

Sleep crept up quickly upon her, and her thoughts dwindled until there was only silence and the eternal darkness that awaited all.

MARK OF ETERNITY

ZACHARY MOULDER

The first instalment of the Mark of Eternity series!

Eve has never seen the light of day, nor known the beauty of a living world. Marooned on the dark side of an unforgiving planet, Eve and her parents, Eli and Nisma, scavenge the remains of their colony ship, the *Eternity*, with the hope of building their own means of escaping their post-apocalyptic prison.

But with time running out and constant setbacks and delays pushing everyone beyond their limits, Eve and her family soon find themselves at each other's throats. Will they manage to pull together and flee their living hell? Or would they be doomed to a life of decay in an eternal night?

A FRIENDLY REMINDER

How did you find Child of Concord? Please leave a review!
Good or bad, I'm keen to see what you think.

Spot any mistakes? Let me know! I'm run a one-man
operation so it's inevitable for mistakes to slip through.

Want to remain up to date with any future works? Check out
my socials that I frequent every so often. If you're interested
in receiving an Advanced Reader Copy for future works, then
keep an eye out on there.

Twitter: @ZacMoulder
Email: zachary.d.moulder@gmail.com

ΛFTERWORD

Let me preface this by saying that I never intended to make a sequel to Mark of Eternity.

If you have read my little shpiel at the end of Mark of Eternity—which if you haven't read then I, in my utmost unbiased opinion, do believe you should!—then you would know that it was the product of my growing frustration with procrastination. I started my writing journey in 2012 when I was thirteen and almost ten years later, I had no visible signs of anything even remotely resembling a finished manuscript.

Up until that point, I had essentially danced about between WIPs whenever I was greeted by the lovely embrace of writer's block. I was also deep in my video game "phase" and, paired with my studies, I found the time and motivation to write severely lacking. That changed when I joined the Australian Defence Force and, without studies to bog me down, I could only pin the blame on myself and my lack of discipline.

So, I took a look at my time in Army, namely the basic training phase known as Kapooka. I spent eighty days there which, when you look at it like that, seemed like a long time— and I would agree—but I devised a way to trick myself into thinking that it wasn't as long as I thought.

I divided it up into single days with a small calendar. Now, it wasn't a single block of eighty days but eighty single days that I can cross out every day. That was where I drew my writing discipline from. I looked at the roughly 75000-word count of novels, broke them up into manageable sizes— generally 1000 words a day depending on workload—and ran with it. All I needed was a WIP to focus on through to the very end and Mark of Eternity, having both a plot figured out and not being a series, was perfect.

And, in what appears to be a rather funny repetition of history, Child of Concord was also a product of this same frustration but this time aimed at the very writing process I had so quickly come to rely on.

While I had the general idea of a sequel to Mark of Eternity in mind (even stating it in my previous afterword), I didn't start writing Child of Concord straight away. That was because there was something else I wanted to write first, Birthright.

Birthright is an interesting story and I'll say that it is the epitome of my new writing style stretched to the limit. I was writing it even while Mark of Eternity was in the latter drafting stages and, by the time of its zenith in size in mid-

2023, it had ballooned to a monstrosity of almost 200000 words—as well as inadvertently ending a relationship I was in ahaha. It was terrible and, even with several rewrites and splitting it up into multiple books, I wasn't happy with how it turned out. Not wanting to devolve into a cycle where I release a book once every decade, I fell back onto a story with a premise still somewhat fresh in my mind, Child of Concord.

I wrote Child of Concord over a period of six months—a stark improvement over MoE's two years!—and I took some lessons I learnt from my first time around.

To start, I emerged from my little writing bubble and started to interact with the wider community on X. There were a lot of writers out there and I really enjoyed talking with them and learning from them. I also got into contact with several reviewers, competitions and the like. I submitted Mark of Eternity to the BBNYA 2023 awards and got in the semi-finals which was a big morale boost for me since Amazon sales were unsurprisingly low.

I was also contacted by the awesome fellows at YourPaperQuest who ran my little book in the first run of their indie book subscription service and they remain my more frequent interactions on the platform—even after I've grown weary of social media in general. So, in hindsight, I should have made my online presence known a lot earlier and this remains my second biggest change in the processes between MoE and CoC.

The biggest change was the introduction of beta readers. As previously stated, I wrote Mark of Eternity in a bubble—which astounds with how well received it is—with the first people to read my story being family members and my editor very late in the book's development stages. I heard a lot of folk on X used beta readers so I gave it a go for Birthright and the feedback they gave concreted my belief in them. When it came to Child of Concord, I sent off my third draft to a beta reader who gave their feedback. I would then make some necessary changes thanks to the input of another human being before sending it out to another reader and making further changes. By the conclusion of the fifth draft following two beta reads, the story was of a much better quality for the editor to peruse than Mark of Eternity was.

But not everything has changed! As you would have undoubtedly noticed, the artwork still remains the same. Doan Trang was kind enough to come back to make a few more awesome illustrations for me to help tie up the two books together and C.K was great at helping me polish off the last drafts.

Unlike Mark of Eternity, all the characters basically remained the same during their development save for Olympia, who was suffering a bad case of Gandalfism. She was powerful, too powerful, but I needed her to be for reasons which I may write in this lifetime. I initially tried to wedge some physical barriers in between her and Eve to bring some sense of stakes back to the story but it was easily picked up as lazy writing by the beta readers. So, I figured I could make her weaker, her detachment from the Taiji having slowly weathered her might from the deity she once was to now a demigod who has to use a bit of their wit. I think it was a decision for the better and even introduced some storylines for a trilogy finale.

As for what I'm writing next? I'm not sure. I've spent a big chunk of this year researching the Golden Age of Piracy with the intent of writing a swashbuckler series as well as piecing together several thrilling standalone stories that I want to write before I move onto other things.

There's even the vague idea of a third instalment to the Mark of Eternity series, one that takes us to the very end of the universe. But we'll see if I can decide to work on that one straight away or fumble about for a few years.

Anyways, thanks for checking my book out.

Until next time,

Zachary Moulder

ABOUT THE AUTHOR

Zachary Moulder is an average bloke who likes to write
stories, paint very small miniatures and enjoy the company of
his friends and family over a few beers. Formerly an M1A1
Abrams Crewman, he is now an Ammunition Technician
serving in the Australian Army. He was born in Brisbane,
Australia, and presently resides in Townsville where he lives
in constant dread for the inevitable arrival of North
Queensland's insufferable summer.